Piano Secrets

GW01072063

Ken Brown

COPYRIGHT

First published in 2013 by Castor Publishing
70 Berry Way, Andover SP10 3XS

Copyright © Ken Brown 2013

Cover Copyright © Ken Brown 2013

ISBN 978-0-9927075-0-7

ACKNOWELDGEMENTS

To Annie, Madeleine, John & Jane who were prepared
to put up with the hardship of visiting Sorrento with me
all in the name of research
and
the wonderful people of Sorrento, Italy.

CONTENTS

PIANO SECRETS

DAY ONE

"Tenika Solange Taylor. You are something else!"

"Look Chanie, you've got to be positive with these guys otherwise they'll be chasing you all day."

The two women stopped at Piazza della Vittoria taking in the warm breeze sweeping across the Bay of Naples. This small piazza, some say built on the actual spot where a Roman temple to the god Venus once stood, is an oasis of everything Sorrento has to offer. Tenika and Chantrea stood by the pillared concrete railing looking out across the bay to Vesuvius as it shimmered in the hazy late morning sun. A small tuft of white cloud hung over the top of the cauldron and a hydrofoil bus ploughed its way across the bay from Naples towards the Marina Piccola way down on the shoreline to their right.

As they looked from their prime cliff top position they could see a very hazy outline of the tip of Capri and, in the far distance, Ischia was a blurry shape on the horizon. The tranquillity of the moment was only penetrated by the noise of children playing on the minute small darkened beach of the Marina Francesco 50 metres below.

Behind them was a small square public garden lined with palm trees 15 metres high. Azaleas and the ubiquitous orange trees adorned the space giving a peaceful resting place for young and old alike. The reddish pink flowers caressed the edges of the garden inviting weary passers-by to rest a while.

"What are those entrances to the cliff face do you think?" asked Chantrea.

"Ah, about three hundred years ago the owners of the cliff-top houses dug stairways down through the cliff to enable stuff from boats to be taken up to their house. These cliffs were the main defence for the town but it was a pain to have to go all the way round to the formal entrances to the town. So they dug their own entrances."

"Sounds like a tough job" replied Chantrea.

"Look we can't stay here all day or we will be late for lunch. Come on Chanie let's get going"

They began to walk down the gently inclined road past the Hotel De La Syrene with its peach coloured walls and palm lined gardens perched on top of the cliff edge. The old road wound its way gently towards the Marina Grande, the tarmacked road giving way to old flagstones and then even older cobbles. The road was leading down to a medieval gateway providing one entrance to the old Sorrento town from the Marina Grande. The road narrowed as the imposing stone walls of properties on either side seemed to press in on the visitor.

Turning steeply down a narrow roadway, Tenika and Chantrea approached the old entrance to the town walls. The old gatehouse, now without a gate, was just big enough for horse and cart and still providing a direct link to the old marina. The stonework still looked good although hundreds of years old. Now reinforced, the structure has the oddity of small terraced properties lining the wall and sitting on top of the gatehouse. It all looked so old in comparison with the modern Tasso Square that defines the heart of modern Sorrento.

As they walked down towards the gatehouse, Tenika and Chantrea passed an open door from which could be heard a woman singing.

Tenika sighed. "I just love it here. I know the top of town is a bit touristy but down here it seems so authentic, the old Sorrento seems to come to life. The walls, the houses squashed together and the wonderful old doors, shutters and tiny balconies."

Chantrea glanced across. "I'm so glad you're relaxed and happy. I'm glad you're away from the mess at home. We've got to keep this up, keep you happy and positive."

As they emerged from the gatehouse, they were greeted with striking sunlight as the full force of the sun glanced off the sea into their eyes. The old steps down to the marina had been replaced by newer easy to tread stones as the small world of the old fishing Marina Grande came into view. Set at the foot of the cliff, and in some places into it, this historic hamlet had its own history and traditions – and, of course its own church. But then Sorrento was full of churches.

Tenika and Chantrea could see the small bay was divided into two by a jetty. Furthest away, the marina had a large volume of small boats tied up at the water's edge with others moored at the outer marina wall. Nearer to them, the marina contained fewer small boats but the main emphasis was on receiving the small number of working fishing boats. Around the marina and set back against the cliff face were buildings ranging from two to five stories of different heights, designs and colours including pink, yellow and white.

The target of the walk came into view, the renowned Trattoria D'Emilia. As the steps wound their way down to the water's edge, the covered platform with wooden tables was visible. Set right on the water's edge of the marina, the main trattoria building was across a small roadway and set back against the cliff.

Tenika marched on purposefully, but then she often did.

"Come on, I love this place."

"What's so special?" replied Chantrea.

"It was opened in 1947 By Emilia and has been run by her family ever since. A strong woman and we sistas have to stick together!"

"And you are one strong sista" muttered Chantrea under her breath.

"I'll just check our reservation and our table."

"Buongiorno. Il mio nome è Tenika, ho una prenotazione con voi."

"Ah sì, questo è ok."

"Dov'è il nostro tavolo?"

"Ci si può sedere ovunque di fuori."

"OK, Chanie, we can sit anywhere outside on the platform on the right."

They positioned themselves to the far side of the platform and at the end of a long wooden table overlooking the extremity of the platform that extended into the shallows of the marina. Water lapped onto the legs of the platform making lapping and gurgling noises underneath them and the sun glistened sharply across the water. Alongside the platform, containing five rows of tables, covered with blue and white checked tablecloths, ran a small roadway leading to the end of the marina. At the end of it a fishing boat was tied up and fishermen, and a lone fisherwoman, were working with nets and doing a general tidy up.

The marina contained a variety of small boats and although this was once a major fishing marina, now a rather slower pace of life seemed to flow across the small community. There was a jetty that led out to the middle of the marina and it contained another restaurant perhaps signalling the changing economic times. The roadway ran from the side of the platform, behind it, past the main entrance to the trattoria and along the marina past the church, small shops and the hotchpotch of properties tied into the cliff. This was once a small self-contained community although now the roadway eventually led up to the main road running through Sorrento.

"Hello, some menus for you."

"Grazie"

"Well, Tee, what do you recommend?"

"I think I am going to have the fish platter with a green salad, some bread and wine."

"Mmm sounds good, I'll have the same."

The waitress returned and Tenika ordered.

"Possiamo avere entrambi il piatto di pesce, insalata verde e una caraffa di vino bianco?"

"Of course." Replied the waitress who clearly spoke English well.

"Oh, and a bottle of still water as well please." added Chantrea.

Chantrea turned back from the retreating waitress and gazed into Tenika's eyes.

"How are you feeling now about your mum?"

"It's not easy. I know people commit suicide for their own reasons and they probably feel they are good ones, but I just feel as if I have been abandoned. I can't shift this pain inside. But at least I am sleeping better."

"And what about your dad?" asked Chantrea in a faltering voice.

"Bastard."

Tenika looked across the marina, her eyes fixed on a point in the distance. She looked back at Chanie, her face stern and hard. Tenika's eyes narrowed.

"As far as I am concerned, it's his fault. Bloody abusing bastard. But don't worry Chanie I am not going to let it consume me. He's not going to do the same to me."

Chantrea reached across the table and held Tenika's hand.

"I am always going to be here for you, you know that."

Tenika looked up into Chantrea's eyes and smiled softly.

"Yes, I know. I don't know what I would have done without you. You are so sensible and calm and I can be so emotional and manic at times."

They gazed at each other with an intensity of care and unspoken understandings. Here was a bond between two women who both understood what it was to bear the pain of having lost a loved one.

"Anyway, here comes the food!"

Each had a large plate with a range of grilled fish and squid landed on the marina that morning. The fish was accompanied by a salad, bread, wine and water. The meal was rustic but splendidly authentic and both Tenika and Chantrea were hungry. Out of the corner of her eye, Chantrea spotted two men approaching them. They were speaking English.

"Mi scusi signore, é libero questo posto?"

"No, va tutto bene. Si può sedere." Responded Tenika with a smile.

"Ah, you ladies are English? So is my friend here."

"I suppose my rubbish accent gave it away?"

"No more than my attempt at the English accent." He said with a grin.

The waitress approached the two men with menus.

"Well I like the look of what the ladies have." Said the Englishman

"Then let us have the same – if you ladies don't mind?"

"Of course not, it's fantastic. I'm Tenika by the way and this is Chanie, well her proper name in Chantrea but I call her Chanie."

The tall dark haired Italian smiled at the waitress.

"Avremo il piatto di pesce, insalata, una birra e una bottiglia d'acqua per favore."

"HI, I'm Luke Adams and this is my friend Rafael Bellomi but he's called Raf by everyone. Where are you from? Are you here on holiday? Are you staying in Sorrento?"

"Yes, were here for a break and staying at Palazzo Abagnale just off Tasso Square. We come from South London although originally I came from Colliers Wood and Chanie here came from the leafy lanes of Chessington. We both live near to each other in Wimbledon. I have a two bed flat down a grotty road whilst Chanie has a rather nice one bed flat on a well to do road."

Chantrea laughed.

"How did you two meet?"

"We were at University together, at Guildford, and I got the job of keeping Tenika on the straight and narrow."

"And you did a good job of that!" laughed Tenika.

Tenika returned her gaze towards Luke's face. He was mid-thirties, average build but with a ruggedness to his face. His short light brown hair had little form to it, more functional than designer, and he had blue/grey eyes. His smile was broad and welcoming and that was something Tenika had noticed.

"And what about you two. Where are you from?"

"I am here on business and Raf is my contact here. He is based here in Sorrento and I live in Tonbridge but I work from an office in London."

"Where are you staying?" asked Chantrea.

"I'm at the Ambasciatori along Via Correale."

"Ah, I know that one, its rather nice sitting up on the cliff edge" said Tenika.

Tenika looked up to see the waitress approaching with food.

"Your food is here, we ought to leave you alone."

Tenika's statement had a tinge of disingenuousness to it but she need not have been concerned.

"Oh that's fine." Said Raf "It's good to talk to someone over lunch."

Tenika noticed that Luke was only drinking water.

"Keeping a clear head for all that business talk?"

"No, I'm on some pills at the moment and shouldn't drink any alcohol. And this is such a lovely place to sit and have a glass of wine. Anyway, Saluti." And the four raised their glasses together.

They chatted as they consumed their fish, bread and wine. Another carafe of wine found its way to the table and the discussion became more animated.

Luke was sat next to Tenika at the table. She was mixed race. Her mother was from Jamaica and married an English man in 1982. Tenika was born in 1984. Luke took in her dark shoulder length hair and piercing dark brown eyes along with her flawless skin. She spoke fast and wasn't afraid of interrupting the two men whom she had only just met. Chantrea, on the other hand, was more reserved waiting her turn for interjection. When it came, it was no less valuable as that from Tenika. Chantrea was a sharp and intelligent woman who came from a background where reserve was the order of the day. Chantrea's mother, Var, was a refugee from Cambodia. One of the intellectuals destined for a harsh life on a rural farm, she managed to survive starvation and torture and was rescued by the Red Cross in 1980. Her husband was not so lucky. He was murdered in April 1975 when Pol Pot's men took Phnom Penh. Perhaps Chantrea had learned from her mother's iron will that enabled her to accept a life of compliance on the farms in order to stay alive and wait patiently for more than four years for that moment when her life could begin again. Chantrea's soft Cambodian facial features were complemented by long brown hair that ran down her back and she seemed to have a constant smile on her face. She had slim features and a warm welcoming nature set against Tenika's often combative orientation. They were both dressed casually but very well and were clearly attentive to their personal presentation.

"So you're an architect?" asked Tenika.

"Yes, and we have a commission to design a special roof for a new building behind Via Degla Aranci. We are at an early stage and I come over fairly regularly to talk with Raf at Dynamo about how we are getting on and to talk specification and stuff. I must admit I don't need a lot of encouragement to come here."

"Do you enjoy your work?"

"Yes, love it. We do commissions around Europe and I love being involved in the overseas work. I love the travel and meeting people like Raf. I really enjoy what I do."

Tenika looked up and Raf and Chantrea were deep in conversation about the location of a restaurant. Her eyes returned to Luke's.

"So do you have any brothers or sisters?"

"Yes, I have one sister, Sasha. She is a teacher at a secondary school in Kent."

"So what about you Tenika, have you brothers or sisters?"

"Yes, two brothers, Claude and Jerome, both younger than me. Jerome works at a bank and Claude is in IT."

Tenika looked across the marina.

"God it's beautiful here. I've been here before and find it enchanting. I just love it."

"I know, Raf brings me here for lunch quite often when I come over. It is a beautiful place, once you've survived the journey from Naples airport!"

"I know, we used the bus. It's cheap but quite a journey. I bet you get a taxi or are collected."

Luke smiled at Tenika.

"Guilty as charged."

Tenika and Luke chatted endlessly about their impressions of Sorrento and where they thought the best places were to eat. Time passed quickly until they were interrupted by Raf.

"I am sorry to interrupt you two, but Luke and I will have to return to work.

"Ah yes Raf, look at the time. Look ladies, it's been a pleasure meeting you both but we shall have to go."

The four rose from their seats to exchange farewells and kisses on the cheek.

"Mmm I do like the European way of saying goodbye." Chantrea said with a huge grin on her face.

All four laughed at this and then Raf and Luke turned and made their way off the platform. Tenika and Chantrea watched as they walked to the restaurant entrance where Raf paid the bill and then on to a white Fiat car parked about 50 metres away. They got in and drove off away from them along the narrow marina driveway.

"Well that was an interesting lunch." Said Chantrea.

"Mmm certainly was" responded Tenika.

"Right let's get the bill."

Tenika gestured towards the waitress.

"Posso avere il conto per favore?"

With payment done, Tenika and Chantrea got up and began to wind their way back up the steps towards the old gatehouse.

"You were getting on well with Luke" said Chantrea to Tenika with a smile.

"Yes, a nice guy. What about you and Raf then?"

"A wife and two children I'm afraid."

"Ah"

"What about Luke?"

"Do you know, I didn't ask."

"A bit slow there then!"

Tenika and Chantrea giggled together as they made their way up the steep incline through the gatehouse towards Via Marina Grande and back towards the Piazza della Vittoria and the centre of town. After ten minutes of slow walking they arrived on the Via San Cesareo, a narrow pedestrianised road parallel with Corso Italia, the main road running through the centre of Sorrento. Via San Cesareo was lined with small shops selling a wide range of goods. Many of the shops had items outside on rails or tables reducing the passing space even more. Whilst many were now geared to the tourist, the road enabled the visitor to imagine what Sorrento was like one or two hundred years ago with narrow streets and a bustle of activity as people come and go buying their provisions. The intimacy of the experience with shopkeepers and fellow shoppers was clear.

Tenika and Chantrea wandered along the narrow passageway barely two metres wide, stopping to look in the shops and particularly the shops selling clothing, leather and jewellery. The old stone paving uneven due to wear over probably hundreds of years added to the sense of history and authenticity. But then Sorrento has been receiving visitors for hundreds of years. The British have made it a favourite destination for almost two hundred years as have literary figures and artists, and the Romans found their way to Sorrento two thousand years ago. If authenticity is perhaps a troublesome concept, the climate, topographical features and friendly Sorrentine culture seem to have been the constant over that long period.

Looking beyond the shop fronts, lights and goods to the architecture in which they stand can be found remnants of very old buildings. Sixteenth century door openings are visible as are ornately decorated balconies still intact after four hundred years. Some buildings still have their square atrium surviving with residential properties on all sides. The stone built buildings were meant to last and there had been a resistance to change. Patching them up has been preferred to knocking them down. That's not to say that Sorrento doesn't have its modern blocks of apartments, because it has. However, on the coastal side of Corso Italia much of the old Sorrento remains.

After what seemed like ages wandering in and out of the small shops, Chantrea realised she had become separated from

Tenika. She began to backtrack checking in shops along the way. Suddenly, she heard the unmistakable South London Italian accent of Tenika coming from a clothes shop.

"Per favore, è per la mia sorella a casa. Lei sarà così felice di ricevere questo."

Chantrea cringed at this old chestnut that Tenika has an ill sister and will be so happy to get a gift – at the right price! As Chantrea moved cautiously into the shop she heard the shop assistant give in.

"OK, Ok, twenty four Euro."

The assistant looked rather weary at the conclusion of the battle.

Chantrea moved up to the side of Tenika and whispered into her ear.

"I think she just wants to get you out of her shop and get on with her life."

Tenika smiled back as they stepped out of the shop.

"They expect it. It's a game. You've just got to be strong and assertive."

"So how much discount did you get in the end?"

"Six Euro. The starting price was thirty Euro and I got it for twenty four."

"You do have some front, you know. I can't hold my nerve like you do. I find it embarrassing."

"Ha-ha Chanie, you just get them to open the door and then stick your foot in it. You must look them hard in the eyes though. They mustn't see any weakness in you or they will stick with their original price."

Tenika and Chantrea wandered back towards Tasso Square and Tenika quizzed Chantrea.

"What shall we do? A coffee in Fauno Bar or back to the hotel?"

"Let's go back to the hotel, I need the loo!"

They emerged from the shaded narrow street into a corner of Tasso square next to the small Ercolano Bar still busy serving coffees and pastries to an eclectic mix of patrons. Passing a couple of shops and the Syranuse restaurant and bar, Tenika and Chantrea came to the imposing gorge which marked the northern boundary to the town for hundreds of years. Corso Italia now crosses the gorge and Chantrea's pace was quickening as her need became greater. Thankfully, the Palazzo Abagnale was only one hundred metres or so along the main road and situated above a Giorgio Armani shop. The stylish building, fitting for the contents of the store, was washed in a warm yellow colour with metallic balconies for every room. Chantrea quickly climbed the stairs to reception where Adriana, the receptionist, greeted them in the usual friendly manner. Then on into the lift and up to the top floor where their 'black and white' room awaited them and for Chantrea it couldn't come soon enough!

The Palazzo Abagnale was a stylish small boutique hotel attracting mainly younger guests from around Europe who were looking for modern design and colour at a reasonable price just a hundred metres from Tasso Square. The two floors having bedrooms had different styles. On the first floor, contemporary lighting and furnishings provided rooms bathed in red, blue and orange whilst the top floor provided rooms with a black and white scheme. Pop art was in abundance on the first floor whilst large black and white pictures of Marilyn Monroe were very visible on the top floor.

Tenika and Chantrea shared a large room with black floor tiling, two single beds each with a large black patterned headboard and a huge white leather sofa. A very clean and stylish black and white ensuite bathroom provided a feel of luxury. Perhaps a key feature for the clientele was the provision of a computer in all rooms and free access to the internet. The double opening doors to the balcony had traditional shutters and fine curtains. Each balcony with its finely designed metal frame was compact yet big enough to sit out on. Both Tenika and Chantrea liked to sit out on the balcony and watch the Sorrentian world go by on the street below as they chatted, laughed and cried.

"What are we going to do this evening?"

Chantrea looked up and laughed.

"I know what you would like to do and that's have dinner with Luke!"

"Well he didn't ask and didn't give his number."

"Well, you know he is at the Ambasciatori" said Chantrea with a wry smile.

"Perhaps, but we came together and we shall stay together. What about taking in the atmosphere at the Fauno Bar tonight?"

21

"Mmm sounds good to me but we had better get there early as it looks like it's the kind of place lots of people want to go to."

Tenika and Chantrea settled down to write some postcards bought earlier in the day. The noise and chatter from the street below subsided as the late afternoon wore on. In Sorrento, this is the lull before the evening awakens and the streets become alive again.

At 7.30 pm Tenika and Chantrea were ready for their evening's entertainment. Tenika was wearing a sleeveless green and orange dress. The colours blending with her silky Jamaican heritage skin tone. She wore matching set of cream coloured necklace and earrings. Her hair, straightened, followed the contours of her face and softly curled into her neckline. Her outfit was completed by white thin strapped sandals. Chantrea was in white. She wore white skinny trousers and a fine white lace top. Her South East Asian skin tone was much lighter than Tenika's and was complemented by a necklace with a silver cross and stud earrings that looked like diamonds although they weren't.

The September evening air was still warm. Tenika chose not to wear a cardigan whilst Chantrea took her white shrug. The walk to the Fauno bar only took a few minutes. Tasso Square was already lively and would become livelier. Chantrea spoke to the smartly dressed waiter with his crisp white shirt and black trousers standing on the street and the two women were ushered to a table in the covered outside area two rows back from the street front.

Fauno bar was quickly filling with a cosmopolitan range of people. It was the time for the locals to dress up and demonstrate their style. Sorrento was not a place for the scruffy.

Tenika turned to Chantrea.

"You know, what I like about this place is that women of all ages seem to have such style. Their clothes are so well tailored. They look so good."

"I know what you mean. The shops here are full of stylish stuff. There's a hint of Paris here ...... the style, the elegance and swagger. I hope I look as good as some of these women when I am their age."

"Oh don't worry Chanie, you will look every bit as good."

"Buona sera signore, good evening. Would you like a menu and perhaps a drink?"

The handsome waiter, about forty years of age, with smartly styled jet black hair smiled at Tenika and Chantrea.

Tenika beamed back.

"Sì, i menu per favore."

"Of course, and to drink?"

"A bottle of white wine, Chanie?"

"Mm yes."

"Ok, una bottiglia di vino bianco secco e una bottiglia di acqua naturale prego."

"Thank you, and your Italian is very good! I will be back for your order in a moment."

"What are you going to have Chanie?"

"I think I might have the chicken pasta dish, what about you?"

"Mm, I'm going for the bass and a salad."

With their meals ordered and drinks arrived, they began to take in the surroundings. It was now about eight o'clock and the bar was practically full. There was a buzz about the place as chatter mingled with the sounds of glasses and cutlery on plates.

The square was alive with people moving this way and that. The shops in Sorrento stay open at this time of year until at least 8.oo pm and people throng the square and streets to see and be seen.

The light had faded and the square was lit by an array of lighting from many sources. The buildings surrounding the square were illuminated revealing the texture and form of beautiful traditional architecture. To the left of the Fauno Bar was the statue of Torquato Tasso, a major sixteenth century poet who was born in Sorrento in 1544. He was largely forgotten in Sorrento at the time because he left Sorrento as a child to be with his father to live and work in Rome, Ferreira and elsewhere. He was brought back into Sorrentian thinking in the nineteenth century as Italy went through its unification process and towns such as Sorrento looked for icons around which its community could focus. For Sorrento, it was Torquato Tasso.

Running south out of the square was Corso Italia, a road containing smart shops, cafes, restaurants and the Sorrento Cathedral. Corso Italia is the boundary of much of what survives of the old town, the entrance to which lies diagonally across from the Fauno Bar along Via San Cesareo.

The buildings on the far side of the square were majestic in their architecture. Although built at different times, there had been an attempt to retain traditional styles. Using hues of brown, pink, cream and yellow to adorn the walls, the buildings were dressed with beautiful window shutters, artistically shaped iron balconies and colourful flower boxes.

Almost immediately opposite the bar was the gorge that provided an effective boundary to the old town against those travelling south from Naples. Now served by steps, a road and a rather hilarious white road train used by tourists, access to the Marina Piccola is granted from which ferries and jet boats can be taken to Naples, Capri and the other outlying islands.

Further to the right is the Chiesa Del Carmine, a sixteenth century church built to commemorate early Christian martyrs. When first built, it was on the northern side of the gorge and, therefore, outside the town. When the fortress walls were removed at this point and the community expanded around Tasso Square, the church found its way into the heart of Sorrento. To the front of the church, and in the road at the point where Corso Italia enters the square, is a statue of Saint Antonino Abbate, the patron saint of Sorrento.

Further to the right, is Corso Italia as it makes its way towards the next commune of Sant Agnello. More shops, amenities, the train station and police could be found along this route.

To the immediate right of the bar is Via Fuorimura that runs over the course of the gorge. The road rises to a gate house bridge that would have given one entry point to the old town through the massive town walls. Today, much of the walls on the eastern side

25

of the town are still intact and the old bridge crosses the gorge above the valley of the mills. More than five hundred years ago flour mills were built in the gorge to take advantage of the water cascading down to the sea. Their remains are still there as a haunting reminder of a long lost past.

Tenika and Chantrea absorbed the hustle and bustle of Tasso Square as people wandered in all directions. Traffic stopped and started as people crossed the square, often not bothering to take a look at oncoming traffic confident in the knowledge that the Sorrentian drivers will always give way. And then there were the motor scooters. Their noise was a constant from the moment the day begins to when it ends. The evening brings them out in their hundreds as their young and more mature owners tumble onto the streets to mingle with friends.

Chantrea looked up at Tenika.

"Have your brothers said anything about your mum recently?"

"Not a lot. I think they have found it every bit as difficult as I have. Jerome has been a sweetie. He always wants to know how I am. I think he feels guilty that I found mum hanging from the stairs and wishes it had been him. Mind you, we all feel the guilt of thinking we could or should have done more or done something that could have stopped her."

Tenika stared down at her plate, her eyes filling with tears.

"I can't help feeling guilty that I didn't stand up to dad more. The abuse went on for years but I never thought it would come to this. I knew things had got worse but mum didn't want me to worry. Whenever I went home she always reassured me that things were ok."

"My mum feels guilt that she was not able to prevent Sengkong from being murdered in Phnom Penh in seventy five. She has carried that with her for the last thirty eight years."

"Didn't her marriage to your dad ease the pain?"

"Yes, I think so for a while, but I am not sure her marriage was any more than a grateful gesture for being rescued. When dad was posted by the Foreign Office to New Zealand, mum didn't want to move again. She needed, or rather craved for stability, and once he had gone a lot of her old feelings returned. I can't imagine what she was put through in those four years on the farms. All I know is that it was brutal and she was scarred for life.

"I am so proud of you Chanie, the way you have supported her and absorbed some or her pain."

"Sometimes I think it's my duty or the role I was born into. It's why I am here. I can't express my anger in the in the ways you do Tee, I sometimes wish I could, but I have to manage it, organise it, file it and too often cry over it."

Tenika took a tissue from her handbag.

"God, we are a pair aren't we! I think we need more wine."

Tenika wiped her eyes and looked up towards the waiters, but the bar was now very busy. Food and drink was moving in all directions and there was a queue of people waiting for a table.

"No-one is noticing us. This calls for direct action."

And with that Tenika stood and walked purposefully over to the waiter who had smiled so charmingly when taking their order. She took him by his arm and he turned with a furrowed brow. Here was a man with many orders to deal with and no time for distractions. Tenika held onto his arm and her other hand reached up and held his. She gazed deeply into his eyes and began to talk to him. He glanced across to Chantrea and his body changed shape to a softer form. He nodded and said OK, and Tenika smiled broadly and gave him a kiss on the cheek.

Tenika returned to her seat.

"What did you say to him? Why did he look at me?"

"I told him you had recently lost your father and that you are very miserable I needed him to help me help you. He couldn't resist coming to your rescue and I think to mine."

"What? You are incorrigible! I haven't just lost my father."

"Well you did."

"Yes, but that was over twenty years ago!"

"Well you had better look miserable because our drinks are arriving."

The waiter arrived and placed a glass of wine in front of Chantrea.

"Signora, I hope you will feel better."

Chantrea looked up at the waiter and thanked him with a tissue held close to her face.

The waiter placed a bottle of wine in front of Tenika and smiled. Tenika smiled back and touched his hand.

"Grazie."

The waiter turned away and the two women looked at each other both holding back a smile but their eyes said it all.

Suddenly music began to play and a trio of musicians had come into the outside seating area and began playing. One middle aged chap with a fine moustache played an accordion, a tall elegant man played an acoustic guitar and a third chap wearing a bright red waist coat played a double bass. All three sang although the guitar player took the lead. With them was a woman, perhaps in her early forties, who wore a stunning white sleeveless dress that hugged her figure. Her job was to entice the customers to part with their cash.

The musicians were very good, and regulars to the Fauno, and they quickly got the patrons involved. Clapping along became the communal involvement and Tenika and Chantrea were only too happy to involve themselves too.

The musicians fifteen minute performance end with raucous cheering and applause followed by the woman in the white dress swiftly moving about the diners with a small red lined oval shaped wicker box into which coins and notes were eagerly placed. This was a regular ritual and diners and drinkers alike happily contributed.

"What do you reckon Chanie, two or three Euros?"

"Sounds Ok to me."

The woman in which approached Chantrea who put the coins into the box.

"Grazie" said the woman and smiled at Chantrea.

"Adoro il tuo vestito" said Tenika.

"I ragazzi non mi possono perdere quando indosso questa!" replied the woman smiling broadly at Tenika.

Chantrea looked at Tenika.

"I didn't quite get that."

"She said that the guys can't lose her amongst the crowds when she wears the white dress."

The three musicians and the woman in white left the Fauno and calm returned.

"You know, what I like about this place is that we are not the only women on their own at a table and we have not had any hassle from anyone."

Tenika smiled.

"Yes, but I could have done with some entertainment tonight. Might have kept us off the morbid stuff."

"Perhaps" said Chantrea. "Tomorrow evening we could try the bar along Corso Italia where the guy stands at the doorway playing the sax."

"Sounds good to me."

The evening wore on and then the patrons began to drift away. The Sorrentians had walked up and down, drank and eaten, talked and laughed. Tenika and Chantrea paid their bill, thanked their charming waiter and began the short walk back to their hotel. Tasso Square was still busy with people and the sounds of cars and scooters. The taxi drivers parked up next to Fauno were keen to find some income from weary tourists finding their way back to their hotels. One driver shouted at Tenika and Chantrea and gestured towards his white Mercedes seven seater taxi. Chantrea smiled but shook her head.

"You've got to have deep pockets if you're getting into one of those" said Tenika.

"Yes, but these guys have to make their money during the tourist season. There aren't many tourists here in winter."

"God, you're so reasonable Chanie!"

"So what are we doing tomorrow? Pompeii, Capri, Positano?"

Chantrea laughed.

"Well, I was thinking of going to the museum along Via Correale. I've been checking up and it has a range of artefacts and art from Roman to near present day."

"So be it Chanie. We shall have some culture."

DAY TWO

The next day began as the last did with an almost clear blue sky and a warm breeze. Their room at Palazzo Abagnale overlooked the Corso Italia, the main road running through Sorrento. There was a gradual build up of traffic and the particular sound of scooters which were found on almost all roads all of the time. Chantrea opened the double doors leading to a balcony and sat outside. She liked to watch the early morning inhabitants make their way to work and the travellers walking to and from the train station. She found it amusing how the travellers so often stood out from the locals by what they wore and even at this time of year, in September, there were still plenty of shorts on show.

"Are we in for breakfast or out today?" asked Tenika.

"Mmm let's try out" responded Chantrea.

They quickly assembled their belongings needed for the day and headed down the lift to reception where they stopped and exchanged pleasantries with Adriana the receptionist and then down the stairs to the front door. They turned right heading past the Armani Shop towards Tasso Square.

"We must go in and have a look round the Armani shop at some point."

"Tee, have you noticed there are no prices on anything and there is not a huge amount of stock in there. That can only mean one thing, each item is very expensive!"

"But we're worth it" retorted Tenika.

Both women laughed as they approached the square. It was now just after nine in the morning and the square was already quite busy.

"Where shall we go?" asked Tenika.

"Why don't we try the Ercolano place over there?"

They walked round the square on the coastal side past the white road train waiting for its first group of tourists wanting a trip round the town centre and down to Marina Piccola. Straight ahead of them on the far side of the square was the Ercolano, a mix of bar and cafe but one that was clearly in favour by the locals. This seemed, on the face of it, to be a cheap man's Fauno bar found on the other side of the square from the Fauno. The cafe was smaller and had much simpler structure and fixtures than the Fauno but no less attention to customers from the waiters. Its menu was also more restricted than that of the Fauno being more of a café than a restaurant. For the purposes of breakfast, however, it met their needs.

Both women chose to have cappuccino and pastries. This was not the healthiest of choices but then they were on holiday and normal rules had been put aside. The Sorrentians seemed to spend half their lives in cafe bars talking to each other or just watching the world go by. For Tenika and Chantrea this was a welcome change to normal daily life in London. They both welcomed the slower pace and a chance to relax and take a slow breakfast and not feel guilty about it. For Tenika this was her first opportunity to get away from London after the tragic events surrounding her mother's suicide. Chantrea had been encouraging her for some time to take a break and get away from the sights and sounds that reminded her so vividly of what she had lost.

Chantrea had felt quite triumphant when they finally booked for fourteen days. Tenika had been insisting she couldn't be away for long citing all sorts of reasons for not doing so. Chantrea had picked off the reasons one by one until Tenika finally conceded her concerns were a form of guilt for her going on a holiday whilst her mother was recently buried.

Tenika and Chantrea sat and chatted for over an hour. They covered a range of subjects from the previous day's lunch to buying presents, work issues back in London and, of course, the weather. As they looked around they could see other young women just like themselves having coffee and relaxing in the warm early autumn sun. Some were tourists whilst others were local.

"You know Tee, I could get used to this. It's such a pleasant way to start a day."

"Yes, although we wouldn't get much work done."

"Well we would just have to do it their way and spread the effort out over the day."

They both laughed and Chantrea thought how good it was to see Tenika laugh after seeing her cry so much recently. They called the waiter over and paid for the breakfast and then began the relatively short journey to the museum. They walked back across the square and turned left on to Via Correale. This took them past the underground car park and cliff top hotels to its junction with Via Califano where the museum was located. Established by Count Alfredo Correale, the collection of art was assembled in a large four floor building having extensive gardens. The items were arranged in chronological order starting with bits of Roman pillar in the garden to nineteenth century paintings and artefacts on the top floor. What caught Chantrea's eye were the seventeenth century paintings of Sorrento showing the bridge over the gorge enabling entry to the town. The colour and detail of the paintings brought home the modest hamlet that existed before proper roads linked Sorrento to the north. She liked its depiction of the romanticism of a bygone age.

They took their time wandering around the large building sometimes together, other times apart. There weren't many other people in the museum so they could sit or stand and look at whatever they wanted for as long as they wanted.

"Chanie, the leaflet says there is a pathway to a terrace overlooking the bay. Shall we take a look?"

"Yes Tee, let's do it."

They came out of the building at ground floor level and entered the garden where a narrow pathway ran from the main house. It sloped gently downward and lying by the side of the path were broken Roman pillars. The path continued through orange trees and the ground around the trees was covered with fallen oranges some of which were well on their way to a rotten state. At the end of what seemed a long pathway, there was a sharp left hand turn and the path descended down to a tunnel, running underneath a road, through which they could see the sea far beyond.

They walked down and into the tunnel and, as they emerged from it, they were hit by the strength of the light being reflected off the sea. Ahead of them was a tiled terrace with open views across the bay of Naples. They headed straight for the railings and took in the magnificent view.

"This is stunning" said Chantrea.

"Mmmm and quite a sun trap too" said Tenika.

They looked across the bay to Vesuvius rising majestically with just a whiff of cloud over its summit. The air was clear, giving good views of Naples, Ischia and the tip of Capri. A warm light wind caressed their faces and Chantrea closed her eyes and took a long deep breath. Tenika, however, was taking in the wider surroundings

"Just a minute, aren't we in the gardens of the Ambasciatori?"

Tenika was looking to her right and could see delightful gardens, a dining area and behind which sat an imposing hotel.

"Are you sure? asked Chantrea.

"Well, it's the only one along here that has this extent of garden. I'll go and ask."

Tenika walked along a pathway and up to a raised platform where she spoke for a few moments with a waiter clearing a table. Then she waived at Chantrea to join her.

"I'm right, this is the Ambasciatori and it's ok for us to be here. I've said we'll have a drink. I also asked if he knew Luke but he said not."

Tenika and Chantrea sat at a table to the side of the dining area which itself was next to a swimming pool. The area was shaded by palms, pine trees, hibiscus with pink flowers, bougainvillea showered with deep purple flowers and plumbago adorned light blue flowers giving colour and texture to the grounds. Their position gave full views across the bay enabling them to watch the range of small craft working their way in different directions across the water. The waiter returned with two orange juice drinks.

As they looked out across the shimmering bay their thoughts wandered back to the lunch at Emilia's and the relaxed discussion had by all.

"I wouldn't mind another lunch like that" said Tenika.

"Yes, I am sure you would" smiled Chantrea.

"A bit of a shame really, here we are at the Ambasciatori and Luke is probably somewhere else with Raf."

Chantrea looked around at the extent of the grounds.

"It's really nice here and I expect very expensive."

"Well a lot more expensive that we pay at the Palazzo Abagnale but then we don't get these views or the grounds."

Chantrea walked over to the nearby railings at the edge of the cliff and looked down.

"Gosh it's a long way down and I think they have their own sea water pool as well. There are a few people down there. I wonder if they have their own secret staircase leading down to the sea?"

Tenika and Chantrea finished their drinks and wandered over to the bar area to pay. There were two male staff on duty, again wearing white shirts and black trousers, who looked after the outdoor dining area. Chantrea thought they were both in their forties but very welcoming and happy to talk. Chantrea took the opportunity to ask whether the hotel had its own secret steps.

"Well there used to be steps but now we have a lift. It makes things much easier. If you go to the end of the garden area where it curves round you can still see some of the old steps sitting against the cliff face."

"Mmm well, I think a lift is my kind of technology" smiled Chantrea.

They paid for their drinks and walked slowly past the empty pool towards the double doors leading into the hotel main public area.

"Wow, this is nice" exclaimed Chantrea.

The public area had a beautiful marble floor and exquisite furnishings. Double-doors to their left led off to an extensive dining room whilst straight ahead was a piano bar. To their right were steps rising to reception and the main hotel doors.

As they approached reception, Tenika moved directly towards a receptionist.

"Buongiorno, sapete se Mr Luke Adams è in albergo?"

"No, non possiamo dire nulla di lui."

"OK, grazie."

"What did he say?"

"I just asked if Luke was in the hotel but he just said he couldn't say anything about him."

"Perhaps he slipped out without telling them?"

"I don't know, well never mind. Let's go."

They passed through the revolving door, turned right and walked along Via Califano, until it reached Via Correale, where they turned right again and walked slowly back to Tasso Square. When they reached Corso Italia they turned left and walked past their hotel in the direction of the train station. They just wandered along looking at the shops and the people.

"It's fascinating Tee, that nearly all the shops are relatively small. There are very few large departmental stores as we have at home. I am sure they will have them, perhaps in the big cities, but I think it adds to the charm of the place. They each have their own distinctive character and presentation."

"Yes Chanie, and they've got everything from the very expensive to everyday prices. They have a lot of expensive clothes shops selling gorgeous stuff but I wonder where do those people go who perhaps don't have the money. Where's the equivalent of Primark?"

"And I am so glad to be somewhere that doesn't have a McDonalds."

"I'm in agreement with you there Chanie."

They wandered up and down the road lined with orange trees stopping off and looking inside and outside of shops.

Eventually, they worked their way back to the hotel and decided it was time for a rest and a visit to the bathroom!

They spent their afternoon looking at guides to Sorrento and chatting about what they might do. Although their aim in coming to Sorrento was to find time to relax and unwind, they both had active minds that needed feeding. Consequently, they both needed intellectual stimulation and both loved exploring other cultures. They looked at the programme for the Tasso Theatre but not much was on whilst they were in town. There was the cinema, a few museums and a host of churches to look at. They considered going further afield perhaps to Amalfi and Positano or off to Pompeii. Tenika fancied getting the ferry or hydrofoil across to Naples, an idea that Chantrea whole heartedly supported. Although in London they were never far away from traditional Caribbean and Cambodian cuisine, they loved to sample food from other cultures. So they spent a lot of time considering where to eat and what they wanted to try. They were keen to eat where the local people dined and for that they would seek the help of Adriana, the receptionist at their hotel, to find new places that might have been established.

Later that evening they had dinner at the Pizzeria Restaurant on Via Francesco only five minutes from Tasso Square. The restaurant's origins were probably as a pizzeria but now offered a much wider range of food for the traveller and local alike. The restaurant had a lot of local people in and Tenika and Chantrea could see that the pricing was very modest compared with some restaurants in Sorrento. They were greeted by a smiling waiter much older than those found on Tasso Square but who was no less charming. Indeed, it seemed that all the male waiters had been on a special charm course to woo the customer into sitting down and parting with their money. To get to the main seating area they had to pass the deserts sitting on tables either side of a narrow walkway. They looked divine and both Tenika and Chantrea were seduced immediately by the look of them.

Tenika ordered a chicken dish whilst Chantrea had sea bass. It wasn't long before Tenika was chatting to the waiters. She loved to use her Italian whenever possible and would try it out on anyone who would listen. There was a delightful ambiance in the restaurant. Diners were chatting, smiling and laughing whilst the waiters were deftly bringing more wine and food as the budget strings eased. For Tenika and Chantrea the highlight of the evening came with the choice of desert. They both giggled their way through the decision making process and chocolate featured heavily in both final decisions. At the end of their enjoyable evening they said goodbye to the waiters and left the restaurant to be greeted by a dark evening with a cool breeze.

They turned left out of the restaurant and walked past the Tasso theatre and Basilica Di San Antonio. They then followed the narrow road up to Tasso Square where they turned left towards their hotel on Corso Italia. The Square still had many people in it drinking and enjoying a late meal. They wandered back to the Palazzo Abagnale, went through the front door and up the stairs to reception. As always there was a smiling receptionist always keen to know what the visitors had been up to and what they thought of Sorrento. It was then into the lift and up to their room where Tenika and Chantrea settled in for late evening relaxation.

"I think I will have a look at the Positano News online service. It might give details of what's on and it has English and Italian versions so I should get everything."

41

As Tenika settled down at the computer, Chantrea was busy sending a message on her mobile phone. The silence only lasted a few minutes.

"Oh my God" Tenika exclaimed.

"What is it?"

"I'm looking at the Sorrento notices on the Positano News, and it says that a body was found early this morning at the foot of the cliffs near the Hotel Corallo at Sant Agnello. Police believe the body is that of visiting English businessman Luke Adams. This is not the first time visitors to Sorrento have fallen to their deaths after a night out."

The two women stared at each other in complete silence until Tenika broke it.

"I don't understand, what was he doing out there? Oh, for Christ's sake that's awful!"

Tears welled up in Tenika's eyes. She had not realised how Luke had got under her skin even though it was a chance encounter of just a couple of hours. Chantrea crossed the room took Tenika from the chair at the computer, sat her down on the sofa and then sat at the computer and looked at the screen. She clicked onto the English version of the story.

"I can't believe this, it's absurd" said Chantrea.

The two women looked at each other in shock.

"But tee, we were sitting next to him yesterday and having a wonderful chat with him and Raf. I find it so difficult to think that he is now dead."

Chantrea could see that Tenika was still struggling to contain her emotions and sat down next to her on the sofa. She took Tenika's hands into hers, an act Chantrea had learned from her mother and aunt. Although she couldn't think of much to say that would be helpful, her mother, Var, believed that taking someone's hands into yours was a way of sharing that person's troubles. She had done this to Tenika many times before, particularly when her mother died, and she knew that for whatever reason Tenika was appreciative of the act and understood its symbolic meaning as much as the physical warmth it brought.

Tenika sat shaking her head as if in disbelief. Then she squeezed Chantrea's hands and looked defiantly at her.

"First thing tomorrow we are going to the Police. I want to know what happened."

"Are they going to talk to us?"

"I don't know. We saw him only hours before his death so we might have something to contribute. Anyway I want to know how he died and why."

"Well Tee, whoever is in charge might not be keen to tell you."

"Then I'll be a right nuisance until the individual does."

"Mmmm, yes, I have a suspicion you might just do that."

43

DAY THREE

The next morning, Tenika and Chantrea were still shocked by the previous evening's news. There wasn't much discussion between them as both had their minds on what might have happened and why. Breakfast was rather a quiet affair too as a veil of seriousness covered them both. Chantrea queried whether the police would talk to them. Tenika was in a rather confrontational mood. She felt the police had to talk to them as they have spoken with him only the day before.

They left the hotel just after nine o'clock and walked the short distance along Corso Italia to the Carabinieri police station on Via Boartolomeo Capasso. Tenika walked first into the rather ordinary building and towards a reception desk.

"What are you going to say?" asked Chantrea.

"That I want to talk to whoever is dealing with Luke's death."

Tenika stood in front of the reception desk and looked at the officer who was writing something on a form.

"Buongiorno, vorrei parlare con qualcuno sul corpo trovato ieri - Luke Adams."

The officer looked up with an expressionless face.

"Buongiorno signorina, vuole confessare?"

"Excuse me?" said Tenika

Tenika's voice was firm and her face expressed annoyance.

The policeman smiled.

"OK, a joke, what is it you want?"

"I want to talk to whoever is in charge of the death of Luke Adams."

"And what is it you want to talk about?"

"We want to know what happened to him. We were with him the other day and he seemed fine."

"What are your names?"

"Tenika Taylor and Chanie Park."

"Please sit and I will see if there is anyone who will talk to you."

The officer picked up the telephone.

"Ciao, ho due donne inglesi qui che vogliono parlare al Soprintendente circa l'uomo inglese trovato in fondo alla scogliera............. Ok."

The officer put the phone down but didn't look up. Tenika got to her feet and moved towards the officer.

"Beh, qualcuno sta andando a parlare con noi o no?"

Her voice was very firm and she looked sternly into the officer's face.

"Yes, yes, someone will come. Now sit down please."

A few minutes later a side door opened and a tall man in a dark suit entered the reception area. He looked towards Tenika and Chantrea and they both stood up.

"Buongiorno signore."

"Buongiorno" replied Tenika.

"You are English?"

"Yes, who are you?" replied Tenika

"I am Inspector Pietro Maldini."

"Are you in charge of finding out what happened to Luke Adams?"

"No, that is my Superintendant but he is not here now. Did you know Mr Adams?"

"We met him two days ago at Emilia's in Marina Grande."

"And did you see him the evening before last?"

"No."

"Then I am not sure you can help us."

"Well, to be honest, I was hoping you could help us. Can you tell us how he died?"

"No, no I cannot say anything at the moment. His sister is coming later today to view the body. We are still investigating. Please leave it to us."

Tenika could feel the frustration rising in her body. She felt she was being fobbed off.

"Do you know where his sister will be staying?"

"The Grand Hotel Ambasciatori but please do respect her loss. Now, I have much to do. Thank you for coming. Ciao."

Chantrea could feel Tenika bristling with frustration at the Inspector's reply. Chantrea moved forward and took Tenika's arm.

"Tee, I think we have gone as far as we can go here."

Tenika looked at Chantrea. Her eyes were narrowed, displaying her annoyance. She held her gaze for some seconds and then let out a breath.

"Ok Chanie."

Tenika turned to Inspector Maldini.

"Grazie Ispettore."

He nodded and turned away. Moments later he was through the door and gone.

Tenika and Chantrea walked out of the police station and into the bright sunlight.

"Chanie, can you remember the name of the company Raf worked for?"

"Didn't he say Dynamo?"

"Yes, I think he did. I wonder if that is the full name or just part of it? Well done Chanie, you're a star."

"Why do I feel our next step is going to be to track Raf down?"

"Spot on Chanie."

"So how do we go about that?"

"I have an idea Chanie."

The two women walked up to Corso Italia and then down to Tasso Square.

Tenika looked across to Chantrea.

"It's time to talk to the taxi guys."

Tenika approached the taxi driver at the head of the line of taxis next to the Fauno.

"Ciao, sai di una società di architetti chiamati Dynamo qui a Sorrento?

"No, mi dispiace."

"Ok."

Tenika looked to Chantrea and told her they didn't know of Dynamo. She moved on to three drivers chatting together and asked the same question. One immediately shook his head but the smallest of the three nodded.

"Sì, lo so. Si chiama Dynamo Progettazione. Si trova a circa mezzo chilometro di distanza. Mia nipote lavora lì."

Tenika turned to Chantrea.

"He says it's called Dynamo Design and it's about a kilometre away. His niece works there."

"I take you there?" asked the smiling driver.

Tenika turned to the drivers, her face hardened, voice shortened and finger pointed.

"Stai cercando di ingannare me perché io sono un visitatore?"

Her fierceness shocked the drivers who all moved backwards. The driver held up his hands as if to surrender.

"No, No, signora. I am honest. I will take you the quick way."

"And no more than ten Euro" demanded Tenika.

"Ok, ok."

Tenika and Chantrea climbed into the white taxi and it swung round and drove inland along Via Fuorimura.

"You can be really scary at times."

"Sometimes it's needed" replied Tenika.

The taxi drove for about five minutes to the outskirts of the eastern edge of the town and stopped outside a redbrick four storey building.

"This is it" said the driver.

Tenika turned to Chanie and whispered to her.

"Chanie, can you check this is the place whilst I take my time to pay him?"

Chanie got out of the taxi and went up to the glass entrance door. On the wall was a panel with names and buttons. She scanned down the names and found Dynamo Progettazione. She turned to Tenika.

"It's ok, it's here."

Tenika paid the driver and walked up to the door. Chantrea pressed the buzzer and a few moments later a female voice crackled out of the speaker.

"Buongiorno."

Tenika moved forward.

"Ah, buongiorno ho una consegna per voi."

"We have a delivery for them?" smiled Chantrea.

The door buzzed and Chantrea pushed it open. On the wall was a list of companies and Dynamo Progettazione was listed as being on the second floor. They took the stairs and arrived at double doors leading to the reception area. An elegantly dressed woman in her early forties smiled at them.

"Buongiorno."

"Buongiorno. E 'possibile parlare con Rafael che ha lavorato con Luke Adams?"

The mention of Luke Adams immediately raised some suspicion with the receptionist. His death had clearly been the talk of the company.

"You are English?"

"Yes."

"Are you journalists?"

"No, no, we are friends of Raf. We just want a quick word with him."

"I thought you had a delivery."

"I am sorry, my Italian isn't very good perhaps I got the wrong words."

The woman was not impressed and frowned at Tenika and Chantrea.

"What are your names?"

"If you tell him that Tenika and Chanie need to talk to him. He will know us."

The woman picked up a white phone and dialled.

"Ah Rafael, ho due donne in ricezione, umm Tenika e Chanie, che vogliono parlare con te. Li conosci? L'sono qui circa l'inglese."

Tenika whispered to Chantrea.

"She's asking him if he knows us and is saying it's about Luke."

51

The receptionist stared down at her desk. Then put the phone down. She looked up at the women but didn't smile.

"He is coming down. Please take a seat."

The reception area had a black marble floor, white walls and the corner sofa Tenika and Chantrea were sitting on was a bright red. The walls had pictures of buildings which they assumed were examples of design work completed by the company. Behind the receptionist was a large colour picture of a bridge. On one wall was a set of pictures showing staff and their names. Chantrea noticed Raf among the pictures. In the opposite corner to where Tenika and Chantrea were sitting there was a corridor that led off from the reception area.

"Not my colour scheme" whispered Tenika.

Chantrea smiled.

"The black and white is a bit like our room at the hotel."

Tenika smiled back.

Suddenly Raf emerged from the corridor. He smiled and held out his hand. Tenika and Chantrea stood up and shook his hand. Raf's smile faded and a more serious look appeared across his face.

"We are sorry to trouble you but we need to talk to you about Luke."

Raf ushered them back to the sofa. They all sat down with Raf sitting on an edge of the sofa with his back to the receptionist. He spoke in hushed tones.

"Look this is not a good time at the moment. Can I meet you a little later? About three o'clock?"

"Of course" said Tenika.

"Meet me at Antonio Cafiero's gelateria and café on Corso Italia. You can't miss it, there is a large ice cream cone outside and there are photos of cakes made by the owner in the window. Go through into the back of the coffee house, down the stairs and I will meet you there at three."

"Ok, we will see you then. Oh and can you get us a taxi back to Tasso Square?"

"Of course."

They all stood up and Raf turned to the receptionist.

"Si può prendere un taxi per le signore per favore. Vogliono andare a Piazza Tasso."

The receptionist nodded but didn't smile.

"Ok, the taxi will come in a few minutes and I will see you later. Bye"

With that, Raf turned and walked out of the reception area. Tenika and Chantrea thanked the receptionist, went through the entrance door and down the stairs. They waited outside the building and within a couple of minutes a taxi arrived to transport them back to Tasso Square. As they relaxed back in the taxi, Chantrea looked at Tenika.

"Well what did you think of that?"

"Well, it has obviously shaken them and the receptionist did seem rather cold."

"Yes, and Raf didn't seem keen to talk in front of her. Do you think something is going on?"

"I don't know Chanie, but I can't wait for three o'clock."

Once back at Tasso Square, Tenika and Chantrea went back to their hotel to freshen up and soon it was time to walk down Corso Italia to the meeting point. They walked through Tasso Square and past shops along the road. Quickly they came upon a large ice cream cone outside a small fronted ice cream shop.

"Well, he was right about not missing it" laughed Chantrea.

They entered the narrow shop. A counter with ice cream and snacks was on the left hand side whilst small tables and chairs were on the right. There wasn't much space in between. Tenika spotted a space further on, down some steps as predicted.

"Possiamo passare? " Tenika said to the young woman behind the counter.

She smiled. "Sì, naturalmente."

Tenika and Chantrea went down three steps to a small area having six small round tables with chairs. They were immediately impressed by the walls being covered with newspaper articles about the shop and the various celebrities that had been there. What looked like many Italian celebrities had been to the shop and elaborate cakes seemed to be a common feature in the photos.

"Look" said Chantrea to Tenika, "The Pope, has he been here too?"

"Well, I don't know about the Pope but behind you is a picture of Geoff Hurst."

"Who's he?"

"He was in the England football team that won the world cup in 1966. I only know because Claude is a bit of a football nut."

The young woman from behind the counter came down the stairs towards them.

"Cosa posso fare per voi?"

"Do you do latte?" asked Chantrea.

"Oh yes."

"We'll have two then. By the way have all these people been here in the shop?"

"Ah yes, all. The owner is famous for making cakes and everyone comes here for them."

"Including the Pope? He has been in here too?"

"Yes, he has been here also."

The young woman turned away and Raf appeared in the shop. He stopped the young woman and asked her something and then came down the stairs to the seating area.

"Hello Tenika and Chanie"

"Would you like a drink Raf?"

"It's ok, I have ordered one."

"This is an interesting place? Are these Italian film stars on the walls?"

"Yes, Chanie, many are – although some are fairly old now. The man who owns the shop, Antonio Cafiero, makes very elaborate cakes and he has been very successful in attracting famous people as his clients. As you can see over there even the Pope has been here."

Tenika brought the conversation back to the main issue.

"Raf, what happened to Luke?"

"I don't know. He got a taxi from our office at 5.00 pm two days ago and went back to his hotel. Then yesterday morning at nine the police arrived at our office to tell us he had been found dead. He had my card in his wallet. That is how they made the link to us ... and me."

Tenika looked hard into Raf's eyes.

"Did he fall by accident or has someone done this to him? If so, who would want to do this and why?"

They hushed their conversation as the waitress brought them their drinks and placed them on the round table in front of them. Raf leant forward looking at Tenika and Chantrea.

"I don't know." Apparently he was found at the foot of the cliff behind Hotel Corallo in Sant Agnello. The hotel is next to a bar which is set on the cliff top. The Police think he might have fallen from there."

Raf looked nervous as the young woman returned with their drinks.

"Aren't there any cameras?"

"There are at the hotel but not at the bar. I think the police are checking at the hotel."

"Did he mention if he had any problems or difficulties with his work?"

"Well our business is very competitive and, in these economic times, some people think Italian contracts should go to Italian companies. Things have been said but no direct threats made. And if they were made, why target Luke? The contract was awarded by us and our clients. If there was a target then why not us? But look, this is madness, we are talking as if Luke was killed by someone. No no I can't believe that."

Tenika was not being deflected.

"Did he mention any other issues or concerns?"

No, nothing. Well, he was helping his sister. She is a teacher in England. I think there were some problems at the school and he has been helping her. He was concerned about her. It made him angry. I think he had been doing some investigations on her behalf but what can that have to do with this? He loved coming here. He was very happy."

"And do you know why he might have been out near the Hotel Corallo? Was there any work reason for that?

"Not for work, no. The project site is in Sorrento over to the east. I think he normally stayed at the hotel in the evenings doing some work and reporting back to his business. Perhaps he went for a walk. Hotel Corallo is on the cliff and can be found easily from the Ambasciatori by walking along the coastal road. It is only about a fifteen minute walk."

Raf put this head in his hand and was becoming visibly emotional.

"The police said his sister was coming to Sorrento today."

"Yes, that is right. She is due to come to the office to talk with our Director perhaps tonight or in the morning. I can't be out long, the police keep asking questions and we are expecting a visit from a senior person from Luke's company also."

Tenika put her hand on Raf's.

"Thank you for coming. I can see this is upsetting for you. Can I ask you one thing? When Luke's sister comes to your office, could you ask her if she will see us? I know she will be distressed but if you could ......"

"Well, I can ask. That's all I can do."

"Thanks, we would be happy to visit her at the Ambasciatori or anywhere else at a time of her choosing. Let me write my mobile number down. Perhaps you can give it to her."

"Ok, I will try. You know, I really liked Luke. I enjoyed his company and he was good at his job. We had been to Emilia's a few times and he really enjoyed it there."

Raf finished his drink and rose to his feet. Tenika and Chantrea did likewise and Raf kissed them both twice.

"Ciao ladies."

He turned and walked quickly up the steps stopping only to pay the shop assistant.

The women sat down again and Tenika turned to Chantrea.

"Why does a guy come all this way to do a job he loves with nice people and fall over a cliff? If he jumped, why? What would cause such an action and if he was going to throw himself off a cliff why would he have been so happy with Raf and as we saw at Emilia's? But if he was killed, then why, for what reason?"

"Couldn't it have been just an accident?" asked Chantrea.

"Well, either he jumped, or he was pushed, or fell accidentally and I want to find out which it was."

"Do you think his sister will see us?

"I don't know Chanie. Perhaps her curiosity to find out what happened will help us. She will probably be around for a few days until the body is released for transporting back to the UK."

"She is going to be in pieces. I do feel for her" said Chantrea.

"Maybe that's our advantage Chanie, we have the T shirt on lost loved ones."

Chantrea smiled back in acknowledgement and they both finished their coffee.

"Come on Chanie, I think I need a walk."

Tenika and Chantrea got up and walked up the steps to the counter.

"Quanto per il caffè?"

"Niente, il signore ha pagato."

"Ah, that's nice. Raf paid for the coffees."

"He seems like a nice chap" said Chantrea.

Tenika nodded in agreement. They wandered through the back streets of the old town down to the gardini pubblici which sat on the cliff top overlooking the bay. Tenika and Chantrea found a seat and gazed out over the still blue water.

"You know Chanie, Raf was in real pain there. He's lost a good friend."

Tenika looked at Chantrea to see tears rolling down her face."

"What's the matter?"

"I couldn't bear the thought of losing you. We've known each other for nearly ten years now and I look upon you as part of my family. Even my mum has said she would be proud to have you as a daughter. You've become such a big part of my life."

"Don't be silly, you're not going to lose me. I'm here for the long term. You know Chanie, I know I can be a bit of a bull in a china shop and I know when we met I could be an aggressive cow. You've shown me how strong someone can be with inner calmness. I do so admire how you stay calm under pressure."

"I get that from my mum. Nothing makes her flap at all."

Tenika put her arm round Chantrea and gave her a long hug.

"Don't you worry Chanie, you're stuck with me and I'm not going anywhere."

"You know Percy was out here a couple of hundred years ago and wrote some stuff when he was feeling a bit miserable. I think I got it my bag here."

"Chanie you always have a poetry book with you. You make me feel like a Philistine at times."

"Hmm here we are, let me just read the ending to you. I know he wrote this near to Naples but not sure where. You never know, he could have been sitting right here with his pad and pen."

Chantrea snuggled up to Tenika so that she could read in a quiet voice.

Yet now despair itself is mild,
Even as the winds and waters are;
I could lie down like a tired child,
And weep away the life of care
Which I have borne and yet must bear,
Till death like sleep might steal on me,

And I might feel in the warm air
My cheek grow cold, and hear the sea
Breathe o'er my dying brain its last monotony.

Some might lament that I were cold,
As I, when this sweet day is gone,
Which my lost heart, too soon grown old,
Insults with this untimely moan;
They might lament—for I am one
Whom men love not,—and yet regret,
Unlike this day, which, when the sun
Shall on its stainless glory set,
Will linger, though enjoyed, like joy in memory yet.

Chantrea shut her book and they sat for a while quietly looking out to sea. Tenika held Chantrea's hand and they sat close to each other. Whilst in certain ways they were opposites in character, they both felt comfortable and relaxed in each other's company. They enjoyed being with one another and both felt each brought security to their relationship.

"Tee, do you realise that people have sat here for over two thousand years gazing out to sea?"

"Is that why this seat is a bit uncomfortable?"

"No, you know what I mean and when the first Romans sat here sipping their wine and guzzling their grapes, Vesuvius didn't look like that at all. Just think what a seat this would have been in AD seventy nine when the volcano erupted. The ash cloud didn't come this way so, had we been sitting here then, we would have had a grandstand view of it."

"You mean Chanie that we could have sat here and watched sixteen thousand people perish under ash and gas."

"Mmmm well you could put it that way. Of course had the wind been blowing in this direction then perhaps it would not be the Pompeii ruins that are so famous but perhaps it might have been the ruins of Sorrento."

"Well Chanie it might have needed a bit of a gale to blow enough ash and gas to bury Sorrento but your point is well made. A fickle wind can destroy or create a fortune."

The women gazed across the bay and then Tenika looked at her watch and Chantrea nodded to her. They got up and began their journey back to Palazzo Abagnale. Chantrea linked her arm in to that of Tenika and they strolled back through the old town towards Tasso Square.

That evening Tenika and Chantrea went back to Fauno bar for dinner. They had forgotten yesterday's conversation about the bar along Corso Italia that had the saxophone player. Their mood was sombre for each had Luke on their mind. To hear of the death of someone unknown or not seen for a long time is one thing, but to hear of the death of someone with whom you had a wonderful lunch just two days earlier was quite something else. The Fauno was busy as usual and they were lucky to get a table outside as they managed to arrive just as a couple were leaving. Within minutes of sitting down there was a long queue at the entrance waiting for tables.

They ordered a bottle of dry white wine and a bottle of still water. Tenika was leaning towards fish and Chantrea was thinking of pasta. They were prompted to a decision by a young male waiter who was charming and polite. In the end Tenika chose a crab salad and Chantrea shell fish with pasta. The drinks arrived and both Tenika and Chantrea looked for a way of diverting their thinking away from the tragedy of Luke and whether his sister would contact them.

"Tee, you know we talked briefly about sharing a flat together, how are you feeling about the idea now?"

"I'm all for it Chanie. It costs us a fortune renting two small flats in south London. It would make so much financial sense to join forces. Gosh it would be so nice to share the cleaning!"

"Look Tee, I agree about the money but I need to be sure we will get on together. We've known each other for years and I think get on really well but we've never lived together. Would we get on alright being together all the time?"

"Chanie, some people think we're an old married couple anyway and your mum treats me like a second daughter. I think it would be fine. You would bring common sense and thoughtfulness to the place and I would scare off all the double glazing salesmen."

Their food arrived via their smiling waiter. It looked and smelt wonderful and they lost no time in beginning to eat. The evening was balmy with just the hint of a cool breeze. Summer clothes were still on show, men in shirt sleeves and women still in sleeveless dresses. They would soon be pushed towards jackets and cardigans as the evenings cooled further and the colder autumn winds blew.

"Do you think it would be good to find a new flat rather than one of us moving into the other's place?"

64

"Chanie, what would you like to do?"

"I think I would like to find a new place that we could sort of start from scratch to build up a shared environment, you know something that represented us both."

"There you go Chanie, so sensible and thoughtful. If only there were more MPs like you. You're right of course, so shall we start looking when we get back?"

"Yes, I would really like to, if you are ok with that."

"Yes, I am really fine about it. In fact I am rather looking forward to it."

They smiled at each other and then focused upon their food and wine. The evening drifted on with conviviality all around them. For a few hours their minds were taken away from the death of Luke Adams but the new day would bring it back into full focus.

DAY FOUR

The following morning Tenika and Chantrea stayed in the hotel room hoping for a call from Luke's sister. The hours dragged. There wasn't any reason for not going out other than a feeling that if they did, and a call came through, they might not be in the right place to respond. From their hotel, they could get to the Ambasciatori in about five to ten minutes assuming any meeting might be there. Chantrea was sitting out on the balcony writing poetry. She enjoyed reading poetry and had written verse from an early age. She found it easier to express her thoughts that way than through other forms of writing. Tenika took the view that Chantrea understated her talent. Tenika constantly encouraged her to bring the poems together into a book and give Percy Shelley a run for his money on a bookseller's shelf.

Tenika on the other hand sat on the white leather sofa with her headphones on listening to music. She liked to listen to female black artists whether it was her usual favourites of Mary J Blige, Stevie Wonder, Jill Scott and Erykah Badu, the romanticism of India Arie or newer artists like Emile Sandé and street rapper Speech Debelle.

It wasn't that Tenika didn't have a more serious side to her because she did. She was troubled by poverty, inequality and discrimination in the world around her. She had a copy of Martin Luther King's speech on a wall in her flat. Her home life had reminded her how badly some people treat others and she had learned from an early age to stick up for herself. Her work at the Kings Foundation allowed her to engage with social policy issues and to contribute in a small way to making a statement about them. Both Tenika and Chantrea were loyal and conscientious workers and although each had their own collection of friends from work, they tended to gravitate towards sharing spare time together. They both enjoyed going out to the cinema or theatre and loved spending an evening at a restaurant just chatting about the day's events. Over the years Tenika had grown close to Chantrea's mother and often had a weekend dinner at her house in Guildford where she and Chantrea would appear as two happy sisters. In fact both had got into a habit of going to one or other's flat at the end of the day just to chill out. They each had a key to the other's flat and with the aid of text messaging were able to coordinate social as well as domestic affairs. When Tenika's mother took her own life, it was Chantrea who provided the support Tenika needed and got her through the darkest moments of her life.

From her position on the balcony, Chantrea looked around at Tenika to speak to her but Tenika was unable to hear her because of her headphones. Chantrea got into Tenika's eye line and waved at her. After some moments she gained Tenika's attention.

"You know Tee that if Luke's sister doesn't want to see us and the police won't talk to us, there is little we can do."

"Maybe Chanie, but let's take one step at a time."

"It will be lunchtime soon. What shall we do?"

"We can go for a coffee and a bite at the Fauna if you like or back to the ice cream place we met Raf."

"Mmm, the Fauno sounds good to me" replied Chantrea.

Suddenly, Tenika's mobile phone sprang into life. Chantrea and Tenika looked at each other.

"Well, go on answer it."

Tenika picked up the mobile phone from beside her.

"Hello."

"Oh, hi Raf."

The room went silent as Tenika listened intently to what Raf was saying.

"Ok, yes I've got that. Thanks so much. Ciao."

"Well?"

Chantrea's voice was impatient.

"Three pm at the Ambasciatori. Her name is Sasha and Raf has told her that we were friends of Luke and want to pay our respects. He says she has seen the police and had to formally identify the body last night. He also said that his company has decided not to speak publicly about Luke and that perhaps we should not go to the office again."

"Sounds interesting. Have they something to hide?"

"I don't know Chanie but we have an hour and a half before the meeting. So let's go to the Fauna for a quick bite to eat."

The Fauno bar was less busy at lunchtime than the evening and the two women were quickly shown to an outside table at the side nearest the statue of Torquato Tasso. They ordered coffees along with a prawn salad for Chantrea and ravioli with crab for Tenika.

"How are we going to play this?" asked Chantrea.

"I am not entirely sure. We had better be very sympathetic to begin with and see if she will tell us what the police have said."

"You know, the fact that his sister has come out suggests he was not married."

"Yes, Chanie, that had occurred to me as well."

Their food arrived and, in comparison to the morning, time now passed quickly. As they ate their lunch they talked about the coming conversation.

"Hope she has asked them lots of questions and pushed them to answer them."

"Tee, she may not be as strong as you and might be in an emotional mess."

"Hmmm, well she is a teacher so she should be good at asking questions."

"But we don't know how much Italian she speaks and whether communication is a problem."

"I don't know Chanie, everyone seems to speak good English here and the Inspector seemed to speak English pretty well."

"Then let's hope she has spoken to him."

Although lunch time at the Fauno was not as busy as the evening, it was still the focus of activity within the square. Whilst the proportion of customers who were visitors to Sorrento was greater during the day, the local population still poured onto the streets for their lunchtime coffee and salads. They watched the traffic policemen in the centre of the square whose job seemed to be less about directing traffic than answering questions from motorists who would stop by him or sorting out tangles of cars who had come to a halt because there was another directly in front. Getting through and across the square seemed to be an art learned from an early age. There was one set of traffic lights but six road entrances onto the square. The locals seemed to be able to move freely onto the square and manoeuvre their way as they wished without collision or temper. At times it looked chaotic but a rhythmical chaos which repeated itself throughout the day.

The waiter who had served them three evenings ago was working in the restaurant and came over to see them.

"Ciao ladies. Are you both ok?"

He looked at Chantrea.

"Grazie, yes were fine and thank you for your help the other night. We did appreciate it."

"Oh it was nothing. I am glad to help."

Chantrea smiled at him.

"What is your name?"

"Lucca."

"Look Lucca, we are in a bit of a hurry, could you get us our bill?"

"Of course, I will arrange it."

Lucca turned and walked to the waiters' station in the middle of the seating area and spoke with a silver haired man who seemed to be orchestrating activity. He in turn looked at his computer screen and called one of the waiters over. Following a short conversation the waiter came over with the bill which Chantrea dealt with. As they left the Fauno, Chantrea made a detour to Lucca who was now on the far side of the seating area. She touched him on the arm as she passed him and he turned his head towards her.

"Ciao" she said.

"Ciao, see you again."

"You're getting very friendly with him."

"Ah, always good to have a friendly waiter on your side."

"Have you ever thought of going into politics Chanie?"

The two laughed as they crossed Tasso Square and began to walk down Via Correale towards the Ambasciatori. Less than ten minutes later they were at the revolving doors of the hotel. Tenika went in first and looked around. There were people sitting on the chairs in the reception area but further away, down the steps, was a woman sitting on her own. Tenika and Chantrea walked towards her. As they approached she looked up.

"Hello, are you Sasha?"

The woman stood up. She was not much older than Tenika or Chantrea, perhaps early thirties. She had shoulder length light brown hair and the same blue/grey eyes of Luke. She had the same oval shaped face and a similar nose. She wore a white blouse and black jeans.

"Yes, which of you is Tenika and which Chanie, if I've got that right?"

"I'm Tenika and this is Chanie."

Sasha gave a nervous smile to each.

"Look, it's a bit public here, shall we find a corner in the garden?"

Tenika and Chantrea nodded and all three went through the double doors into the garden. They turned right past the swimming pool and walked down to the cliff edge and sat at a table in the far corner of the garden.

"We are very grateful to you for seeing us. This must be an awful time for you."

"Thank you Tenika, it is. I must admit it is hard keeping it all together. But then, there is lots to do and people to see. I understand you were friends with Luke. He sent me a text a few days ago to say he had met you at a restaurant. He was very complimentary of you both."

That comment hit hard with both Tenika and Chantrea. They could feel emotion rising in their heads and Tenika put her hand onto that of Chantrea.

"Yes he was a lovely man. We had a very enjoyable time" responded Tenika.

Sasha looked over the railings and across the bay. She stared for a while before returning her gaze to Tenika and Chantrea.

"It's lovely here isn't it. I wanted to stay in the same hotel as Luke to be as close to him as I could. Sounds rather silly really when he is in the basement of the hospital."

"No, I think it's wonderful that you want to be so close to him. I am sure he knows that. Tenika and I would do the same thing."

"I guess you've had a busy time since you arrived?" asked Tenika.

"Yes, the first dreadful task was to identify Luke's body. At least he looked serene and at peace. I think they put some make-up on his head to hide his injuries. I was ok in the room with him but as soon as I walked out I couldn't handle it any more. I cried and cried."

Sasha stared down at the table.

"That's only to be expected" said Tenika.

"Have you ever lost anyone so close to you?" asked Sasha.

"Yes, I lost my mother unexpectedly a few months ago."

"I'm sorry. I shouldn't ask you such a question."

"It's ok. Have the police said anything about Luke's ....."

"I met with them this morning. They have been very good. They sent a police car to the hotel to collect me."

Chantrea looked across to Tenika. She sensed Tenika was beginning to sharpen her language looking for precision in the answers that might be forthcoming.

"They said that an autopsy was carried out two days ago. Death was caused by multiple injuries resulting from falling fifty metres from the cliff top. He had drunk alcohol and the police seem to think that it might simply be an accident resulting from drinking. They said this was not the first time that tourists had fallen from the cliff top after drinking. They said his body became wedged between rocks and was the reason why it was not carried out to sea."

"Did the police actually use the word tourist?" asked Tenika softly.

"Yes, I am pretty sure they did."

Now it was Chantrea's turn to dig for information.

"Sasha, when we were at the restaurant the other day, Luke didn't drink any wine he only drank water because he said he was taking some medication."

"Yes, that's right. He's been taking amoxicillin for a lung problem. He probably could have had a small drink but he has been trying to avoid alcohol because it can interfere with the antibiotic."

"Did you mention this to the police?"

"No, it was just a haze. I wasn't thinking straight. But as I say, he could have had a drink if he wanted to."

Tenika returned to role of questioner.

"Raf told us that there had been some issues regarding Luke's company having the contract here. Did you know anything of that?"

"Uhm, well Luke had said there had been comments made here and I think they had been in the press. Some of the Italian competitors were unhappy that the contract had gone overseas. I know that it had been discussed here in Sorrento and back in London but I think Luke thought it was all hot Italian air."

"Had there been any threats?"

"Not that I know of .... if you mean personal. I think Luke's company had advised him to keep a low profile when out here, you know not to court attention. But perhaps you can find more from the papers here. I am sure Luke said things had been in the press."

"Can I ask how your meeting went at Dynamo this morning?"

"Yes Tenika, that was quite good. A chap from the British Trade and Investment Office in Naples turned up as has one of the Directors from Luke's firm, Andrew Hillsom. They have all been very sweet. Luke's firm will take care of returning his body to the UK when it has been released and they are also meeting my expenses here. They all thought we should not make any public comments but just leave things to the police to sort out. They all seem to have been as helpful as they can and I couldn't have asked for anything more."

"And what of the chap from the Embassy, did he say anything?"

"Not a lot. He said they would provide assistance where they could with regard to the repatriation and would monitor the situation but also said they couldn't get involved with the police investigation."

A waiter approached them and asked if they wanted drinks. Tenika took Sasha's hand.

"Sasha, we have been asking you these questions. Do you want to stop? If so, that's fine."

"No, it's ok. Strangely enough it feels good to get this stuff out. Perhaps I need to talk about it as much as you need to hear about it."

"Ok, then let's have some drinks. I'll have an orange juice. Chanie, what about you?"

"A latte for me."

"And you Sasha?"

"Yes, I think I'll have a latte too."

The waiter smiled and walked off to the garden bar to get the drinks. Tenika, although being as soft in her manner as she could, was not letting the opportunity pass.

"What do you do back in Kent Sasha?"

"I teach in a secondary school."

"Do you enjoy that? How is it going?"

Sasha smiled.

"I don't know if Luke said anything to you but it's been a bit of a nightmare to be honest. We have had a new head teacher, Suzannah Boswell, for two years now. Her mission in life is to improve the pass rate for the school in order that we move up the ladder for local schools. She wants to be top dog and we have to give her the figures to do it. The targets we have been set are extremely difficult to achieve and it has caused all sorts of upset. I am in charge of Geography and so if any of the teachers in my department don't meet their targets then it's my fault.   Not meeting targets also impacts on pay progression as well so many people have been unhappy. We are always being reminded of our contractual obligations for this and obligations for that and the senior management team use open emails to all staff to name and shame those who haven't done this or that. Sometimes it does feel like public humiliation is the key management approach."

"It doesn't sound like a happy place to be" said Chantrea.

At that moment their drinks arrived and Tenika smiled at the waiter to acknowledge the service.

"No, Luke had been getting increasingly frustrated with what he thought was bad management. I just think he didn't like them having a go at me. During the last summer term I had a conversation with Suzannah Bosworth, the Head, in which she said to me that if I couldn't give her the improvement she wanted then perhaps I needed to take my career in a different direction. I was very upset and spoke to Luke on the phone. He was livid and wrote to the chair of governors. Suzannah wasn't impressed with that. The last time we spoke about it he was intimating he might write to the press to see if a bit of publicity could get the governors to draw back a bit. He had been doing a bit of background research on Suzannah to see if there was any ammunition he could use. More than a dozen staff left at the end of the summer term. Many couldn't hack it any more. Good people too."

"He sounds so supportive of you."

"Yes, always been a protective big brother. As soon as he got a car he used to ferry me about or collect me in the evenings from my friends or places I had been. I didn't ask him, he just wanted to know I was safe."

For a brief moment a smile appeared on Sasha's face as her memory wandered back to a happy place. As the memory faded so did Sasha's smile. She looked up at Chantrea.

"So where are you two staying?"

"The Palazzo Abagnale, it's on Corso Italia just a short way up from Tasso Square. You can't miss it because it is over the Armani shop. It's not quite as nice as this but a very friendly place and a really good location for Tasso Square."

"You know, Luke was very lucky to stay here. The hotel seems really nice and the views are breathtaking."

Both Tenika and Chantrea nodded in agreement as the three women sipped their drinks and took in the wonderful view from their cliff top table.

"So Sasha, how long are you staying?" asked Chantrea.

"Well I have been given a few days compassionate leave and I am hoping that the police will release Luke's body soon and then it's back to England and a funeral to arrange. What about you two?"

"Well we arrived five days ago and we are here for two weeks so we have some time yet" responded Tenika.

With their drinks finished the discussion drew to a natural conclusion. Sasha looked at her watch and smiled at Tenika and Chantrea.

"It's been good meeting you two. I think I needed the chat."

"What comes next for you?" enquired Tenika.

"Well tonight I am having dinner with Andrew Hillsom from Luke's firm. And then, we shall see what tomorrow brings."

The three women rose from their seats and walked slowly back towards the hotel's main building. They entered through the double doors and Sasha accompanied Tenika and Chantrea up the steps to the revolving doors. Tenika kissed Sasha on the cheek.

"Thank you for meeting with us."

"No, thank you for caring about Luke."

Chantrea stepped forward and also kissed Sasha.

"Chanie sounds an interesting name. Does it mean anything?"

"Well, my full name is Chantrea but Tenika calls me Chanie and yes, Chantrea means moonlight. I was born on a night with a full moon."

"That's lovely."

Sasha then turned to Tenika.

"And Tenika, I can see why Luke took a shine to you. Thank you for giving him that feeling."

Tenika smiled and then she, and Chantrea, moved through the revolving door onto the street outside.

They walked quickly along Via Correale and then cut through Piazza Angelina Lauro to reach Corso Italia and then turned right to walk to their hotel. Once inside their room, Tenika turned to Chantrea.

"I need a shower and then perhaps later we might talk about all of this. I need to get my head round it all."

"Sure."

Whilst Tenika took a shower, Chantrea sat outside on the balcony watching the Sorrentine world go by. Corso Italia was a little quieter now in the late afternoon. Some shops still close during the afternoon and the number of people on the main streets reduces as many prepare to re-emerge in the evening. The sound of scooters was much reduced, although still to be heard, as was the passing traffic. When Tenika emerged from the shower it was Chantrea's turn and that was to be followed by the nightly conversation of what would they wear and where would they have dinner. That evening, Tenika and Chantrea decided on the

L'Antica Trattoria on Via PR Giuliani. It was a short walk through Tasso Square and then down Via San Cesareo until they reached the old church on the left. They then turned right into Via Giuliani and walked down about two hundred metres along a narrow street that gently fell away downhill towards the cliff. The restaurant was on the right hand side and they took a table in the outside area at the back that was sheltered by a wooden lattice framework covered with vines and other climbing plants. As they settled in to their seats, Tenika pulled pen and paper from her handbag.

"You have come prepared!" exclaimed Chantrea.

"Yes, there's a lot to this situation. I might need to make some notes. Now Chanie, we've heard a lot of interesting stuff today. Let me start with the obvious question. Why might a chap who seemed to love life, was in the middle of supporting his sister through bad times and enjoyed his job, throw himself off a cliff?"

"Well, if you put it like that it doesn't seem to make any sense" replied Chantrea.

"No it doesn't. Unless there is something else going on that made him feel desperately unhappy with himself, that his sister or Raf knows nothing about, then I don't believe suicide applies here."

"Well the police seem to have suggested to Sasha that it was an accident. He drinks, he gets tipsy and over he goes."

"Yes Chanie, but the problem is the alcohol. With us he declined alcohol because of his medication and Raf confirmed he had done this before. So why did he drink alcohol that evening? If he just wanted a drink why not take it from the mini-bar in his room? And why was he more than a kilometre away near a hotel?

81

"I'm not sure Tee but could it be that when he was in working mode he remained dry to ensure no negative interaction with his medication but once away from work he fancied a drink and walked a while to somewhere he wouldn't be recognised and also where it wouldn't appear on his room bill? I suspect that Raf and Luke had tried a number of restaurants here and by going into the next commune he avoided any recognition of his indiscretion."

"Mmmm, and another thing Chanie, why is there a desire of Luke's company to deal with repatriation of the body with the aid of the British Embassy? Might there be an issue here whereby there is desire to deal with the problem quickly to avoid problematic questions about local competitors who didn't want a foreign business to have an Italian contract?"

"But Tee, if that is the case you are suggesting Luke might have been murdered by a disgruntled Italian competitor."

"Yes Chanie, its possible. The murder would send a clear message to others who might be considering offering contracts abroad. The police have suggested that his body being wedged between rocks was a chance happening. If it hadn't been then perhaps the body might have been washed out to sea and not found for some time."

"Then where does the alcohol come into it?"

"I don't know Chanie, I don't know. Perhaps it was an insurance policy just in case the body was found. But if the police decide it was an accident, then the body will be released soon and flown back to the UK. Problem solved."

"It might suit the Italian authorities to take such a view to avoid awkward questions."

82

"Exactly Chanie."

Tenika scribbled notes on her paper trying to make some sort of pattern from it all.

"But Tee, I still don't see what difference we can make to this. After all, we don't know what stance the police are going to take."

Tenika stopped and stared at her paper. She exhaled slowly.

"Ok Chanie, you are right. You see why I need you with me, your calmness to counter my desire to tear off into something. It would be good if we could talk again to Sasha to know what the police are doing."

"But isn't she going to think something is odd if we keep stalking her? And she does need space and time to grieve."

"Of course you're right Chanie. Perhaps though a short call to her tomorrow to just see how she is?"

"I can see you are getting your teeth into this."

"Yes I am Chanie and I want to get to the bottom of it all."

DAY FIVE

The following morning after breakfast, Tenika and Chantrea were in their hotel room wondering how to spend their time. Chantrea was sitting out on the balcony taking in the warm early morning air and watching Sorrento come alive as people and traffic increased in volume and noise. Tenika was sitting on the leather sofa with her paper from the previous night's meal.

"We could go and have a look round the wood carving museum, you know I like the smell of wood. Perhaps the cathedral, we haven't done that yet. Or maybe a bus out to the old roman villa and listen to the sirens."

"Yes, Chanie, I don't mind what we do. I can't sit here waiting to ring Sasha."

Suddenly the phone in the room burst into life. Tenika jumped up and picked up the phone.

"Hello."

"Oh yes, put her through."

"Good morning Sasha, how nice to hear from you."

Tenika looked across to Chantrea but her eyes were already fixed on Tenika's face. There was silence as Tenika listened intently to Sasha.

"I see. So when do you think things will get moving?"

"Look Sasha, it's very kind of you to let us know and it would be nice to see you again before you leave. We don't want to intrude but if you have spare time?"

"Ok, that's fine. Thanks once again. Bye."

"Well?"

She has seen the police this morning and it was the chap we met, Pietro Maldini. He went to the Ambasciatori to see Sasha. She says they have decided to treat the death as an accident. Apparently he said there was no evidence of others involved and there was little more they could do. Apparently he was seen on a camera outside the bar next door to the hotel. It was after midnight but was alone. That's where they think he went over."

"So they are going to release the body?"

"Yes, fairly soon, probably in the next couple of days. The Director from the company is liaising with the Embassy chap over arrangements."

"So, Tee, what are we going to do?"

"Hope you don't mind Chanie, but a change of plan. It's off for coffee at the Hotel Corallo."

"Somehow that doesn't surprise me!"

Tenika and Chantrea retraced their steps to the Ambasciatori via Piazza Angelina Lauro, through the small garden beyond then right past the car park towards the museum they visited the other day. Via Califano descended gently past the old abandoned hotel until the Ambasciatori was reached.

"Ok Chanie, let's keep an eye on the time to see how long it takes to walk."

As Tenika and Chantrea left the Ambasciatori behind, the road bore sharp right for one hundred metres or so until it joined Via Rota, the main road leading to Sant Agnello, the next commune. The road wound its way past some large gated houses perched on the cliff top, then round a tricky right and left bend having little space for walking. They turned left onto Via Cocumella and when they reached the junction with Corsa Crawford, they could see the sea again and the end of their journey.

They walked towards a sharp right bend as the road reached the cliff edge. Ahead was a square building set back on the cliff edge and next to it on the right was the Hotel Corallo.

"Where to first?"

"Straight ahead I think, Chanie."

The square building sat on its own promontory. As they walked towards the building it sat at the end of a well laid out tiled area with two trees and seating provision. The building had three green doors with the remainder of the wall covered with vine. The underlying colour of the building was terracotta.

The promontory was edged with good quality and well maintained iron railings. As they rounded the building to be on the seaward side of it they could see the building was, in fact, a bar with wooden benches that drinkers would sit on along with a main entrance. It was closed, perhaps too early in the day.

Tenika and Chantrea moved to the edge of the cliff and moved to the far side of the railings where the Hotel Corallo came into full view. In the corner, the two women stopped and peered over the edge to the rocks below.

"Well this looks like where it happened Chanie."

"Yes, and look, there is only a narrow parapet under the railing as well. If you go over it's straight down to the rocks below."

Tenika and Chantrea stared down at the rocks more than fifty metres below. The gentle wash of waves over the rocks seemed to reduce the danger for anyone falling so far.

"I wonder what time this place closes?" Mused Chantrea.

"Good question Chanie."

"Right, let's go into the hotel and ask about room prices, cameras and when this place opens."

Tenika and Chantrea walked back to the road, turned left and fifty metres along the road found the entrance to the hotel.

"No Italian, Chanie, it's time to keep my little secret to myself."

The hotel entrance lobby was reasonable, clean and with some brown covered chairs. Tenika went up to the reception desk where a dark haired woman was looking at her computer screen. Behind her was a screen split into six small screens showing images from security cameras. One of them showed the outside rear of the hotel including the corner of the patio area of the bar next door where they had just been standing."

"Hello, my friend and I are in Sorrento and we are looking at hotels for a future visit. Do you have details about the Hotel Corallo?"

"Buongiorno, of course we have a leaflet here and it has the room rates on the card inside."

"Thank you. My friend here can be a little anxious at times. Do you have security here all the time?"

"Yes, reception is open 24 hours and we have security guards at night."

"Any cameras?"

"Yes, inside and out."

"Do they film constantly?"

"Inside yes but outside they take a picture every twenty seconds, a bit like a web cam."

"That's fantastic. Do you mind if we take look around?"

"No, please do. There isn't much space outside because we are so close to the cliff."

"Grazie."

"Ciao."

Tenika and Chantrea moved away from reception and through the public area. They looked into the dining room and checked the lifts.

"Better make sure we look as if we are looking around."

"Agreed Chanie."

They came across a door leading out onto a small patio area with tables and chairs.

"Not a lot of room out here Tee and the view is a bit restricted too."

"Look Chanie, we are slightly below the corner of the bar and really all you can see is the corner where we stood. I can't see how any camera is going to see much more than that even if it is higher up on the hotel building."

They made their way back into the hotel and through to reception.

"Thank you very much" said Tenika to the receptionist.

"You're welcome."

"Oh, by the way, what time does the bar next door close?"

"At this time of the year it is midnight."

Tenika smiled at the receptionist again and they walked out of the hotel. They turned right, went past the entrance to the promontory with the bar and began to walk back along Corso Crawford.

"By the way Tee, how long did it take to walk here?"

"Twenty minutes Chanie."

"Chanie, the more I think about this, the more I don't see it adding up. Why the police are going to close the case and just say it was an accident is beyond me."

"Perhaps because there is a possibility that it was and they don't have any evidence for anything else?"

"I think we need another conversation with Inspector Pietro Maldini.

"Well can we have lunch first and I am going to need the loo soon!"

Tenika and Chantrea made their way back to their hotel, stopping off briefly before going on to the Fauno bar for lunch. Once settled at a table with a drink and some food, Chantrea expressed some concerns.

"Now look Tee, are you sure you're doing the right thing?"

"Yes Chanie, I want to know why the police are not investigating further. It all seems too convenient to say it was an accident."

"Inspector Maldini is not going to be impressed with you challenging him."

"I don't care what he thinks. I owe it to Luke. Look Chanie you don't have to come with me and I am conscious this business is turning our break here upside down. I don't want you to get into trouble."

"It's ok, I am coming with you. Anyway, you need me to look after you. Who knows what you might say once you get excited."

"So what are you going to do if they say he is not there or he is busy?"

"Sit and wait for as long as it takes. Eventually they will want to get rid of us and will want to give some sort of account."

"They might just pick us up and throw us out!"

"Let them try."

"Oh God Tee, I thought you might say something like that."

Tenika looked up at Chantrea and smiled. She reached across the table and took Chantrea's hand.

"Don't worry I won't do anything daft."

"Have we got the telephone number of the British Embassy on us?"

"I think we probably have. Why?"

"Just in case you get us arrested."

Tenika laughed out loud.

They continued with lunch until all the food and drink was consumed. Then Tenika looked up at Chantrea.

"Ok, are we ready for battle?"

"I think so Tee."

"Then let's pay and go to the police station."

It was only about a ten minute walk to the police station. Tenika and Chantrea didn't talk much on the way. They both had a sense of the seriousness of what was about to happen. They arrived and walked into the reception area. The same policeman as before was behind the desk. He looked up and his face indicated an acknowledgment.

"Buon pomeriggio."

Tenika stood close to the counter looked directly into the eyes of the policeman.

"Buon pomeriggio. Vogliamo vedere Ispettore Pietro Maldini.

"E 'per l'Englishman?"

"Si."

The officer lifted the phone and asked for the Inspector. He listened for a moment and then put the phone down. He then spoke to Tenika in English.

"He is not here. I am sorry."

"That's ok, we'll wait."

With that, Tenika and Chantrea turned and sat on the bench seat in the corner of the reception area.

"No, no he is not here!"

"We are going to wait."

Tenika was firm in her voice. She took her gaze away from the officer and spoke softly to Chantrea.

"Don't look at him. Don't give any sign of weakness."

The officer held his hands up with exasperation and returned to his paper work.

So time began to pass. People came and went. Some looked at Tenika and Chantrea and some didn't. Black women were still a rarity in Sorrento and some seemed just curious to look. The first hour went quickly, the second more slowly and the third even slower. Throughout the time Tenika and Chantrea chatted away looking happy and unconcerned about the time.

At three hours and ten minutes a very well dressed man with silver hair entered the reception area. He turned and looked at Tenika and Chantrea. The officer behind the desk got up of his stool as if standing to attention. They spoke together in hushed tones and, at one point, the officer looked over at Tenika and Chantrea. Then the well dressed gentleman moved off into the hallway over at the far side of the reception area and the officer made a telephone call. About five minutes later, Inspector Pietro Maldini appeared from the hallway. He did not look happy.

"Ladies, what are you doing?" he said in a voice displaying his annoyance.

Tenika and Chantrea stood up, their faces looking very serious.

"We've come to talk to you about Luke Adams."

"I am sorry but this case is finished. There is nothing to talk about and I am busy. Please go back to Tasso Square and have an afternoon cup of tea."

Tenika felt herself tense with the patronising comment but remained calm but firm.

"I am sorry too Inspector, we have much to say and will stay here until you have time to talk to us."

And with that Tenika and Chantrea sat down and took their gaze away from him.

The Inspector turned his back on the women and looked at the officer behind the reception desk who raised his eyebrows in a dismissive way. The Inspector put his hands on his hips and began muttering in Italian.

He turned back towards Tenika and Chantrea and growled at them.

"Ok, five minutes and only five minutes. Is that clear?"

"Of course" said Tenika calmly.

"Come this way."

Inspector Maldini led Tenika and Chantrea into the hallway leading into the heart of the building. A short way down the hallway he opened a door into what seemed to be a rather bare interview room with a table, four chairs and little else. Tenika and Chantrea quickly sat down and Inspector Maldini had a resigned look on his face suggesting he realised this conversation would take longer than five minutes.

"Inspector Maldini, can you please tell us why you have decided Luke Adam's death was accidental?

"Because ladies we have no evidence that it was anything else."

"Are you aware that Luke was taking medicine and not drinking alcohol here in Sorrento?

"Yes, because the medicine showed up in the autopsy tests but he was an adult and could go out and have a drink if he wished."

"When we were with him he declined to drink and Rafael from Dynamo confirmed he had not seen Luke drink at all."

"Perhaps Mr Adams wanted to have a drink in privacy, away from work and work colleagues."

"If that was the case, why not just have one in his hotel room from the mini-bar? Why walk for twenty minutes to Sant Agnello?"

"Perhaps to get out and have a walk, get some fresh air."

"Did you check the cameras at Hotel Corallo?"

"Of course we did. The outside camera at the Hotel Corallo shows Mr Adams next door at the corner of the bar patio area. He is looking out to sea. One moment he is there and the next he is gone. No one else is shown by the camera. Also his wallet was still in his jacket and it had his credit cards and cash so there is no evidence of a robbery."

"Do you know there is a twenty second delay between photos on the outside cameras?"

"Yes, we know that. More importantly, how do you know? Have you been there?"

Inspector Maldini was becoming agitated but seemed determined to see the conversation through and get the women out of the police station.

"Did you check where he had a drink?"

"Well he did not have the drink at the hotel or the bar next door. We asked the staff, so I don't know where he drank."

"Have you considered the threats made about the award of the design contract to Luke's company?"

"What threats?"

"We understand there have been competitors who were very unhappy about the situation and have made their feelings known."

"It's just talk. People are going through hard times. They complain that is all."

"So as far as you are concerned, a man who is on medication and has demonstrated in front of people a desire not to have alcohol, ignores his mini-bar, walks a kilometre to have a secret drink, gets tipsy and falls over the edge of the cliff?"

"The evidence we have suggests that because we have nothing to suggest anything else. We have spoken to Mr Adams' sister, Dynamo and a representative of the British Embassy, they have all agreed to this."

Up until now, Tenika had asked all the questions. Now Chantrea intervened.

"Inspector Maldini, just how much alcohol did Mr Adams have in his system?"

"The equivalent of about two glasses of wine."

"That doesn't sound much to become sufficiently drunk to fall over a cliff."

"Alcohol affects people in different ways and it might have reacted with his medicine causing instability."

There was a pause in the conversation.

"Now ladies, I must ask you to go now. I have much to do."

"Ok Inspector, Chanie and I will go now but we may wish to talk to you again."

Inspector Maldini looked astonished at the suggestion. He let out a long breath.

"Please leave this case alone. You do not understand the system here. There is nothing more you can do. I appreciate the concern you have for Mr Adams but it is done."

Tenika and Chantrea stood up and Tenika squared up to the Inspector.

"Oh there is more we can do Inspector, we can find out who killed Luke Adams and we are going to do so."

Pietro Maldini looked bewildered at this statement but led Tenika and Chantrea back to reception and through the main doors onto the street.

"Goodbye ladies."

The comment was made with particular emphasis on the word 'goodbye'.

Tenika turned and looked at him.

"We will be seeing you again Inspector. Oh by the way, whilst we were in reception a very well dressed gentleman with silver hair came in and went down the hallway. Do you know who that was?"

"It was Alexander Albero, the Mayor. Now please."

Inspector Maldini gestured towards the direction of Corso Italia.

"Thank you."

With that Tenika and Chantrea turned and walked up toward Corso Italia and Inspector Maldini returned into the building.

Tenika and Chantrea walked past the school on the right hand side to the junction with Corso Italia. Neither said a word just as if they thought someone might be listening in. They arrived at Palazzo Abagnale and went straight up to their room with barely an acknowledgement of the receptionist.

Tenika placed her bag on the bed.

"Chanie, you're a star. What a fantastic question!"

"What, you mean the alcohol?"

"Yes, since when does someone fall over a cliff after two glasses of wine? And look, suppose Luke did go out and have a drink. Would the man we met at Emilia's who wouldn't touch a drop have had two?"

"Mmm, and not just that Tee, did you notice how the conversation between the Mayor and the officer at the desk seemed to lead to Inspector Maldini seeing us?"

"Yes, that was all rather odd."

"It was that look the officer gave us. It was creepy."

"Yes Chanie it was. This whole thing is creepy. There is something not right here and we need to plan our next steps."

"Where do we start?"

"Well, I think we need another conversation with Sasha. I think we need to check if she really is happy with the decision to assume accidental death as Inspector Maldini said."

"I am going to ring her at the Ambasciatori."

"Take care Tee, she will still be fragile."

"Ok, ok."

Tenika stood by the double doors leading on the balcony and gazed out over the street below as she rang the hotel.

"Buon pomeriggio. È Sasha Adams nella sua stanza? "

"Un momento."

A few seconds later, Sasha picked up the phone her room.

"Hello."

"Ah Sasha, how nice to speak with you again. How are you?"

"Hi Tenika, bearing up I guess."

"Chanie and I were wondering what you were doing for dinner tonight?"

"Well Andrew Hillsom, from Luke's company, has asked if I would like to have dinner with him again."

"Ah, well that's ok, but we wondered if you were at a loose end whether you would like to have dinner with us?"

"Do you know Tenika, I think I would like that."

"We would really like that. Where would you like to go?"

"I don't know if it is far, but I would like to visit Emilia's where you met Luke."

"No it's not far at all. We can walk it. It will only take ten to fifteen minutes from Tasso Square."

"That's fine. I like walking and probably need the exercise."

"Ok, is seven thirty fine with you?"

"Yes, it is."

"Then let's meet outside the Ercolano bar in Tasso Square at seven thirty. When you get into Tasso Square stay on the seaward side and you will see the bar on the far side of the square."

"Ok, Tenika. I look forward to seeing you and Chanie."

"Bye Sasha."

Tenika turned to Chantrea.

"Right Chanie, can you make a booking with Emilia's?"

"Of course."

"I need to think about the meeting. It's time to start sorting this mess out."

"Do you need some paper?"

Tenika looked up at Chantrea and smiled.

"Yes please."

Light cloud had drifted in from the sea but the air was still warm needing just a cardigan or light jacket. Tenika and Chantrea left their hotel early to make sure they got to the Ercolano bar before Sasha. Tasso square was already livening up with cars and scooters arriving for another night out.

Chantrea pulled at Tenika's arm.

"There she is" pointing across the square to the figure of Sasha walking quickly towards them.

Tenika waved to catch Sasha's attention through the increasingly crowded square. She noticed Tenika and waved back.

"Hello Tenika, hello Chanie. This is quite a place in the evening isn't it?"

"Yes it certainly is."

"I am sorry for looking a little dowdy. I didn't know what to bring to Sorrento and was in a complete daze when packing. I just kept saying to myself don't take bright colours, it won't look good. So I have brought a case load of black, white and blue."

"Don't worry, we are at the other end of the scale. We only brought bright colours so have some difficulty looking sombre."

"So, which way do we go?"

"It's this way, Sasha, we must first go past the little shops."

"I think I can cope with that."

The three women walked at some pace past the shops, stopping occasionally to peer into the windows. Their exchanges were small talk, weather, clothes and food. No one seemed to want to grasp the nettle of Luke's death.

They reached Piazza della Vittoria and stopped to look over the gulf. The lights of Naples shone on the far side of the gulf and they could spot the lights of boats moving across the water in the dark. They stood there for some moments taking in the lights then Sasha turned to Tenika and Chantrea.

"I hear you have been upsetting the police."

"Um what do you mean?"

"I had a telephone call this evening from Inspector Maldini. He said that you two had an idea that Luke had been killed and that the idea was not helpful to me in my time of grief. He suggested I did not listen too much to your ideas."

"Ah Sasha .... yes we did see Inspector Maldini today....

Sasha took Tenika by the arm and looked her firmly in the eyes.

"Now listen to me Tenika, I will make up my own mind about what ideas to listen to. I am as keen to find out what happened to Luke as anyone, perhaps more so. Luke saw something in you and I think I can see it too. I am not the strongest woman in the world and sometimes I wish I was a lot stronger, particularly at work, but I can make up my own mind. So, if you have ideas I am willing to listen."

Tenika smiled at Sasha, kissed her on the cheek and they continued their walk down Via Marina Grande towards the restaurant.

As they emerged through the old gatehouse and descended into Marina Grande, they were greeted with an array of lighting throwing shadows across the roadway and water's edge. A few brave souls were eating outside at Emilia's using candles to enhance the atmosphere. Whilst the September air still had warmth to it, a breeze off the sea brought a chill to the air. The restaurant resting on the wooden platform in the middle of the marina was well lit and sounds of music from it echoed around the marina.

Chantrea led the way towards the door of the restaurant.

"We've booked a table inside. I hope you're ok with that?"

They entered the compact restaurant and went down six steps. To the left was a small bar area, at the back the kitchen and then seven tables for diners. The walls were adorned with nautical artefacts, memorabilia reminding diners of the history of the restaurant and along with alcoves containing bottles of local wine. The restaurant was already filling and the smell of food was heavenly.

"Buonasera. Avete una prenotazione?"

"Sì, il mio nome è Chanie Park."

"It's for three, yes? I remember the name."

Tenika looked across to Chantrea.

"Mmm very impressive with the Italian Chanie."

"Maybe, but a rather limited vocabulary I'm afraid."

The waitress showed them to a table set against the right hand wall and gave each a menu.

"This is nice, kind of rustic but then I like that. Were you two inside or out when you were here with Luke?"

"We sat outside" said Chantrea.

Sasha gave a reflective look and then set about examining the menu. Quickly they decided and chose their dishes, sea bass for Tenika and Sasha whilst Chantrea chose pasta. Then it was down to business.

"So I gather from Inspector Maldini that you have a number of ideas about Luke's death."

"Well Chanie and I have been giving it a lot of thought but can I ask you a question first."

"Of course."

"Are you happy with the decision to categorise the events as an accident?"

"I'm not sure what to think to be honest. When Inspector Maldini sets out the case for an accident it does sound convincing but I am sure I am not in the best of mindsets to analyse it for myself. The Andrew Hillsom from Luke's company seems happy enough as does Dynamo. It has all gone so fast since I have arrived that I am sure I haven't grasped it all."

"Well that's interesting because Chanie and I also feel the decision has been taken very quickly with little consideration of alternatives."

"So what do you think are the alternatives?"

"Well we have ruled out the idea that Luke took his own life. His commitment to you and his work just don't fit with someone who wants to end it all. That leads us to the possibility that someone else was involved."

Sasha looked at both Tenika and Chantrea and spoke in hushed tones.

"You mean you think he might have been murdered?"

"Well we don't accept the neat picture from Inspector Maldini that Luke decided he wanted a drink but, choosing not to use the mini-bar in his room, he walks for twenty minutes to St Agnello finds somewhere to drink the equivalent of two glasses of wine, takes a look over the edge of the cliff, loses his balance and .... well that's it."

"The inspector said the camera from the hotel shows Luke on his own by the cliff edge."

"Yes, that is true but the camera takes pictures every twenty seconds so it is possible someone else was there but was missed by the camera."

"And Luke didn't get a drink at the hotel or the bar did he?"

"No, the inspector told Tee and me they had checked both and he had not been seen."

"Tee?"

"Sorry Sasha, I always call Tenika Tee."

"Sorry, obvious!"

"Sasha, what do you know of the issues about Luke's firm getting the contract and some people here not being happy about it?"

"Well Tenika, he did not say too much about it but I did get the impression that it had ruffled some feathers here. I think there was comment in the papers, something along the lines that any work going should go to Italians. He always reassured me that nothing would come of it. It's just business, he would say."

"Do you know how Luke's firm got the contact?"

"Not in detail. I think they have salesmen whose job it is to search out tender opportunities and clinch deals. Luke contributed to the tender but I remember him saying that others had the job of sealing the deal here in Italy."

"Sealing the deal?"

"Yes Chanie, I remember him using that phrase although I don't know what he meant by it."

There was a pause in the conversation as they all ate their meal. Tenika then took a different line of approach.

"Sasha, when we spoke at the Ambasciatori, you said that Luke had been doing some background research on the Head teacher. Do you know if he found anything?"

"No, I don't. He just said he was dealing with it and that if we applied a bit of political pressure we might get Suzannah Bosworth, the Head, and the governors to back off a bit. He could be a bit like a dog with a bone, very determined to complete something once started. In this case I knew he was just trying to protect me but he wasn't the kind of person to let go easily. But look, I can't believe the school had anything to do with this. It's one thing to bully staff who are not giving the numbers required but it's quite another to start killing staff family members. On that basis half the staff should be terrified. Anyway, how would they know he was here? I haven't told anyone and, in fact, I didn't know

107

Luke's precise travel arrangements because it was arranged at short notice."

Tenika raised her hand to stop Sasha.

"No, I am sure you are right. I suppose what is nagging away at me is that if this is not an accident in which Luke acted entirely on his own, then there may be some pattern of behaviour or actions that have led us to where we are. Perhaps I am grasping at straws."

"I understand Tenika and I am sort of grateful that you and Chanie are thinking about this as hard as you are even if I am rather alarmed at the ideas in your heads."

A waitress came and cleared their plates away and brought them coffee. The conversation stalled again as each sipped their coffee.

"Ok, so how can I help you two, if I can?"

Chantrea put her cup down, she had an idea.

"Do you know if Luke had a laptop computer with him?"

"Yes, he did. I know that because I have seen his room and it is on his bed. I think the police took it away to look at it but it has been returned now the decision has been taken. I have asked if I can pack his things and Inspector Maldini has said that is ok and I will do so in the morning but I suspect Andrew Hillsom from Luke's company will take the laptop at some point. The hotel has told me to let them know when I want access to Luke's room and they will open it for me."

"Sasha, do you think we could look at it?"

"What about the password Chanie?"

"Ah well there is no problem there because it was something of a joke between us that he always used a nickname of me from when I was a child. He said it reminded him of me when he used it."

"So Sasha, what do you think? Would you let us take a look?"

"Well it will contain his work stuff and perhaps some personal items as well."

Sasha hesitated. She sipped from her coffee cup and Tenika and Chantrea looked at each other.

"You can see that I am not used to breaking rules" sighed Sasha.

"Well we aren't going to pressure you Sasha. It's your decision."

"Chanie, If I did let you look at it I don't want it taken out of the hotel. I couldn't cope if Andrew Hillsom turned up, wanted it back and it wasn't there. Would you be willing to look at it in the morning in my room? I don't want to let it out of my sight."

"Of course Sasha, I would do exactly as you say. Thank you we really appreciate this."

Tenika reached out across the table and put her hand onto that of Sasha.

"Thank you Sasha. You really are a fantastic woman. I bet Luke was so proud of you."

The comment hit a nerve and emotion welled up inside Sasha. She quickly pulled a tissue from her handbag and dabbed at her eyes."

"I hope so" Sasha said in a frail emotional voice."

"Right, we have a plan. Tomorrow Chanie, you look at the laptop and I will use the computer in our hotel room to look for evidence in the press of complaints about the award of the contract. Let's see if we can chew on the bone every bit as hard as Luke would have."

The women finished their drinks and gathered themselves whilst Tenika paid the bill. Then the women climbed the steps back into the cool night air. The clouds had moved away and a clear sky greeted them. As they climbed up towards the old gatehouse, they stopped to look across to Naples to take in the twinkling lights lining the shore.

"This is a special place and I am glad you brought me here. Thank you."

Tenika and Chantrea hugged Sasha and then the women turned and walked up the steps, through the old gatehouse, then up onto Via Maria Grande and back towards Via San Cesareo that led in to Tasso Square. Although after ten o'clock, the square was still lively and the restaurants and bars were working hard to meet the demands of late diners and drinkers.

"I can walk back to the Ambasciatori from here. You two don't have to come with me."

"Wouldn't think of it" said Tenika.

"No, we will walk with you all the way. It's not far and we can take the short cut via Piazza Angelina Lauro on the way back" added Chantrea.

So the three women walked quickly along Via Correale and then Via Califano until they reached the Ambasciatori. They stopped at the door and hugged again.

"What time should I come in the morning?"

"Is nine ok for you?"

"Yes, that's fine."

"Night then."

Sasha turned and went through the door whilst Tenika and Chantrea began the walk back towards the centre of Sorrento.

"Inspired thinking about the laptop Chanie. Let's hope he hasn't added a bunch of numbers onto the password."

"And let's hope the files are organised in a logical way with folders that have sensible titles. At least that way I might be able to eliminate files and focus on things that might be helpful."

"Let's hope so Chanie, let's hope so."

DAY SIX

The next morning both Tenika and Chantrea were up early. Chantrea opened up the double doors and sat out on the balcony whilst Tenika attended to her hair. It was another warm day with only patchy cloud in the sky. Down below, the early risers were making their way to work and the sound of scooters was already beginning to build.

"I think this is quite an important day Tee, if we don't find any helpful information that gets us somewhere we may not get much further."

"Yes, I know Chanie but I feel we will be lucky. Something will turn up."

When Tenika had finished with her hair, they went down in the lift to the breakfast room. It was mainly white, walls and tables with clear see through chairs and black table coverings. On one wall was a television screen showing an Italian breakfast show. Against a wall furthest from the doorway was a buffet breakfast containing cereal, boiled eggs, ham, fruit, bread for toast and a range of pastries. There was an urn of hot water for those who wanted tea and a separate urn of hot coffee. Tenika had discovered, however, that cappuccino was available to those who ordered it and she had every morning.

Like most things at Palazzo Abagnale, breakfast was a relaxed affair but with good quality produce and an attentive and friendly service from the elderly waitress. The majority of those staying at the hotel were relatively young and from different parts of Europe. The decor of the hotel was perhaps too contemporary for some but for those, like Tenika and Chantrea, the lack of fussiness and friendly disposition of all staff was perfect for a relaxing visit. Well that is how it had started.

"Right Chanie, I am going to stay here and get on the computer. I will start with the Positano News and see where that gets me. I think you have the more difficult job, assuming you can get into his computer, to try and find something amongst what could be a lot of files."

"Well assuming the password works and he hasn't encrypted everything, I will try to get to grips with the file structure and to start with may try some searches using particular words. I'm not sure how long it will take."

"And you don't know how long Sasha will give you."

"True."

"Let's keep in touch during the morning and then meet up when you are done."

"Ok Tee."

Tenika and Chantrea finished their breakfast and went back to the room to freshen up.

"Ok, I am off."

Tenika and Chantrea hugged each other.

"Good luck Chanie."

"Same to you."

Less than fifteen minutes later, Chantrea was at the reception desk of the Ambasciatori.

"Good morning, my name is Chantrea Park and I have come to see Sasha Adams. She is expecting me, could you call her room?"

"Of course."

The receptionist phoned through to Sasha's room.

"Good morning, there is a Miss Park in reception to see you. .... Of course, I will tell her."

"She says you may go up to her room. It is room 512. You can take a lift which is behind you on the right."

"Grazie."

Chantrea walked down the steps towards the lift on the right hand side. She looked at herself in the large mirror on the lift wall and just hoped she would find something of use. The lift door opened and Sasha's room was on the landing just to the right. She knocked on the door and waited. There was a pause of about ten seconds and then the door opened and Sasha ushered her into the room. Sasha closed the door and took Chantrea's arm.

"Good morning Chanie. I've had an early morning call from Inspector Maldini. He says Luke's body will be released today and that we can take him home. I have also spoken to Andrew Hillsom this morning and he says he can arrange a special flight for tomorrow morning but wants to collect Luke's things today to be forwarded to the carrier in readiness. He mentioned the computer too. He said he would collect it today with Luke's belongings and then keep it to save me the problem of returning it to him. He wants me to let him know when Luke's things are ready for collection."

"Right then we had better get on. Where is the laptop?"

"I have it here. I got it last night and hid it in the wardrobe. I don't know why!"

The room was large and sea facing. It had a balcony overlooking the bay straight across from Vesuvius. The furnishings were lush and the furniture of high quality.

"This is a lovely room."

I know, it's beautiful. Luke had a similar one down the hall."

"Luke's company looks after it's people very well."

"Well, interestingly, I found that Luke's room is being paid for by Dynamo. I asked at reception when I first arrived. I was worried about what the bill would come to."

Chantrea settled herself down at the table in the corner of the room. Opened the laptop and turned it on."

"Ok, Sasha we are at that moment when I need the password."

"It's wabblebot. Not particularly flattering I know but it comes from a time when I was over-weight as a child and it stuck."

Chantrea was not particularly taken with the lack of sensitivity contained in the word. She chose not to respond.

"Ok, let's try with some numbers attached."

"There you go, wabblebot001. Good we're off."

"I am going to leave you to it. I am sure you don't want me to look over your shoulder."

Chantrea began looking at the file structure on the computer hoping that it was well organised and that folders and files had clear meaningful titles. Luck was in, Luke had been very ordered separating work folders from personal ones. Thankfully, it didn't seem as if he used encryption on his files as well.

"So, Chantrea what do you and Tenika do for a living?"

"Tenika works as a researcher with the Kings Foundation and I work at Surrey University on the student support department. My mum works at the University and she let me know when they were looking for people with languages to cope with the rising international student population. I speak Khymer and so got lucky."

"You two seem to get on so well. When did you meet?"

"We gravitated towards each other at University. It's strange really because we have never really talked about it that much. We just get on very well and seem to complement each other. We like being in each other's company."

"You're both very attractive women. I suppose you have chaps running around after you all the time."

"Hahaha, not exactly. Tee has had a couple of admirers but she tends to frighten them off. She is a very strong woman."

"Yes I can see that."

"And as for me, forever alone I think is the phrase. Well, that's not really true. I am constantly surrounded by people at work, I have my mum and Tee so there isn't a lot of time for other distractions."

"What about you Sasha do you have anyone?"

"Well, I am single. I've had a long term relationship but it fizzled out and now I am consumed by school work. I don't seem to have any time for anything else and with the difficulties we've been having at school, I haven't been in the mindset for much else."

Chantrea took out her notebook and began to write things down. Time passed and Sasha made coffee for them both whilst Chantrea continued to search.

"How are you getting on? It's getting on for twelve and I think I will need to contact Andrew Hillsom soon."

"I'm fine. In fact probably done. Do you think there is any chance that I can copy two documents from the laptop?"

"How would you do that?"

"Well, It's a bit of luck really, because I knew we had a computer in our hotel room I brought a memory stick to Sorrento with me."

"What do the documents say?"

"Well, I am not sure how important they are but I would like to show them to Tee."

"Well we have come this far."

"Thanks Sasha."

With that, Chantrea took out her memory stick and saved the two documents onto it. She closed down the laptop, unplugged it and replaced it into its bag.

"Will you let me know what you and Tenika do next?"

"Yes, of course. I will need to go back and see how she has got on. Have you got a mobile here?"

"Yes, I have. Let me write down the number for you."

"And you don't happen to have a photo of Luke do you?"

"Well strange you should ask because I have one in my purse along with one or two others.

Sasha picked up her hand bag from the bed and pulled out her purse. In it was a small passport sized photograph of Luke.

"It was taken last Christmas."

"I don't suppose I could borrow it, could I?"

"Yes, it's ok. It's a copy and I can easily replace it."

"Sasha, you are so lovely. Thank you."

"Mmm I don't think my head teacher thinks that."

"So Sasha, you will be leaving tomorrow?"

"Yes, that's the plan. I will travel back with Steven and Luke's body. I should know later what time."

"Ok, then let's make sure we catch up later on."

Chantrea collected up her things but before leaving went through the doors onto the balcony. Although there were some fluffy clouds in the sky, it was warm and the view around the coastline and across to Vesuvius and Naples was breathtaking."

"This is a fantastic view Sasha."

"Yes it is. In different circumstances I could happily sit out here and drink a glass of wine."

"I know. Well, thanks for the coffee and talk to you later."

"Ok, Chanie, it's been good to see you today."

Chantrea walked back through the room to the door and then made her way via the lift back to reception. As she did so, she stopped at reception.

"Buongiorno, I just wonder what the rate is for a room similar to 512?"

"Yes, that is a Premier room and the rate is three hundred Euro a night with breakfast. Can I give you a brochure?"

"Mm yes please,"

"Grazie"

Chantrea went through the revolving door into the sunlight cascading down onto Via Califano. She took out her mobile phone and rang Tenika."

"Hi, I'm done here and on my way back. Should be about fifteen minutes. How have you got on?"

"Fine Chanie, found some interesting stuff."

"Oh, good. Well I have copied two documents that are also interesting but tell you more when I arrive. By the way, Luke's room is three hundred Euro a night. It's fantastic, Dynamo were being very generous. Anyway, see you soon."

Fifteen minutes later Chantrea arrived back at Palazzo Abagnale and quickly went up the lift to the room. Once in, she disappeared into the loo. She called to Tee.

"So how did you get on with the newspaper?"

"Good actually, I've had a long chat with a reporter with the Positano News and looked through their articles on this particular contract and other general stuff"

Chantrea reappeared from the bathroom and sat down on the sofa. Tenika sat at the table facing her."

"Ok Tee, you go first. Tell me all."

"Right, well things first begin to appear in the paper in March when the award of the contract was made public. A company based in Naples called FP Ingegneria was very unhappy about the award and its managing director, a chap called Francesco Giardiniere, wrote to the paper saying how the award

120

was unpatriotic and uneconomic. He did not believe there were not companies locally or regionally that could do the work. He said bringing in a British company was a waste of money. He also said that Italian companies and the authorities needed to do something to stop this behaviour."

"Mmm sounds interesting."

"Yes Chanie, but I haven't got to the best bit yet. I then spoke with a reporter at the Positano News and he said there had been rumours of inducement payments and companies battled to get this and other work. He said there was no concrete evidence which is why they couldn't say too much, however Francesco Giardiniere believed that some dodgy dealing had taken place to ensure Dynamo gave the work to Luke's company. This is, of course, all off the record."

"So Tee, you are saying there is some belief that bribes or inducements were used to secure the contract?"

"Yes."

"Well that's interesting because I have something to show you."

Chantrea got up from the sofa, took the memory stick from her hand bag and connected it to the computer.

"There's a couple of things I want to show you but the first one is quite interesting."

Chantrea pulled up a two page document onto the screen.

"This internal document marked Confidential is from someone called Suresh Sharma and is a briefing document to Luke and his colleagues talking about the situation prior to winning the contract. The important paragraph is down here. Look:

.......The promotional budget is now in place and our negotiators are applying it to the situation. We are confident that its application will lead to a successful result offering reciprocal benefits that our overseas staff have enjoyed in the past. I can assure you that all effort is being placed into winning the contract and that our negotiators are applying the maximum economic leverage available. ......

So, what do you think of that Tee?"

"I think you have hit gold Chanie. This seems to be an implied statement that the promotional budget is being used for inducement purposes. They clearly went out to win the contract and used money as part of the process. What do you think they mean by 'reciprocal benefits' Chanie?"

"Well, I have thought about that and I wonder whether as part of the deal overseas staff, such as Luke, are provided with high quality accommodation by the main contractor."

"Well, it all fits doesn't it?"

"Chanie, there's something else that's been bothering me."

"What's that?"

"Well, you remember Inspector Maldini said the name of the Mayor was Alexander Albero?"

"Yes."

"What do you think the name of the managing director of Dynamo is?"

"Well, I guess you are going to say someone with the same name?"

"Luciano Albero to be precise and he is the brother of the Mayor. My contact at Positano News confirmed it. What do you think about that?"

"Let me try and get my head around this. There is a suggestion here that inducements or bribes were used to secure the contract and that somehow that has led to the death of Luke perhaps at the hand of a disgruntled competitor. That causes alarm bells to ring at the town hall where the Mayor doesn't want any scandal to become public so it becomes helpful if Luke's death is treated as an accident and the case is closed as soon as possible."

"Well Chanie, there are pieces of a puzzle that do seem to fit together."

"Now Chanie, you said there was a second document?"

"Yes, I am not sure how relevant it is in the light of the other stuff but let me get it on screen for you. I found it in Luke's personal area and it looks like a draft of a letter to Sasha's head teacher. Here it is."

Tenika looked at the letter. It wasn't in a finished form but set out some interesting issues.

"Mmm, what does it say here ....so Luke was preparing to write to, or had written to, Suzannah Boswell accusing her of past deeds. Apparently before she left her last post there was an assertion that she had acted improperly towards a female member of staff and that she had resigned before any actions were taken. Gosh, he says he has a statement from the member of staff and intends to make it public if she does not pull back from her bullying position with staff. He says also that Sasha would be prepared to make a public statement as well."

"Strong stuff eh?"

"Yes Chanie it is but did Luke do anything with this and, even if he did, does it have any relevance to matters here?"

"Oh, and Sasha gave me a small photo of Luke. It's here if I can get it out."

Chantrea handed the photograph to Tenika who gazed at it for a few moments.

"Good work Chanie it might come in use."

Tenika put the photograph onto the table next to the computer.

"What's next then?"

"Well Chanie I think it is another conversation with Inspector Maldini and I think it might be helpful if we check if Sasha really was going to make a statement for Luke."

"Right so shall I ring Sasha? She has given me her mobile number?"

"Yes, I will ring Inspector Maldini once I have found the number and you can ring Sasha but then I shall need some lunch. Look, it's gone two now. I can hear the Fauno calling."

With that, Tenika rang down to reception to ask if they had the telephone number for the local Carabineri and Chantrea rang Sasha.

"Oh hello Sasha, it's Chanie here. How are you getting on?"

Hi Chanie, I'm fine. The luggage is being collected at three o'clock."

"Oh I see, that's in about forty five minutes or so?"

"Yes, and the flight has been arranged for ten in the morning."

"Oh good, look Sasha I've got a question for you. It's about Luke's support for you with your school. Did you ever make a statement for him? You know, something that could be used at a meeting?"

"Well, I didn't write a statement but I think he did from comments I made to him. I seem to remember we sat down some months or so ago and I went through it all in detail and he wrote it all down. Why do you ask?"

"Well we're still looking at all angles. Did you agree for him to use it?

"Umm I think I said he could if pushed. I was in a rather unhappy state and felt my time at the school was coming to an end. I thought I was going to be pushed at some point so I didn't think it mattered if Luke used the statement. If I was going to lose my job it didn't seem to matter how it came about."

"Sasha, there was something on Luke's laptop which suggested there may have been inducement payments to Dynamo. It's not really clear and I wouldn't say anything to Andrew Hillsom but Tenika wants to talk to Inspector Maldini again. Oh, and don't worry she won't mention you."

"Ok, well let's see where that takes us. Good luck and do remember to keep me informed."

"Yes, don't worry I'll ring again this evening."

"Thanks Chanie, bye for now."

"Bye."

Chantrea turned to Tenika who was sitting on the sofa.

"So Tee, it looks like Luke produced the statement based on testimony from Sasha and she did give him permission to use it, if pushed was how she put it. How did you get on with your calls?"

"Well I got the number for the Carabinieri from reception but then got a call from Raf. He wants to see us at Dynamo. I said we need lunch first but he says they will provide something and are sending a taxi over to get us."

"That's rather interesting. Did he say why and what's the urgency?"

"No he didn't and you're right it does sound a little odd."

"By the way, there's quite a breeze outside giving a chill to the air. I'm going to wear my thick cardigan."

"Right Chanie, in which case it is on with my special matching scarf and hat."

About ten minutes later the telephone rang informing them that a taxi had arrived. Tenika and Chantrea quickly went down in the lift and found the taxi parked outside on the street. The driver said nothing as the car sped through Sorrento and within a few minutes had arrived at Dynamo.

"I wonder who is paying" Tenika said to Chantrea.

"No payment. Dynamo is paying" replied the driver.

Tenika and Chantrea climbed from the taxi and pressed the buzzer for Dynamo.

"Buongiorno" crackled from the speaker.

"Buongiorno, Tenika Taylor e Chantrea Park per vedere Rafael Bellomi"

"Vieni in."

The door buzzed as it opened and Tenika and Chantrea climbed the stairs to the reception area. As soon as they entered the receptionist smiled at them."

"Hello, please take a seat. Rafael will be here in a moment."

As good as her word, Raf appeared moments later.

"Hello Tenika, hello Chanie. Thanks for coming so quickly. Please come this way."

Raf walked off in a purposeful way and Tenika and Chantrea had to move smartly to keep up. Moving through a door in reception, they found themselves in an open plan area with numerous work stations. At the end of the area they went through another door into a corridor. They came across two people walking in the opposite direction. One, a short man in his thirties, whilst the other was a stylish woman in her forties. She was slim with dark wavy hair cascading over her shoulders.

"Ciao, siamo in riunione domani mattina?"

"Sì, non ti preoccupare."

The woman smiled at Raf.

"Ciao, io non ti vedo da un po."

"Ciao Maria."

Raf kissed her on the cheek.

"e chi sono i tuoi amici?"

"Mi dispiace, questo è Tenika e questo Chanie. Sono amici di Luca."

The woman looked at Tenika and Chantrea.

"Ciao" she said.

"Ciao" responded Tenika.

"Do I spot a British accent in there?

128

The woman smiled.

"Well done! I have lived here for many years but I still carry a bit of an accent."

"Your Italian is very good Maria. Where did you come from originally?"

"My family came from sleepy Bournemouth." I came here to have better weather and a more interesting life."

"I am sorry Tenika, we must move on."

Tenika waved goodbye to Maria and they continued to walk along the passageway and then took stairs up one floor.

"Does Maria work for Dynamo?"

"No, she provided business English training for our people. Some have group work, others have one to one. She has been with us for many years now."

The floor they were now on was rather quieter with smarter looking offices.

"Please, we are here."

Raf gestured to Tenika and Chantrea to enter the room. Inside to their left and sat at a desk was a heavily built man in his late forties. Straight ahead was a table with six chairs and to their right was a dresser containing a range of food and drink.

"My name is Luciano Albero. Thank you for coming. You must be Tenika and I think you are Chanie. Is that right?"

Tenika and Chantrea took turns to confirm their identity and shake hands.

"I think we prevented you from having a late lunch so we have got some things in for you. Please take what you wish."

They looked round to see a range of items. Paninis, fruit and drinks along with fine plates, cutlery and napkins. Tenika removed her hat and scarf, hanging them on a coat stand in one corner.

"Someone's making an effort for us" whispered Chantrea.

"Yes, and I wonder why" responded Tenika.

Luciano Albero, Raf, Tenika and Chantrea all sat at the table. Coffee was served to them all.

"Can I say Mr Albero that your English is very good."

"Please Tenika, call me Luciano. For me English is a necessity not a luxury and I am flattered you think my English is good."

"Now I asked Rafael to invite you here today because I wanted to talk to you about the sad events of the past few days. I am aware from Rafael that you were friends of Luke and I wanted to share with you our sadness of his death. He had worked with us for some time and we had grown to like him a lot. The work he was doing with Rafael was excellent and it is so sad that such an accident has happened."

Tenika and Chantrea looked at each other both sensing they were being invited to comment. Tenika took the plunge.

"We agree with you. It is such a sad loss to us all and, in particular to his sister whom we have met here. Accidents, of course, do happen but in this case the circumstances do seem a little odd."

Luciano Albero raised his eyebrows.

"In what way might I ask?"

Tenika sensed danger but carried on.

"Well, it just seems a little odd that a man who was on medication and who chose not to drink with Rafael and ourselves should then go out, drink and fall over the cliff."

"Ah well Tenika, people are very complex creatures and when they are away from home they may behave in ways that are different and unusual. The police say there is no evidence of any other matters and that is why they have released the body for transportation to the UK. Is that not so?"

"Yes you are quite right Luciano." Tenika conceded.

Chantrea also sensed the need to tread very carefully.

"Perhaps it is the fact that the death and its manner was so shocking to us that causes us, and perhaps anyone who knew Luke, to be curious about the circumstances. Perhaps we have been shocked into pondering about the word 'why'."

"Chanie, I applaud your philosophic considerations and your desire to help Luke's sister. You are both excellent friends for anyone to have. The problem is that such matters are unsettling and ultimately we must all get on with living and our daily lives. Do you know that I have had a reporter on the phone to me today asking questions about Mr Adams and the project. I was even asked if I had any comment about those old allegations from FP Ingegneria about impropriety concerning the contract."

Luciano laughed out loud and gestured to Raf to join in. He seemed less inclined to be so excessive.

"You see ladies such sad events cause questions to be asked that are irrelevant and, well, harmful if not stopped. I assured the reporter that nothing illegal concerning the contract had taken place and I know the police agree with me. I told the reporter to go and talk with Inspector Maldini or Superintendent Mosta."

"This food is lovely. You are very kind Luciano."

Chantrea was grasping at straws to change the conversation.

"It is our pleasure. Tell me, for how long are you in Sorrento?"

"Another seven days" said Tenika.

"Ah well do take your time to see the sights and soak up the atmosphere. Make sure you try our many good restaurants. Try to relax if you can. I know it won't be easy with these matters on your mind but do try to. How did you get to Sorrento from Naples airport? Bus or train or taxi?"

"We came by bus, it is very good value."

"Ah but it is very slow. I want to show you how grateful we are at Dynamo with your concern for Luke and, if you will let me, we will provide you with a Mercedes car to take you to the airport when you leave. Just let Rafael know the time and he will arrange it."

Luciano looked across to Raf.

"Is that ok Rafael?"

"Yes of course."

"Now ladies, it has been a pleasure to meet you but I have to leave for a meeting but please stay here with Rafael, have more food and drink and when you are ready he will get you back to your hotel."

Luciano Albero left the room and the atmosphere relaxed just a little. They all took more coffee and Chantrea helped herself to more fruit. Raf looked at Tenika and Chantrea in an uncertain way. He wasn't sure how the meeting had gone.

"Please try to understand the impact of Luke's death on the company. It is easy for those who want to make negative comment to do so. Also, when two foreign ladies ask the questions they ask, that too is noticed."

"Are we being warned off?" Tenika asked rather firmly.

"No, perhaps not in the way you mean."

Raf lowered his voice and leant in towards Tenika and Chantrea.

"I am in a difficult position, I want to be helpful to you but the company is firmly supportive of the police's decision that it was an accident. It does not want its business raked over."

Sensing Raf's door was slightly ajar, Tenika probed further.

"Does the company have anything to hide?"

"It insists it has done nothing illegal."

Tenika decided it was time for the big question, come what may.

"Raf, were there any financial payments made to Dynamo to secure the contract?"

"No, none."

That answer brought the discussion to a halt and all three looked away from each other as they drank their coffee. Tenika gazed out of the window whilst Chantrea held her coffee cup in her hand. Both were thinking what should come next. Chantrea put her cup down and looked at Raf.

"Raf, were there any considerations made in respect of the relationship between Dynamo and Luke's company that were enhanced through some sort of financial assistance?"

Tenika looked at Chantrea rather amazed at the sentence. She then looked at Raf.

"If there were considerations, or arrangements if you mean, I cannot see how they relate to Luke's death."

"But there were considerations or arrangements?"

"The relationship between companies is always a complex one. Each helps one another. It has always been so."

Tenika now felt the door opening wider and had her own question."

"And was the provision of accommodation at the Ambasciatori part of those considerations?"

"We were very happy to provide the accommodation. We wanted to treat Luke and any of his colleagues well."

The door to the office opened and a woman dressed in a rather formal grey suit entered.

Raf looked to both Tenika and Chantrea.

"This is Mr Albero's secretary. I think it is probably time for us to leave."

"Ciao, stiamo per partire."

"Bene, spero le signore ci lasceranno soli ora?"

There was a flicker on Tenika's face but she held back from anything more.

"Sì, hanno capito cosa intendevamo."

They all rose, collected their belongings and left the room. Raf led them back to reception and then down the stairs. No one spoke on the journey. At the bottom of the stairs Tenika turned to Raf. Her face was stern and her eyes narrowed.

"Can we trust you Raf?"

Tenika's question was sharp edged and Raf's body language was that of a man who expected the question. Raf took his time to reply as if not sure what to say.

"As I said before, I want to help but I also have a family to feed. Please enjoy your time in Sorrento but take care of what you ask and who you ask. And don't forget about the car, just let me know when you need it."

"I think we understand Raf. Thanks for helping us so far. Ciao."

Tenika and Chantrea both shook hands with Raf, turned and left the building. Outside was the same taxi waiting to take them back to their hotel. They got in and were greeted by the driver.

"I hope your meeting went well?"

Tenika gripped Chantrea's hand firmly and looked at her.

"Yes, it went very well. They are nice people and a nice company."

"What are you going to do now? I mean where shall I take you?"

"Oh we're going to enjoy our holiday. Could you drop us at Tasso Square?"

"Of course."

The taxi sped its way back through Sorrento to Tasso Square where Tenika and Chantrea were dropped off next to

Fauno bar. As before, the cost was met by Dynamo. Tenika and Chantrea walked across the square towards their hotel.

"Sorry for grabbing your hand like that but I had a feeling the driver was fishing for information that would find its way back to Signor Albero."

"Yes, I got the feeling something was up and when you said enjoy our holiday, well I knew something was up! By the way, what did the secretary say to Raf?"

"She said that she hoped we would leave the company alone now."

Mmm Tee, did you know the reporter was going to ring Luciano?"

"No, I didn't. Perhaps a bit naive of me."

"Well things are certainly starting to happen. What's next?"

"I think we should talk again with Inspector Maldini. I'll ring him from the room."

Tenika leaned over to Chantrea to talk quietly into her ear."

"Oh, by the way Chanie, your question about considerations was fucking brilliant. It's opened up the box even though we don't know what the considerations were."

"Other than the accommodation at the Ambasciatori" responded Chantrea."

"Quite so."

They arrived at the hotel and went up the stairs to reception. Standing there was a policeman. The receptionist gestured towards the women.

"Signorina Taylor e signorina Park?"

"Yes."

"Please come with me. I must take you to the police station."

Tenika and Chantrea looked at each other. Tenika smiled.

"Well, we wanted to go!"

They hadn't noticed the police car parked along the road. They were both ushered into the back of the car and within a couple of minutes were in the back car park of the police station. They got out of the car and the officer beckoned them to follow him. They entered the police station at the back and followed the officer along a corridor that turned left and then right. Finally, a door was opened for them and they entered another interview room. The officer pointed towards the chairs at a table and Tenika and Chantrea sat down. The officer stood by the door. After about five minutes the door opened and Inspector Maldini entered. He nodded towards the officer and he left. Both Tenika and Chantrea got up.

"Ciao Ispettore Maldini."

Tenika held out her hand. It was ignored.

"Please sit down."

The inspector seemed to be furious.

"What do you ladies think you are doing?"

"I don't know what you mean?" replied Tenika.

"When we last met, I asked you to leave this matter to us and yet you have been asking questions and upsetting people in Sorrento."

"Who exactly have we been upsetting?"

"You spoke with a reporter from the Positano News who has spoken to Signor Albero and raised issues about corruption and its link with the death of Mr Adams. Now there is no evidence of a link. The only evidence we have is of an accidental death. The body of Mr Adams is being flown out tomorrow with his sister and you must accept this is the end of the matter."

Tenika could feel her combative side rising. She looked hard and straight into the eyes of Pietro Maldini.

"So we have upset Luciano Albero have we? And why are you concerned with that? Is it anything to do with the fact that the Mayor is his brother?"

The inspector was struggling to remain composed.

"You cannot come to this country and disrupt the lives of people with no evidence. Do you understand?"

The inspector's voice was loud and near to shouting. Chantrea felt she had to try to calm matters.

"Inspector, we don't want to disrupt the lives of anyone and we accept that evidence is key to this matter. However, we feel we have found something that is important. We now understand that some consideration was made between Luke Adam's company and Dynamo for the award of the contract. If this is true then there is reason for Dynamo to cover this information up and, more importantly, there is motive for someone to try to prevent such action taking place again. The death of Luke Adams could be a warning against such considerations happening with overseas firms in the future."

"What are you talking about? Consideration? What consideration? What does this mean? What are you talking about?"

"We think some sort of financial benefits were transacted between Dynamo and Luke's company to facilitate the award of the contract. The provision of accommodation by Dynamo to Luke and his colleagues was one element of that consideration."

"Miss Park, if you are saying bribes were taken for this contract then I need evidence. Do you have any?"

"We think it was a lot more subtle than a bribe but I have to admit I don't know exactly how it worked."

"So you don't have any evidence!"

"Ispettore, Rafael Bellomi as much as admitted it to us today and we have been warned off by Luciano Albero from asking any more questions. We think we are getting close to the truth and we need your help."

"Miss Taylor, I am sure that Signor Albero merely wants to get his business back to normal and doesn't want journalists asking damaging questions which have no basis in fact. If people believe you are spreading untrue rumours about them, they may take legal action against you. People might decide you are unwelcome here. Do you understand?"

Tenika was furious at this. She went on the offensive.

"What I see is a questionable death and authorities who seem to be taking an easy way out even when there is evidence to suggest questions need to be asked. What's the matter with you? Are you afraid of big business and their political allies?"

Chantrea put her hand across and placed it on Tenika's arm, however Tenika did not flinch from her stare at Pietro Maldini.

Pietro Maldini drew in breath although visibly shaking.

"Miss Taylor, I think you have said enough. You have questioned me for the last time."

The Inspector stood up and opened the door. He roared out a name and in seconds a uniformed officer was at the door.

"Escort these women out of here. I have had enough of them."

With that, Inspector Maldini walked out of the room. Tenika and Chantrea got up from their chairs. Tenika was still full of anger and just stared ahead."

"This way ladies."

The officer led the way and in moments they reached the front door. They walked out into the chilly air turning left towards Corso Italia. Tenika let go.

"Those fucking idiots. What are they doing? Why is he so frightened of the Alberos? If he thinks I am going to be frightened off by them then he is very wrong."

Tenika clenched her fist as she threw her comments out.

Chantrea kept quiet, she knew from the past that this moment the best tactic was to let Tenika let off steam and, when done, a conversation could begin. It didn't take long to walk back to the hotel, Tenika marched off with Chantrea struggling to keep up. The silence continued up the stairs and into the lift. As they entered the room Tenika took off her hat and scarf and threw them onto the floor and slumped onto the sofa. With her elbow on the arm of the sofa, she held her head under her chin and stared ahead.

"I'll get us some coffee" said Chantrea in an emotionless voice.

She walked to the table and telephoned down to reception for two cappuccinos. After about five minutes of silence there was a knock on the door and their coffees had arrived. Chantrea took the tray and placed it on the computer table. There was still no sound. Chantrea opened up the doors to the balcony, took her coffee and sat outside. After a couple of minutes Chantrea saw movement behind her from the corner of her eye.

"Chanie"

Chantrea got up, went back inside with her coffee and sat on the sofa next to Tenika.

"I'm sorry. I'm really sorry. I just lost it."

Chantrea smiled.

"It's ok, you're such a fighter. It's what makes you such a strong woman and I do admire you for that. You do things that I can't do and I love you for it."

A tear rolled down Tenika's face and she reached across for Chantrea's hand.

"I am so lucky to have you with me. I can't imagine what mess I would get into without you."

"You would conquer the world whoever you were with."

"Oh Chanie, where do we go now? Is this the end of the matter?"

"I don't know but let's drink up."

About an hour later the telephone rang in the room. Chantrea picked up the phone.

"Hello .... oh I see, ok I'll be right down."

"There's a delivery for us. I'll go and get it."

Minutes later Chantrea returned with a small envelope.

"What is it?" Queried Tenika.

"I don't know. The receptionist said it was left by some scruffy chap in jeans."

"Does it say anything on the envelope?"

"Yes, just Signorina Taylor and Park."

"Well open it then."

Chantrea opened the envelope and pulled out a single sheet of paper. It just had three words written on it.

"What does it say?"

"Albero Carità Mayoral"

"That's the Albero Mayoral Charity. Let's get it up on the computer."

Tenika quickly powered up the computer and found her way to the website for the Mayor's charity.

"Hmm let's have a look at what it says. The charity supports disadvantaged and poor families in Sorrento and Naples where Alexander Albero was born."

"Well that's not surprising. Don't most Mayors have a charity of some sort?"

"Yes, Chanie but this one is funded by communal and business donation and part of the programme is the development of a sort of social housing programme."

Tenika looked at Chantrea.

"The consideration" they said almost simultaneously.

"So Chanie, let's think this through. Luke's firm pays money into the charity to support the worthy objective of building social housing. Mayor Albero is the hero, is re-elected and continues in power. That aids brother Luciano who just happens to be in the development business. In return Dynamo provides lovely accommodation to Luke and colleagues. Can it be that simple?"

"And someone out there doesn't like the ethics and makes a point through the death of Luke?"

"Quite possibly Chanie, quite possibly."

"Is it possible to check if such a payment was made?"

"Ah Chanie that is the question and I don't know the answer to that but I know a man who does although I don't think this is the time to ask him!"

"No, I don't think it is."

They both laughed.

"It's good to see you laugh again Tee. Who do you think sent this?"

"Raf but I don't think he will admit to it."

"This has been quite a day."

"It certainly has Chanie. I wonder what tomorrow will bring."

"Well before then I must ring Sasha to see how she is and fill her in on today's events although I think she should get a shortened version."

"Yes, keep it low key. Don't raise her expectations. She is probably anxious about the flight home and all that will come after it."

"Yes, I agree. I'll ring her after dinner. And when we go don't forget your hat and scarf it is still quite chilly outside."

They decided to dine at the Ristorante O'Parrucchiano on Corso Italia. A little more expensive but an interesting restaurant set in layers up a central staircase. At the top and back, where Tenika and Chantrea had a table, the diners are set in amongst a range of colourful foliage including the upper reaches of trees intertwined with the dining area. They decided to try to talk about other things than Luke's death. Not an easy task given the passions of the day. However, they had thought about little else for some days and now was an opportunity to talk of other things. In fact to try to return to the original reason for visiting Sorrento in the first place – to relax and get away from emotional pain.

Their discussion ranged from clothes, repairs to their flats back in Wimbledon, latest films, new theatre shows, art collections and, of course, the weather. They laughed and, for a time, lost themselves in a simple world of social pleasure. They were for a couple of hours no different from all those who had travelled to Sorrento for hundreds of years to relax, take in the climate, the food and the ambiance of the local population.

When the meal ended, they were as satisfied as the Romans and the romantics who had sat and ate at the table of wonderful Sorrentian hospitality. They wandered back to Palazzo Abagnale refusing to think about other matters. They looked in shops, took in the happy faces in the bars and waved at Lucca in the Fauno bar. Chantrea linked her arm into that of Tenika. Laughter turned to giggles as they wished a traffic policeman a very good night and he returned the compliment. These two young vivacious women of the twenty first century were as one as they skipped across Tasso

Square arm in arm although this would be the last time they would ever do so.

Once back in their room Chantrea telephoned Sasha.

"Hi Sasha, I'm just ringing as I said I would. Are you all set for tomorrow?"

"Hello Chantrea, yes all set. The luggage was taken this afternoon and I am just left with a small case for the plane. Andrew Hillsom has chartered a private jet to take us back and everything is arranged for Luke's body to be taken to an undertaker from the airport. I am very grateful to them for everything they have done. How did you get on? Any progress?"

"Well we have had another conversation with Raf and Inspector Maldini. I think it is fair to say that things are ongoing."

"Well look Chanie, if Luke's death was an accident then so be it. It would be nice to know the precise circumstances but you and Tenika have lives to get on with so don't spend all your time on this. Be prepared to let it go because I know I shall have to."

"I understand what you are saying and we shall only go as far as the road takes us. I think Tenika wants a word."

"Yes, put her on."

"Hi Sasha, I shall be thinking of you tomorrow. I really hope everything goes well."

"You are so kind Tenika and let me say again how grateful I am for the care and concern you and Chanie have given to Luke. I will never forget it."

147

"Well we won't forget you either Sasha. I hope you will keep in touch regarding funeral arrangements. I am sure we would like to come if we are back by then."

"Don't worry I will do that."

"I hope also that things improve at your school. There is enormous pressure on you at the moment so try not to let them get you down."

"I had a text today from the school asking me when I was returning!"

"It doesn't stop does it?"

"No, but I have learned some lessons from you. I know I must be stronger and be prepared to kick back when necessary. Well I must let you go. Thank you once again for all you have done. Love to you both."

"Yes, take care of yourself too. Bye."

"Bye Tenika."

"I'm whacked Chanie. I need to have a shower and go to bed."

"Ok, you go first cos I need one too."

Tenika went into the bathroom to take her shower and Chantrea sat on the sofa with her book of poetry. She had always liked poetry from an early age and had written poems herself. She read a poem by Robert Browning, The Englishman in Italy – Piano di Sorrento. Chantrea focused upon a particular part of the poem:

"No seeing our skiff
Arrive about noon from Amalfi;
  Our fisher arrive,
And pitch down his basket before us,
  All trembling alive
With pink and grey jellies, your sea fruit;
  You touch the strange lumps,
And mouths gape there, eyes open, all manner
  Of horns and of humps,
Which only the fisher looks grave at,
  While round him like imps
Cling screaming the children as naked
  And brown as his shrimps"

Chantrea closed her eyes and thought back to Emilia's and the fishermen (and woman) working on their nets. She thought what a wonderful place this must have been all those years ago when the world was a simpler place and where the fisherman's basket of squirming fish could bring such joy to children.

DAY SEVEN

"Buongiorno."

"Buongiorno, it's me again. I am in need of your help once more."

"What is it this time?"

"I have another problem that needs resolving."

"Is it linked to the Englishman?"

"Yes."

"What is this problem that needs resolving?"

"There is a woman here as a tourist who is asking too many questions and may find the secret of the Englishman's death. I need to stop her."

"How do you know she will find anything?"

"She is resourceful and very determined. She has already received encouragement to stop her questioning from other sources but does not want to listen. She keeps going to the police and soon they might listen to her."

"What do you want me to do?"

"Eliminate her."

"When do you want this to happen?"

"As soon as possible. I want it to look like a robbery on a tourist."

"And what is the name of this woman?"

"Tenika Taylor."

"Where is she staying?"

"Palazzo Abagnale on Corso Italia."

"Is she alone?"

"No she is with another woman called Chanie Park"

"What does this Tenika Taylor look like?"

"She is a black woman, aged about thirty, with straight black hair about one metre 68 centimetres in height. Oh, and she has a distinctive matching purple scarf and hat. She is no fool."

"Well this is possible, there are not many black women in Sorrento. I can find her but at a price."

"I will give you five thousand Euro, the same as before."

"No no, this time it will be ten thousand Euro."

"But last time I did the difficult part of the work, you only helped me."

"I know, but this time you want me to do the whole job and so the price is higher. It is your choice."

"Very well. Just make sure you do a good job."

"And you will pay me the same way as before."

"Ok."

"Remember the job will only be done after you make the payment."

"Then I will do it straight away."

"You will tell me when the job has been done?"

"Yes."

This was not the only conversation taking place that morning. Earlier a car containing Andrew Hillsom had arrived at the Ambasciatori to collect Sasha Adams and take them both to Naples airport. The journey of about an hour was only occasionally punctuated by conversation. Sasha was too saddened and reflective of her loss whilst Andrew Hillsom spent much of his time on his mobile phone.

They arrived at Naples Capodichino airport and moved swiftly to a special gate for business passengers with a boarding pass. As they passed through security, Sasha was waived through but Andrew Hillsom was stopped by a smiling security officer who asked him to go with him for some formalities regarding the 'consignment'. Sasha turned back towards him.

"It's ok Sasha, just some formalities. You go through to the Eccellenza private lounge and I will meet you there in a few minutes. You have the entry pass with your boarding card."

"Ok, I will see you there."

Andrew Hillsom followed the security officer through a door out of the security area and down a short passage. The officer stopped and opened a door and beckoned Andrew to go in."

"Buongiorno Mr Hillsom."

Andrew Hillsom stopped and looked surprised at the figure standing in the room."

"Uhm buongiorno Ispettore Maldini. This is a surprise."

"Please take a seat. I don't want to hold you up. I know your flight is in less than an hour."

"Well what can I do for you?"

"Well, after all of the sadness of this case, I wanted to come personally to thank you for all you have done. Your efficiency in dealing with organising the transportation of the body is so much appreciated as has been your assistance to us and to Dynamo."

"Well to be honest Inspector ..."

"No please call me Pietro."

"Ok, well Pietro as I was saying, you need not have come. I did what needed to be done. He was our employee and we accept our duty to deal with the situation."

"Well it was first class, as you say, and I am sure that Miss Adams has been very reassured by your presence here."

"I hope that she has, yes."

"You know Andrew, I am one of those who welcome the involvement of business from Britain or France or Germany. It has always been the Sorrento way. I know there are those who might have it differently, but I think it broadens our view of the world. You bring new ideas to us, new ways of doing things. It helps our small commune become part of a much bigger world. Do you know what I mean?"

"Uhm well yes I do and, of course, we are delighted to join with the commune of Sorrento in its development and look to continue doing so in the future."

Andrew Hillsom looked at his watch and hoped this conversation would come to an end soon.

"Steven, I think the people of Sorrento are so grateful for the contributions of companies such as yours to the support of those in need."

"Sorry, I am not sure what you mean."

"Oh, I am just referring to the contribution you have made to Mayor Alexander Albero's fund. It is so good of you to do so."

"Well, er, I am not sure I can ...."

"Oh Steven, don't worry this is an informal chat, not formal. I met with the Mayor the other day and he was so happy with his funds."

"Well, uhm we have tried to do our little bit to help and we wish the Mayor all the best in his endeavours. We hope our contribution will be a small help."

"Well Steven, I will not keep you any longer. Have a safe journey home. The officer outside will take you to Sasha and ensure you collect your flight."

The two men stood up.

"Thank you for coming and let's hope we don't have the same reason for meeting ever again."

"Yes, let's hope so."

The two men shook hands and Andrew Hillsom left the room and was escorted by the security officer to the VIP lounge where Sasha was waiting.

"All sorted?"

"Well I think so. I think I have time for a quick coffee before boarding."

Back in Sorrento Tenika and Chantrea decided to think about what their next move might be. To help with that process, they turned their attention to spending some time looking for presents to take back home with them. They had already spent some time in Via San Cesareo looking in the shops trying to think of some items that would be interesting but not shouting tourist to the recipient. On this basis they rejected the ubiquitous lemon drink that Sorrento is famous for.

Tenika thought about a belt each for her brothers, Claude and Jerome. There were many sellers of leather goods and good quality too. Tenika wasn't sure about whether such a gift might be too simple or, if she went down that route, what colour and style to get. Chantrea was looking particularly for her mother and had visited clothes shops and jewellers. She was particularly taken with some coral jewellery but no decision had been taken.

They wandered back to Tasso Square and over to Fauno bar for coffee. Lucca spotted them approaching and beckoned them to come his way. They waved and walked straight in towards him.

"Buongiorno."

"Buongiorno Lucca" replied Tenika.

"Outside table?"

"Si Lucca."

They were given a table near to the front of the street tables giving them an excellent view of morning life in Sorrento."

"What can I get you?"

"Do you do a ham and tomato Panini?" asked Chantrea

"Of course, anything for you."

Tenika and Chantrea laughed.

"Ok, let's have two Paninis and two cappuccinos."

"Straight away" said Lucca.

Today's weather was a better day than that previously. The wind had fallen and there were only a few clouds in the sky. The temperature was still in excess of twenty degrees celsius providing a very pleasant environment.

"Well Tee, Sasha will be airborne now."

156

"Yes and the poor woman has some dark days ahead of her."

"Do you think we will make the funeral?"

"Well Chanie it depends on when it is. These things normally take a week or so to organise and we will be just back then. So maybe."

Lucca arrived back with the coffees and Paninis.

"For my favourite ladies."

Lucca smiled at both Tenika and Chantrea but perhaps the smile lingered just that bit longer for Chantrea.

"Grazie Lucca." Chantrea smiled at Lucca warmly.

Tenika and Chantrea began to consume their Panini and coffee whilst looking onto the square.

"Tee, have you noticed how some of the elderly ladies walk across the square? They just step off into the road with their eyes fixed ahead and don't flinch at any cars coming their way. The traffic seems to just come to a halt around them. It's like an assertion that people came before cars and they still have ownership of the space. It is the car that must give way, not the person."

"Yes Chanie you're right and have you noticed that dog over there sitting on the side of the road by the Ercolano bar? I noticed him the other day. He just sits there watching the world go by and sometimes moves just into the road as if to get a better view of what is going on. I feel I am watching him watch us watch the goings on in the square."

Even at this time of the year, there were many tourists in Sorrento. They came from all over the world. A keen ear could make out accents from Japan, Germany, USA, France and, of course, Britain. Still a strong tourist destination, there were always Brits close by.

"I wonder whether there is a short-cut way of getting above the town in order to get a panoramic view?"

"Haha Chanie, I know just the man with the answer."

With that, Tenika waved at Lucca who spotted her and came over."

"Lucca, is there a way of getting above the town to get a good view?"

"Do you mean by walking or taxi?"

"Walking."

"If you go up Corso Italia all the way to the Capodimonte hotel, you will see it on your left at the bend of the road, you will then come to steps leading up into the hill. If you take these steps they lead through the olive groves and up to a road above the town. You will get very good views from there."

"Grazie Lucca, you are so kind."

"No, it is my pleasure."

"He is so nice Tee."

He is, but he is also working hard for a tip."

"Are you up for a walk when we are done here?"

"Yes Chanie, I think I am. It will give us a good time to think."

Tenika and Chantrea took their time to eat their Panini and drink their coffee and, when done, paid Lucca – with a handsome tip – and set off walking up Corso Italia. In moments they reached the cathedral and then passed the Parrucchiano restaurant they visited the night before. They passed an eclectic range of shops from expensive fashion stores, straight forward tourist shops selling post cards and the usual tourist paraphernalia, specialist wine shops, a delicatessen, foreign exchange merchants and a pharmacy. They reached the busy junction with Via Degla Aranci which took traffic coming from the south onto a one way system. Opposite the junction was the Sorrento hospital and ahead what appeared to be a sheer cliff face.

The road had largely been flat to this point but now began an upward incline. The road began to turn to the right and as Tenika and Chantrea moved round the bend and the incline become much steeper, the Capodimonte Hotel came into view one hundred metres ahead. As they passed the Capodimonte, the cliff face seemed far too steep for anyone to climb but then the steps came into view.

"Right Chanie are you ready for this? I think it's going to be a bit steep."

"let's do it."

They began to climb the stone steps which zigzagged their way up the cliff face. Soon they were above the Capodimonte hotel and other buildings sitting on the Sorrentine plateau. The cliff gave way to a steep hillside on which was a sea of olive groves. Hidden away could be seen small old shacks used by farmers, many of which were in ruinous form. The steps gave way to an ancient stone paved pathway climbing at about thirty five degrees through the groves. The hillside was thick with olive trees and nets still waiting for harvest time. As they climbed higher they began to see trackways between the groves that led to properties hidden away on the hillside. Although the day was warm and the sun was flooding the hillside with light, the path was a dappled pattern of light and shade as the olive trees gave protection to the traveller.

Into view came an elderly woman walking slowly down the pathway. She was carrying a bag and probably making her way down to the town for a spot of shopping. This was the way it had been for centuries as people made their way up and down the hillside pathways to the town below. As the woman approached Tenika and Chantrea, they could see she was of some age. Her face was tanned and lined. She wore a scarf to protect her head from the sun and a patterned dress.

As they got close to each other, the woman looked at Tenika and Chantrea and greeted them with a warm smile. Tenika and Chantrea responded likewise. The climb was hard going and a half hour passed before the pathway reached a roadway cutting across the hillside. They climbed from the path onto the road and could see, just a short way up the road, the Aminta hotel.

"Ah Chanie, this looks like a good resting place."

They walked across the road and up the steps to the main doors. Inside, the floor was marbled and sparkling. The female receptionists were very welcoming.

"Buongiorno."

"Buongiorno. Possiamo avere considerazione l'hotel e prendere un caffè?"

"Of course, if you go up the stairs, there is a terrace and you can get a drink there."

"Grazie."

They made their way up the stairs onto a landing and through double doors which took them onto a terrace at the side of the hotel. To their right, the terrace opened up into a large area having a terraced pool which was cut into the hillside. There were plenty of people sitting by the pool and a few in it. The main benefit of the terrace, however, was the magnificent views down and across Sorrento. From the vantage point, they could see all along the peninsula. It was, simply, a breathtaking view and worth every moment of their effort to get there.

"Buongiorno. Can I get you something?"

Tenika and Chantrea turned quickly to find they were confronted by a young male waiter smiling at them."

"Uhm yes please. What shall we have Chanie, coffee or something cold?"

"Mmmm I think orange juice for me."

"Ok, two orange juices please."

"With ice?"

"Yes, why not."

"Ok, please take a seat and will bring your drinks."

"Grazie."

Tenika and Chantrea sat down at a table with stylish rattan chairs having deep cushions. They settled in and looked at the view across the bay. The waiter returned quickly with their drinks."

"Are you residents?"

"No, visitors."

"Then that is six Euro please."

"Chantrea retrieved her purse from her shoulder bag and paid the waiter."

"Grazie, enjoy your drinks."

"What a view Chanie."

"It's wonderful. You can see just how flat the plateau is on which Sorrento and the other communes sit. It's almost as if someone a very long time ago dug it out of the hillside."

A warm breeze swept across the hillside whilst Tenika and Chantrea took in the sight and sipped at their drinks.

"Tee, do you think we are going to get anywhere with Luke's death? Thinking something has gone on in the background is quite different to proving it. In that respect Inspector Maldini has a point."

"Yes, Chanie I know. Look we now know that Luke's company gave money to the Mayor's charity and whilst that is probably not illegal, it is the ethics of the relationship between the Mayor, his brother at Dynamo and the award of the contract that scream out. We know also that others did not like the contract being awarded in this way and it is possible that others found out about the donation to the Mayor's fund and have put two and two together and come up with corruption."

"You said that Francesco Giardiniere at FP Ingegneria – have I got that right? - was very unhappy about the situation but even if he found out about the donation and believed it influenced the award of the contract how do we prove he or they had anything to do with Luke's death?"

"Yes Chanie, that question has been running through my mind. Without any evidence other than the photo of Luke by the cliff edge on his own, we are struggling. I accept that. I had wondered whether the reporter that had spoken with Luciano Albero had found anything, but then the reporter does seem to go in rather bluntly and news of his questions find their way back to us rather quickly."

"Inspector Maldini's reaction last time we saw him suggests people are getting very upset with being asked questions. The problem is we are not sure if their anger is because we are wasting their time or because they are trying to cover something up."

"Chanie, I am sure they don't want the donation to be common knowledge. Even if it had no connection to the award of the contract the fact that the Mayor is the brother of Luciano Albero would raise eyebrows – even here! We're missing too many bits of the puzzle."

"If only we knew where Luke had some alcohol we might understand why and it might also answer the question whether anyone was with him at the time."

"Indeed Chanie. Anyway, I am going to take some photos with my phone."

Tenika and Chantrea spend some time taking photos, sitting on the wall by the side of the terrace and taking in the spectacular views. Then it was the gentle walk back to Sorrento down the same path through the olive groves. It was a lot easier going down than up and both agreed the journey down was very pleasant. As they got closer to the town the sound of cars and scooters became ever more distinct. Finally, they reached the bottom of the steps and were back onto the road leading into Sorrento town centre.

"Shall we stop off at the supermarket and get some bits for a late lunch?"

"Sounds good to me Chanie."

They stopped at a small store on the junction of Corso Italia and Via Degli Aranci. They bought some bread, ham, cheese and tomatoes. Then they wandered down Corso Italia briefly looking in shops along the way but increasingly needing a rest, some food and the loo. They reached the hotel and climbed the stairs to reception. The receptionist, Adriana, was as friendly as normal and a moment was passed sharing the morning's experiences. Then into the lift, up two floors, and finally they reached the comfort of the room. This time it was Tenika who was first into the bathroom whilst Chantrea opened up the doors to the balcony to allow air, light and the sounds of Corso Italia below flood into the room. As soon as Tenika emerged from the bathroom, in went Chantrea. Tenika began the task of preparing lunch with the items from the shop and minutes later they were both having lunch sitting out on the balcony.

Even in September the noise and bustle of Sorrento town centre died down from the middle of the afternoon as some shops close and people have a quiet afternoon in preparedness for the evening opening period. Chantrea settled in to read her poetry book whilst Tenika wrote post cards bought on their first day in Sorrento. It was quiet and they were relaxed, two women completely as one in each other's company.

As the early evening began to draw in, Tenika and Chantrea broke out of their afternoon's activity.

"Tee, I am going to go back into town to look at some bits and see if I can find something for my mum. I might go back to the jewellery shop and look at the coral stuff."

"That's fine Chanie. I've got a bit of a head so I'll stay here."

"That's fine, I'll see if I can pick up something to eat for later on. I might go to the restaurant on Via San Francesco, you know the one with all the cakes just inside the door. I might get us a treat."

"That would be nice. Thank you Chanie."

Chantrea began to prepare to go out and stepped out onto the balcony to see what the temperature was like.

"Tee, that chilly wind is getting up again. Can I borrow you lovely scarf and hat?"

"Of course you can. You will probably look more stylish than me."

"I doubt that Tee."

Chantrea gave Tenika a hug and then left the room. She stepped out onto the street as the sun was going down and headed straight for Via San Cesareo where the jeweller was located. Of course the problem was what to buy. Even though Chantrea was leaning towards a necklace, there were many of different styles, colour tone and prices. She spent quite a time before making a decision on a beautiful necklace with an exquisite colour and a price to match. Once the purchase was competed, Chantrea wandered off further down the narrow street in search of an historical book about Sorrento. She found a book shop a little further down the street but couldn't find quite what she wanted. Most books took an overview of the peninsula and included other places such as Positano and Amalfi. So on went Chantrea looking here and there at all sorts of items. She loved looking at the white blouses and shirts containing lace. They were very different to what could be bought in South London and Chantrea adored the style and tradition of lace making on the peninsula. Again, the problem was one of choice and she found herself moving from one shop to another and then back to the first shop again. Finally a decision was made and another purchase completed.

Time was pressing on and Chantrea decided to go across to the restaurant to make sure she could pick up some cakes. She cut through an alleyway to Via San Francesco and walked across to the restaurant located on the edge of the piazza containing the Tasso theatre and the statue to San Antonio Abbatte. She went in and smiled as she immediately came across the range of cakes and pastries just inside the door. A smiling waiter approached.

"Buonasera, do you think it is possible for me to buy a selection of cakes? You know little pieces of each of them?"

The waiter smiled.

"Of course, what would you like?"

"Chantrea felt quite empowered as she pointed to different cakes and the waiter cut small portions off."

"How is that for you?"

"That's great. Can you put them in a box?"

"Si"

Chantrea walked behind the waiter round to the pay point. He disappeared into the kitchen whilst she paid for the cakes. Moments later he reappeared with the cakes in a box neatly tied up.

"Grazi."

"Ciao signora."

Chantrea walked back to the front door of the restaurant and back out into the dark piazza. The clouds had covered the sky and the small piazza seemed quiet and peaceful. She walked to her left towards the entrance to the sometimes used theatre and, to its side, the dark entrance way to the old Basilica. As she passed the entrance she heard what seemed to be a cry from the shadows. Chantrea stopped and looked. The cry, if that is what it was, was heard again. Chantrea went over to the shadowy entrance and could see the figure of a person huddled in the corner.

"Are you ok?"

"Help" came the reply in strange muffled sound.

Chantrea bent over to see better and suddenly a hand reached out grabbed her arm and pulled her down. At the same time a sudden pain seared through her body. She gasped, trying to take a breath but nothing happened. She felt as if she was being punched again and then a third and fourth time. On each occasion pain tore through her body. The violence was dramatic and frenzied. She slumped to the ground gasping for breath but her lungs responded weakly. She wheezed as she tried to force oxygen into her lungs. A wave of dizziness engulfed her and all she could see were shades of light and dark. She reached out but no one was there to find her outstretched hand. Then calmness began to possess her although her body convulsed at intervals. Chantrea tried to call for help but only a strange gargled noise came from her mouth. She tried in vain.

"Tchee ....Tcheeee....."

With that, the pain eased and she fell unconscious lying in a pool of her own blood.

Tenika was looking at her watch and wondering where Chantrea had got to. She thought Chantrea might be a couple of hours but it was now more than three hours since she went out. She had finished her cards and done some washing in the bathroom sink. Her head had also cleared and was hoping for the luxury of the cakes.

"She must be looking at every shop in town."

Suddenly there was a knock on the door.

"At last! Where have you been?" Tenika called out as she went to open the door.

"Ispettore Maldini."

Tenika looked at him quizzically.

"Good evening Miss Taylor. You must come with me."

"I'm sorry, what have I done now?"

"No, no it's Miss Park. There has been an incident and she has been taken to the hospital. Please quickly, we must go."

Tenika was stunned by this. She took a jacket from the wardrobe and picked up the key. She followed the Inspector into the lift. He looked very solemn."

"What's happened and where?"

Tenika's voice was being affected by the adrenalin pumping through her body.

"I cannot say now, it is not clear. Let us get to the hospital."

"Is she badly hurt?"

"We will know more when we arrive."

They rushed down the stairs and into the waiting police car. It sped off down Corso Italia and as it did Tenika had visions that Chantrea had stepped off into Tasso Square without looking and had been hit by a car. Moments later they arrived at the hospital and quickly got out of the car. Tenika followed the Inspector into the hospital. He called a hospital staff member over and spoke quickly to him. Tenika was reeling from all that was happening and didn't catch what was said. The staff member led the Inspector down a hallway, then turned right arriving at reception area to some sort of medical area.

"Noi siamo qui per vedere Chantrea Park, la donna inglese."

"Sì, mi segua."

The nurse led them to a side room and ushered them in.

"What's going on?" Tenika asked with a voice now showing clear emotion.

"Someone will come" replied the Inspector.

A female doctor opened the door and beckoned the Inspector to go outside. Tenika got up.

"No, please wait here a moment" said the Inspector in a calm and almost soothing voice.

Inspector Maldini returned a few minutes later. He pulled a chair round towards Tenika and sat down in front of her. His eyes fixed on Tenika's and he spoke softly.

"Miss Taylor, I am very sorry to tell you that your friend Miss Park has died."

Tenika stared at him and then a huge wave of emotion filled her body. She began to shake but consciously forced herself to control it.

"What? Tell me what's happened."

"I don't know all of the details, but it seems Miss Park was attacked in Via San Francesca shortly after visiting the restaurant to buy cakes. My officers are working on this right now."

Tenika was fighting emotion every second.

"Can I see her? I want to see her."

"I think so in a little while. It will help me also if you identify her."

"I need to see her. I've got to see her."

Tenika's voice was gaining strength and becoming demanding.

"I understand. They are making preparations for this."

Inspector Maldini stared at the floor whilst Tenika stared past him at the wall. Neither spoke. After what seemed like an eternity passing but was, in fact, a matter of minutes the door opened and the female doctor appeared again. She looked at the Inspector and nodded.

"Ok Miss Taylor, we can go now."

Tenika and the Inspector followed the doctor along a corridor and then to the right. They went through double doors and then came to a further door. The doctor turned and spoke in very good English to Tenika.

"The Inspector and I will come in with you. I am very sorry but you cannot touch anything. Are you ready?"

Tenika nodded and the door was opened. Ahead in the centre of the room was a bed with someone lying on it. The body was covered to the neck with a white sheet that had been folded very precisely. Tenika stepped forward with the Inspector on one side of her and the doctor on the other. As she got closer, she saw it was Chantrea. Tenika gasped and felt her whole body wanting to explode with emotion. Tears welled up in her eyes and she could hardly breath. Tenika put her hand over her mouth and stared at the body of her dearest friend.

"I am sorry to ask, but I must, is this Miss Park?"

"Tenika nodded, still paralysed by the shock."

"I am going to step outside and leave you for a moment."

The Inspector stepped backward towards the door and beckoned to the doctor to move back also. She did so and stood by the door leaving Tenika standing at the bedside.

"Oh Chanie, why didn't I come with you? I would have protected you."

Chantrea looked peaceful and there were no marks on that part of her face visible to Tenika. It looked as if someone had brushed her hair so that her dignity had been preserved. Tenika so wanted to hug Chantrea or at a minimum hold her hand and stroke her cheek. Tenika turned to the doctor.

"Will I be able to come back and see her again? I want to hold her hand."

"Yes, we will be able to arrange it if the Inspector agrees. There is procedure."

Tenika turned back towards Chantrea.

"Ok Chanie, things to do but I will be back I promise."

Tenika turned and walked back through the door and found Inspector Maldini sitting outside.

"I want to know how she died."

"Miss Taylor, I would like us to go down to the police station so that we can talk about this. It will be better there."

"Can't you say anything?"

"I think it would be better at the station. I will tell you everything we know."

They began to walk back along the corridors to the hospital entrance. Suddenly Tenika stopped.

"What is it?"

"Chanie's mum. Who is going to tell her?"

"Well we would not do anything yet until we have identified the person. Normally, in this case, we would contact the British Embassy to notify them and they might contact the family but they may be agreeable to you making the call if you wish. Let us take one step at a time."

As they reached the police car, Tenika's emotions were changing. The emotion of grief was being replace by one of frustration and anger. The new emotions were no less powerful and flooding. They arrived back at the police station within ten minutes and Inspector Maldini led Tenika into the building and into one of the interview rooms she and Chantrea had already been into.

"Would you like a coffee? I think I need one."

"Yes, thanks."

"How do you take it?"

"Just with milk, no sugar."

Inspector Maldini stepped out of the interview room and another uniformed officer stepped in. A few minutes later the Inspector returned with two coffees. The uniformed officer stepped out of the room.

"So, Inspector, what happened?"

"From what we know so far, Miss Park went into the restaurant and bought some cakes. She came out of the restaurant and was attacked by the entrance to the Tasso Theatre. There is no performance on today so it is all quiet there. We know Miss Park paid for the cakes and used a purse because the restaurant remembers her getting a purse out to pay. However, there was no purse with Miss Park when the police arrived."

"So it was a robbery?"

"Well it looks like that at the moment."

"Did you notice anyone following you this morning?

"No, I can't say I did."

"And nobody came up to you and asked questions?

"No."

"Did you or Miss Park get money from a cash machine?"

"No, Ispettore how did she die?"

Tenika's voice had become emotionless, yet firm and was increasingly demanding.

"Well there will be an autopsy tomorrow but we know Miss Park was stabbed probably with a knife."

Tenika's mind began to race. Suddenly her eyes and body moved as if a realisation had come upon her.

"Oh my god!"

"What is it?"

"When Chanie went out tonight she wore my scarf and hat. Although she has a lighter skin tone to me, both of us have black hair and in the dark she could easily have been mistaken for me. Someone may have tried to kill me!"

Tenika's eyes were darting about and she was clearly becoming agitated.

"Miss Taylor we don't know that."

"Ever since we first met I have told you that something has been going on in the background to cause Luke Adam's death. You have not believed me, you have told me to go away. You have not listened to Chanie or me when we have tried to give you evidence. You have not listened when we told you about the donation to the Mayor's charity and how this could result in a scandal if found out. You have not given consideration to another firm wanting to make a point that no more contracts should go overseas.

Tenika's voice was becoming louder and she more agitated.

When we saw Luciano Albero a couple of days ago he warned us off asking questions and even Rafael warned us about asking questions and what might happen if someone found out.

Tenika stood up smouldering like a volcano about to explode.

"And now the most precious person I know has been stabbed to death on your street wearing my clothes. I should be in the hospital not Chanie. It's you who have failed like so many miserable men who have no balls."

And with that Tenika launched herself at the Inspector slapping him full across the face. He grabbed her by the arms but was surprised by her strength. They fell against a wall with Tenika snarling in his face.

"Somebody" shouted the Inspector.

One uniformed officer and then another ran into the room and pulled Tenika off the Inspector.

"Take the bloody woman away and put her in a cell" he roared.

Tenika was still struggling. She wasn't going anywhere quietly.

"Get your fucking hands of me."

Tenika kicked one of the officers who squealed in pain. With that the officer took a very firm hold on Tenika and she cried out in pain as they frogmarched her away. The Inspector looked down at his dishevelled state in disbelief. He was covered in coffee and his shirt was torn.

Two hours later, Inspector Maldini was sitting in his office when the door opened and in came Superintendant Mario Mosta.

"Buonasera Pietro, I heard about the English woman and thought I would drop in and see how things were progressing."

"The preliminary report from the pathologist says that she was stabbed four times with a long knife probably 150 millimetres long. Her wallet is missing and the only camera image is very poor showing a dark shadowy figure walking away from the scene."

"So, is this a robbery that has gone wrong?"

"It could be but I am troubled by it. If it was a robbery, why stab her four times? Why stab her at all? We don't get this kind of crime here. It is not consistent with our experience. The knife used was also very big. Most knives used on the street are relatively small, designed to harm but not kill. This knife would kill with one thrust."

"Do you think there is more to this Pietro?"

"It is too soon to say. However, the murdered girl was wearing a scarf and hat of Miss Taylor. There is a possibility of a miss-identification."

"Why would anyone want to target the other woman unless you are thinking about the death of the Englishman? You know we have spoken about this and I don't want any movement on that unless you have concrete evidence."

"Earlier this morning I spoke with Andrew Hillsom at the airport to wish him goodbye. During the conversation he confirmed that his company had given some assistance to the Mayor's charity."

"Ah, was it a formal conversation?"

"No, informal."

"Then it is of no use to you."

"Yes, but at least I now know that there could be a motive for the death of the Englishman and also now know there could be a motive for silencing Miss Taylor."

"That's a lot of 'coulds' Pietro. You know we can't take action on a 'could' we need something certain. This is a sensitive situation."

"Yes, I know. Don't worry."

"By the way Pietro, I hear you had a little trouble with the other English woman and she is in a cell? Is she being charged with assault?"

"She is in a great deal of pain following the loss of her closest friend. With your agreement Mario, I would like to deal with her my way."

"Well it's up to you. You are in charge of the case and I am off home. Ring me if you need any help."

"Buonanotte Mario."

"Buonanotte Pietro."

Pietro Maldini sat calmly in his office reflecting on the evenings events. He got up and walked down to the cells on the ground floor. He spoke to the custody officer and asked to see Tenika. The custody officer collected the keys and they both walked along a narrow corridor to cell three. The custody officer opened the small shutter in the door to see where Tenika was positioned. She was sitting on her bed with her head in her hands. The custody officer opened the door and the Inspector entered the cell.

Tenika looked up. She had been crying and looked very forlorn. Pietro Maldini sat on the end of the bed. Tenika stared at the floor. She spoke softly.

"I am sorry, so very sorry for what I said. It isn't your fault. It is the fault of the bastard that killed her. I feel I have tarnished her reputation with my behaviour."

"Miss Taylor, two years ago my wife was killed in a car accident that was not her fault. Afterwards, I was very angry. The pain of losing her was so great. I struggled to go home at night and see my children. I had to learn to control my pain and my anger and so will you."

Tenika looked up at Pietro and saw a soft face offering some compassion. Tenika's eyes filled with tears.

"It hurts so much."

"I know it does."

Tenika finally let out the sadness bottled up inside. She sobbed uncontrollably. Pietro Maldini simply sat with her letting her know someone was there to share the moment. He gave her his handkerchief to mop up the tears which she accepted. When the cascade of tears was over she sat up as if somehow a weight was off her shoulders.

"I kicked your policeman. I guess you will charge me with all sorts but I would like to apologise to him. Is he still here?"

"Yes, he is here all night."

"Could you get him for me? Please?"

The inspector got up and went outside the cell. He came back moments later.

"He will come down. His name is Constantino."

A few moments later Constantino appeared at the door.

The Inspector beckoned him in.

"It's ok Constantino, the lady wishes to talk to you."

Tenika was still struggling to hold back tears.

"Buonasera Constantino. I want to apologise to you for what I did. I hope I have not hurt you. I had just lost my dearest friend and took it out on you. I am so sorry."

The Inspector looked up at Constantino who seemed to understand the politics of the moment.

"Ok, I accept your apology. You remind me of my mother. When she is angry she frightens me as well."

"Thank you Constantino" said Pietro with a smile.

Constantino trudged off with another tale to tell his friends down at the bar on his day off. Pietro turned to Tenika.

"Miss Taylor, I am not going to charge you with anything if you agree to something."

"What's that?"

"That you work with me and not against me. Let me tell you something. This morning I spoke with Mr Hillsom from Andersons. In that conversation he confirmed a contribution to the Mayor's charity. That is evidence, of a sort, Miss Taylor that can help us move forward."

"So do you believe me now?"

"What the evidence now tells me is that it is possible for there to be a motive for the death of Mr Adams and that, if you are right and that Miss Park was targeted instead of you, then you could now be in danger. But these things are just possibilities, nothing is proven. We must investigate Miss Park's death and see if any link exists. But please work with me on these matters."

"I feel rather foolish and ashamed."

"Please don't feel like that. You are fighting for the people you love. That is a noble cause. We just might get somewhere if we work together."

Tenika looked up at the Inspector and knew there was no alternative open to her.

"Ok, I agree. No more fighting."

"Good, then I will have you taken back to your hotel and my officer will speak with the hotel staff. Here is my card. It has my office and mobile number should you need it. Now, I need to go home .... and buy a new shirt!"

"Mmm let me give you my mobile number so we can keep in touch. Oh, by the way what about informing Chanie's mother?"

"Ah yes, we have spoken to the British Embassy in Rome and they are happy for you to do this if you wish. Alternatively they will inform the police where Miss Park's mother lives and ask them to inform her. We just have to tell them what help is needed."

"Well it is nearly midnight here so it is nearly eleven in Guildford. The question is whether to call tonight or first thing in the morning. My worry is what support is available for her tonight. Perhaps a coordinated call with the Embassy first thing tomorrow is better."

"As you wish, we can arrange that in the morning. Ok, let's go."

Tenika was taken back to the hotel in a police car. She was still suffering from the shock of seeing Chantrea's body. The image kept returning to her mind as she stared aimlessly out of the car window. At the hotel, she was escorted to reception by a police officer who said he would talk to the hotel manager. The manager offered Tenika a different room if she wished but Tenika insisted on staying in the same room. Tiredness began to swarm over her and she asked to go to her room. The officer escorted her to the door and made sure it was shut behind her.

She threw her bag on the sofa and sat on her bed. She felt tired and alone. She could just muster enough energy to close the curtains and go to the toilet before curling up on the bed fully dressed. Thankfully sleep saved her from more of the images of earlier that evening.

Elsewhere in Sorrento a telephone rang.

"Ciao"

"The job is done."

"And done as a robbery?"

"Yes, don't worry. It went ok, the woman squealed like a pig for her friend. I thought you would like that."

"Good, let's hope I don't need your help again."

"Ciao."

DAY EIGHT

Tenika awoke early to the sound of a scooter passing by on the street below. It was Sunday and the noises outside on Corso Italia were much more subdued than normal. She looked around the room to see Chantrea's items reminding her of the exhausting and shattering previous day. She sat up on the bed, reflected a while and then spoke to the room."

"Chanie, I am not going to hide you away. Your things can stay where they are for now."

Although Tenika knew the awful truth that Chantrea was never going to knock on the door or come through it lighting up the room with her smiling face, leaving her items where they were gave the impression that such an event might just happen. It allowed Tenika the comfort of feeling that Chantrea was with her and that gave her strength. Suddenly she thought of Chantrea's mum and looked at her watch. It was seven thirty. She had some time to spare but not much. There were things to do.

Suddenly the telephone rang and Tenika leant over to pick it up.

"Buongiorno, this is Sophia from the breakfast room. Would you like me to bring breakfast to your room this morning?"

"Oh, uhm that's good of you. Could you bring cereal, some melon and orange if you have any, uhm a croissant and coffee at eight o'clock?

"Yes, ok."

Tenika got off the bed and headed for the bathroom. She wasn't sure what the day ahead held for her but suspected it would be another busy one. Showering had an urgency to it because the thought of speaking to Chantrea's mother was firmly established in Tenika's head. She needed a plan and time to execute it. She was out of the shower and in her wardrobe when there was a knock at the door. She opened it to find Sophia, the elderly woman who looked after breakfast, standing there with a tray. Tenika greeted her.

"Buongiorno."

The elderly woman looked up and Tenika could see there were tears in her eyes."

"Buongiorno, I am so sorry, so sorry."

Tenika took the tray from her and smiled. Grazie was all she could say and the woman turned and got back into the lift. It was a reminder of what was to come both here in Sorrento but also on return to Wimbledon. There would be a lot of faces and a lot of questions. Tenika had entered a new chapter in her life and one that she had no knowledge of its length.

Tenika took the tray to the table with the computer on it and sat down. She took sips from her coffee and reached for her mobile phone. It was time for the first part of the plan. She found a name on the contact list and pressed the call button. It took a good thirty seconds for the phone to be answered.

"Good morning Sokhong, It's Tenika here. How are you?

"Hello, Tenika. How are you and how is Italy? Are you two having a good time? It's very early, can't you sleep?"

Sokhong was Chantrea's aunt. She often couldn't sleep because memories of her time on the farms at the hands of Pol Pot's army were still vivid. Her husband had also been murdered in the early days after Phnom Penh had fallen and she had not found it easy to cast off that period of history.

"Sokhong, I need your help."

Sokhong heard the change in Tenika's voice and instinctively knew something was wrong."

"What's the matter? Has something gone wrong?"

"Chanie has been hurt and is in Hospital in Sorrento. I am going to ring Var at half past nine this morning and I would like you to be there to support her if she needs it. Owen will probably have gone to work and I would rather she is not alone. The British Embassy might also ring shortly after."

"Now Tenika heard a change in Sokhong's voice. She was small in size, perhaps only just over five feet tall, but a woman who had become extraordinarily strong from her experiences in Cambodia all those years ago. She was also astute and knew that the British Embassy would not ring for a cut finger.

"How bad is she?"

"She's not good and I can't ring Var if you are not there."

Tenika was determined to keep her voice under control but Sokhong had heard this kind of conversation before.

"Don't worry, I will be there. It will only take me half an hour to get there. Be strong Tenika."

Those last three words cut straight through Tenika. She took a long breath and took some time to compose herself again.

"Thanks Sokhong. You won't say anything about this call will you?"

"No, don't worry."

"I must go now. See you soon."

"Ok Tenika, I will hold one of Var's hands and one of yours."

Tenika pressed the end of call button and tears filled her eyes. She knew this was going to be a difficult morning but had to get through it. Whilst working her way slowly through breakfast, Tenika next took Pietro Maldini's card from her purse and rang his mobile number.

"Buongiorno."

"Buongiorno Ispettore. I am sorry to trouble you on a Sunday morning."

"Ah, Miss Taylor, don't worry about that. I shall be working today. I hope you had a reasonable night?"

"Well, I got through it. I am going to telephone Chanie's mother at nine thirty this morning and I wonder whether you could arrange for the Embassy to ring at nine forty-five?"

"Ok, I will speak with them. If there is a problem I will call you back."

"Grazie Ispettore."

"No problem, Ciao."

"Ciao."

The die was cast and now Tenika had to prepare herself for the call. She reflected back to when she called her brother Jerome after finding her mother's body. That was a horrible occasion. She wasn't able to get much detail across to Jerome, she simply broke down in floods of tears. That had been sufficient for him to know something was terribly wrong. This time she wanted to be better controlled. It was Var who needed support. It was she who would be receiving a terrible pain.

Tenika picked her way through her breakfast constantly thinking about what she would say. Was there any way of telling a mother that her only daughter was dead that could be anything other than brutal? She finished breakfast and got herself dressed. Tenika then began to tidy the room but made sure Chantrea's items were placed in an orderly way on her bed side table and on the larger table in the room. Clothes were put away in draws and on hangers in the wardrobe. Again, Tenika made sure everything was ordered and carefully placed.

As the time approached nine thirty, Tenika sat on the sofa and calmly stared across the room. This was no time to lose control of her emotions. She needed to convey the information clearly. Sokhong would do the rest.

On the stroke of nine thirty, Tenika pressed the call button on her mobile phone.

"Hello."

"Hello Var, it's Tenika."

Hi Tenika. This must be a special day. I have Sokhong here and you have rung me."

"Var, I need to tell you that Chanie has been killed in an incident here in Sorrento."

There was silence down the phone for a few moments.

"Did you say Chantrea had been killed?"

"Yes, I am so, so sorry Var."

Tenika could hear Var breaking down at the other end of the phone and saying things to Sokhong. She came back onto the phone clearly in tears."

"How? What happened?"

"The police are still investigating but it looks like a street robbery that went wrong."

"Were you with her?"

"No, she had gone out to do some shopping."

Tenika could hear muffled conversation between Var and Sokhong. Then Sokhong came onto the phone."

"Tenika, when did this happen?"

"Yesterday evening."

"Do they know who did this?"

"Not yet, the police are investigating. I was with them until midnight."

"Are you ok Tenika?"

"I'm getting through it. Can you tell Var that the Embassy in Rome will ring at nine forty five to offer support."

"I will tell her. Look, leave her with me for a while. Perhaps we will talk again later."

"Ok, Sokhong, love you."

"Bye Tenika."

With that, the call was over and Tenika felt some relief that the deed was done. She was confident that Sokhong would support Var well. She felt a little guilty that she had not considered more the likely feelings of Chantrea's step-father Owen who was a buildings engineer with Surrey County Council. There was a special bond between Chantrea and Var. Chantrea had the visual looks of a Cambodian woman and was very attached to her Cambodian roots. She was bilingual and had been back to Cambodia with Var on more than one occasion. For Var, Chantrea represented the continuation of a Cambodian family torn apart by Pol Pot and his army thirty five years ago. So many family members had died. Chantrea was one sparkling star that had emerged following the darkness of those days. It gave Var a meaningful life and a new purpose. Owen was a good man, a very good man who had supported Var following her divorce from Ronald. He acknowledged that he could not comprehend all that had gone on in Cambodia although knew that it had affected both Var and Sokhong to the core of their being. He loved Var and he loved Chantrea and perhaps that's all that mattered. He would be devastated too but perhaps in a different way.

Tenika opened the doors to the balcony, stepped out and gazed upon the people going about their business on another warm early autumn day. It was a reminder that life goes on no matter what and that she must go forward too. Her mobile phone rang. It was Var.

"Hello Var."

"Tenika, the Embassy in Rome has just called and offered support. I have so many questions but I must thank you for calling. It must have been very difficult for you. I know how close you two are. Sokhong says she is still holding your hand and won't let go. I will let you know what we are going to do, whether we are coming out and, if so, when."

"That's fine Var, you can let me know at any time."

"I will let you go now Tenika as I am sure you have many things to do. Our love is with you,"

"And mine with you."

Tenika looked out of the doors to the road outside. Var's voice had changed. She seemed to have moved into a state of emotional control that she had had to master in Cambodia. Those who lost control of their emotions usually died and Var, along with Sokhong, had learned how to survive.

Tenika had a desire to get out. She needed a walk. She thought about visiting the spot where Chantrea died but couldn't face that yet. Instead her thoughts returned to Luke and his fall from the cliff outside the bar next to the Corallo hotel. She collected her things, put Luke's photo in her purse and left the room. Tenika's mind was buzzing and she couldn't take in much around her. She was slightly conscious of faces looking at her as she went through reception and thought that people were looking at her as she walked through Piazza Angelina Lauro. Everyone in Sorrento knew of Chantrea's death and everyone was looking at Tenika or so it seemed. She kept her eyes fixed towards the ground and marched on towards firstly the Ambasciatori and then the road to Sant Agnello. After half an hour she was back at the spot outside the bar where Luke had fallen to his death. She stood there and gazed out across the bay. Tenika closed her eyes and felt the warm breeze on her face and listened to the waves gently rushing over the rocks below.

Tenika was unsure how long she stood there. It was quite a time. She then went back to the main road and began to walk slowly along Via Cappuccini past hotel Corallo. She could see the bay on her left through gaps between the large buildings. On her right were large rather grand residential buildings which, if you had an apartment high up in the building, would provide magnificent views over the bay. There was a degree of aimlessness about Tenika's journey. Her mind was still recovering from the shock of Chantrea's death whilst trying to ask questions of why and how. She was struggling with the idea that it was linked to Luke's death because that would mean Chantrea was targeted deliberately to stop their questions. Worse still, was that if the killer thought it had been herself walking alone last night then she should be dead.

Tenika was caught between wanting yesterday's events to be a simple robbery gone wrong and wanting it to be a clear statement that she and Chantrea had caused Luke's killer to come out of the shadows. This latter thought, of course, rested on the assumption that Luke had a killer and that remained uncertain.

Tenika got to the junction with Viale Dei Pini and turned right. She thought that if she kept turning right at junctions she should return to her original route. Then another thought entered her mind, she needed the toilet. A short way along the road Tenika came across the Hotel Alpha. It was not a particularly inspiring name but perhaps beginning with the letter 'A' found its way near to the top of the list of hotels in the telephone book. The sign on the outside said it was a four star hotel, it looked clean and Tenika's need was growing.

She entered the hotel through large glass doors to a bright open area having marble tiled flooring and a magnolia colour to its walls. Perhaps a little bland but bright and with a good feel of space. Tenika enquired at reception and was pointed off to her right to a ladies room in the lounge area. Her first impression was a host of black circles found on the back of the lounge chairs. The area was simply furnished but with some sophistication. Behind the bar was a barman formally dressed in a black suit with bow tie. He smiled as Tenika passed him to the ladies room which was clean and sparkling with the strong lights. A range of toiletries were on offer to the visitor and when compared with Tenika's criteria for acceptable toilets, this one passed the test.

As she returned past the barman a random thought occurred to her. She stopped and spoke to him.

"Hello, my friend suggested I come and look at this hotel. He was very impressed with the service in the bar."

"Thank you, was your friend here recently?"

"Yes, about a week ago. I have a photo of him, not that I expect you to remember you must get lots of guests here."

Tenika showed the picture to the barman who thought for a moment.

"Yes, I remember him because he was here with a woman."

Tenika suddenly became very aware of what was going on in front of her. Adrenalin began to pump through her but she remained very calm."

"You have a very good memory."

"Well the lady had very dark hair, long and a little wavy, rather like my sister. It could have been her from behind."

Tenika reminded herself of her agreement to work with the Ispettore. This was not the time for a grilling of the barman.

"He was very complimentary of you. Thank you so much."

"You are welcome."

Tenika walked back through reception into the fresh air outside.

"Thank you God."

Tenika felt a doorway had opened in front of her. She thought of the words from Inspector Maldini. This doesn't prove anything about the detail of how he died but it does now prove he was not alone on the night of his death. Tenika now had a spring in her step and decided to walk back the way she came. She wanted another look at the scene of death. Had Luke walked back this way alone? Who was the woman with black hair? What had they talked about? Had the mysterious woman walked with him to look over the cliff? Had she pushed him over it? Tenika was conscious her thoughts were running away with her. As she returned to the bar which was now open for lunchtime, she began to feel a little fear running through her.

The possibility of Luke having been murdered had moved forward one step and that, in turn, moved the same conclusion about Chantrea one step forward as well. Tenika suddenly felt vulnerable and began to walk back towards Sorrento quickly. She looked around her to see if there was anyone else to be seen. There wasn't but it did not lessen her speed of foot.

As Tenika approached the Ambasciatori she pulled out her mobile and rang Inspector Maldini.

"Ah ciao, Ispettore."

"Ciao Miss Taylor."

"Are you in your office?"

"Yes, Miss Taylor. Why?"

"Can I come and see you for a few minutes. I have some new information."

"Miss Taylor, what have you been up to now?"

"Nothing, nothing but I have some news. Please?"

"Ok, but just for a few minutes."

"Ok, I will be there soon. Ciao."

"Ciao."

Within five minutes Tenika was standing at the reception desk at the police station. The officer behind the desk recognised her immediately and did not smile. Her reputation had spread across the station.

"Buongiorno, I've come …….."

"Yes, I know. Please sit down."

The officer pointed to the bench seat in the corner and she went over to it. The officer made a telephone call and looked at Tenika as he said a few words to someone. About a minute later Inspector Maldini appeared.

"Ah Ispettore Maldini."

"Miss Taylor. Please come this way."

Tenika followed the Inspector to the first interview room she and Chantrea had been into. Tenika sat down as did Inspector Maldini."

"Are you ok Miss Taylor?"

"Yes Ispettore, thank you. This morning I needed a walk after speaking with Chanie's mother and I couldn't go anywhere near Via San Francesco so I went back to Sant Agnello. I don't know why, my mind was spinning this morning. There was just too much going on in it. I stopped off where Luke fell and then just walked further on into Sant Agnello. I needed the toilet and found myself at the Hotel Alpha. I am not sure what road it was on. Anyway, I used the toilet and was taken by a smiling barman and, I don't know why, but I spoke to him and made up a little story."

The Inspector raised his eyebrows.

"No, no Inspector it's ok, I told him that my friend had recommended the hotel to me and I was passing so I thought I would drop in. I showed him a photograph of Luke not thinking for a moment that he would recognise him, but he did. He said he was there with a woman with black wavy hair who looked, from behind, like his sister. So you see, Ispettore, there was someone with him on the night of his death."

"And why are you telling me?"

"Well, I thought you might go and interview the barman and see if he could remember any more."

"You mean you did not interrogate him?"

"No Ispettore, I remembered what I agreed with you. It was just a couple of questions and that was it."

"You realise Miss Taylor that the barman might be mistaken, it might have been a different night and, even if it was the correct evening, it does not prove any link to his death."

"Yes, I understand all of that. Until now, there has been no evidence of anyone else involved with Luke on that night. Now, there is the possibility of evidence that there might have been someone else there. If we could find the woman and find out what they spoke about it might shed some light?"

The Inspector leaned back on his chair and looked thoughtful.

"I will see what can be done but I cannot promise anything. Do you understand?"

"Tenika had the urge to challenge the lack of immediate action but held her fire.

"Of course Ispettore, I understand. Is there any news on your investigations into yesterday?"

"We have searched the area but have found nothing of use. A post mortem examination on Miss Park is being undertaken today."

"Will you tell me the results of that later?"

"I will see what I can do."

"Thank you for seeing me and, uhm, I am sorry about your shirt."

"Don't worry about it. It was an old one anyway."

They got up from the chairs and Tenika extended her hand towards the Inspector. He hesitated, looked at her, showed a glimmer of a smile and shook her hand. A bridge if not rebuilt was now under construction.

As Tenika walked back to the Palazzo Abagnale, she began to have a more focused view in her mind. The key issue was whether Luke's death was linked to that of Chantrea. If it was, how did the woman with the black hair fit in? Also, if they were linked and Chantrea was murdered by mistake, then Tenika could be a target in the future. Tenika began to feel a sense of cold resignation to the battle that lay ahead. She was convinced something was behind Luke's death and was beginning to believe Chantrea was killed deliberately. It fitted Tenika's version of events, if not that of Inspector Maldini.

Across the road from her hotel, there was a small shop that sold, watches, clocks and knives. It was open even on a Sunday trying to attract the tourist market. Tenika went in and bought a 100 millimetre long knife that could be concealed in her hand bag.

"Right, two can play at that game" Tenika said to herself as she came out of the shop.

This was no longer an intellectual game. It was real and very dangerous. Tenika felt vulnerable and a little fearful, but determined to find the answers to her questions. If someone has shown their hand through the brutal murder of Chantrea and were going to show themselves again in an attack on Tenika, she was ready, come what may.

Tenika made her way back to her room and sat on the sofa. She felt safe in the room but opened the doors to the balcony and looked out. Were there any individuals loitering about? Were there individuals sitting in cars looking up at her room? Was she becoming paranoid?

Across town, Inspector Maldini had left the police station and made his way to the Hotel Alpha in Sant Agnello. He had spoken to the hotel manager and asked for complete confidentiality in the conversation that was to take place. This the manager readily agreed to. The barman identified by Tenika was summoned to the manager's office where he too agreed to the confidential nature of the discussion.

"Do you remember the conversation with a woman this morning who showed you a picture of a man?"

"Yes I do."

"have you seen the man before?"

"Yes, he was here some days ago."

"Can you remember which day it was?"

"Yes, it was last Sunday evening because I remember it was rather quiet that night and we were able to do a lot of restocking on the bar."

"Was the man alone?"

"No, as I told the young woman, he was with a woman who had long black hair similar to my sister."

"How old was the woman?"

"I am not sure, forties I suppose, but attractive."

"Now I want you to think carefully about this question. Can you remember what they drank? "

"It is hard to remember. There have been so many people and so many drinks since then. I think she had wine and I seem to remember him having water with lemon."

"Are you sure? Take your time."

"Yes, I think that is what they had."

"Did they arrive together?"

"Well they came into the bar toqether."

"And what time was this?"

"Uhm quite late. After eleven and they left after midnight because it was the same time I was cleaning down the bar."

"And they left together?"

"They left the bar area together but I can't see where they went after that. I don't think she was a resident."

"Why do you say that?"

"Well I only saw her that one time. She or they could have been here for one night but the hotel register will show if that is the case."

Inspector Maldini looked across to the hotel manager who looked at pages on his computer screen.

"No, we had no single women booked in here on that night."

"Did they seem happy, sad, argumentative?"

"Well it is some time ago, but I would say happy. I am sure I would have noticed if there had been any argument between them."

"Did she speak Italian?"

"She ordered the drinks in Italian, yes."

"And she was fluent rather than a tourist?"

"Yes, fluent."

"Thank you both. Can I remind you that I do not want this conversation to be told to anyone else. It is very important that you say nothing. If anyone asks, just say I came to warn you about pickpockets in town."

Inspector Maldini turned to the hotel manager.

"Just one last thing. Do you have cameras in the bar area?"

"Yes, just one."

"Can you get the tape for that night?"

"I am not sure if we go back that far. I will check for you but it may take a little time."

"Well, as soon as you can."

"I must go, thank you both once again."

Inspector Maldini knew his next meeting would be with his Superintendant and he also knew it would not be an easy meeting. He drove straight back to the police station and rang the Superintendant at his home.

"Ciao Mario, I need to talk to you urgently."

"What is the problem? That English woman hasn't been giving you trouble again has she?"

"No, no but it is linked to the Englishman who fell from the cliff. We now believe he met a woman at the Hotel Alpha at Sant Agnello. I have been to see the barman and, as far as he can recall, the Englishman drank water not wine. Only the woman drank wine. He also says they left the bar after midnight."

"Oh Pietro, this is not what I want to hear."

"I know and I also know this does not prove that the Englishman did not fall of his own accord but I gives us a problem of where the alcohol came from that was in his body."

"What of this woman? What description did he give you?"

"Black hair and in her forties."

"Not much to go on."

"I know."

"Look Mario, I must be honest with you. I now feel something is wrong about this and I am beginning to feel Miss Taylor may have been right in believing that something happened that night involving others. I don't want to change any decisions about the death but I would like to find this woman if possible. More importantly, Mario, if there is a connection between the death of the Englishman and Miss Park last night, then Miss Taylor might be in danger."

The Superintendant was frustrated and his voice reflected deflation.

"Oh Pietro, Pietro, what are you doing to me?"

"I am sorry Mario."

"Ok, look I am probably going to have to say something to the Mayor but leave that to me. Can you continue your quest quietly?"

"Yes, I will be as discrete as I can be."

"What will you do about Miss Taylor?"

"I am not sure yet but I will need to talk with her."

"Ok, Pietro, carry on. I don't want three dead English people here. Just think what it would do to the tourist trade!"

"Oh, by the way, when will we have the autopsy report on Miss Park?"

"It should be here later today."

"Good, do let me know what it says as soon as you can."

"Of course."

Across town Tenika was having a quiet time in her room. Although the woman with the dark hair provided something to work on, she felt alone and vulnerable. This was not a feeling Tenika was used to. She was a strong woman who always felt she could take on whatever challenges the world threw at her. Now in a more reflective mood, she had a mixture of sadness and apprehension about what lay ahead. She was determined to move forward but unsure how to do so.

The hotel staff were very supportive providing her with coffee and lunch in her room at no charge. It enabled Tenika to avoid going anywhere near the fatal spot where Chantrea met her death. It was a respite although Tenika knew she would have to face the streets around Via Francesca again. It was as if Tenika's body needed to absorb all that had happened and adjust itself back into a stable equilibrium of rational thought, emotion and energy.

The afternoon was drawing on when there was a knock on the door.

"Who is it?"

"Ispettore Maldini."

Tenika opened the door and invited the Inspector in.

"Thank you Miss Taylor. I need to have some more words with you."

"Of course Ispettore."

Tenika sat down on the sofa and the Inspector sat on the chair by the computer table.

"I have spoken with the waiter at the hotel Alpha."

"What did he say?"

"Well, he confirmed what you told me about Mr Adams and the woman with the black hair. Now, importantly, he also said that as far as he can remember Mr Adams did not drink any alcohol."

"I knew it!" exclaimed Tenika.

Tenika's eyes drilled into the Inspector. She wanted to hear more.

"The barman believes they arrived together and left together just after midnight."

"And the bar next door closed at midnight, didn't it?"

"Yes, that is correct."

"So, if they did then go round to the rear of the bar they wouldn't have been seen."

"Well, Miss Taylor, we must not go too fast here. We don't know what happened when they left the hotel Alpha. The woman might have gone one way and Mr Adams another. We still don't know how the alcohol got into his body. Did he have some before he arrived at the hotel Alpha? Was that with the woman or on his own?"

Tenika was staring ahead, her brow furrowed as she thought through the issues.

"And Ispettore, why were they together at all?"

"Yes, of course, but I have to think of all possibilities."

"What do you mean?"

"Well, one possibility is that Mr Adams was away from home and perhaps wanted the company of a woman. He had a drink before meeting her, perhaps to raise his courage, then after meeting her at the hotel Alpha went to the bar. It was closed and private ...."

"Sorry, you mean she might have been a prostitute and somehow in the act of passion he fell over the cliff?"

Tenika looked at the Inspector incredulously.

"As I say I must think of all things, not just the ones you wish me to."

"And are there a lot of forty something prostitutes in Sorrento?"

"No, no but it is a possibility. However, I agree that because Mr Adams may have chosen not have had alcohol at the hotel Alpha, this is a problem for us. I also accept that there is the possibility of a link between the deaths of Mr Adams and Miss Park although we still have no clear proof of that. Nevertheless, as I say, I need to think of all things possible. I have spoken with the hotel manager who tells me that the two other rooms on this floor have been vacated today and there are no new guests due until tomorrow. He has agreed to my putting a female police officer into one of the rooms on this floor. She will stay in the room overnight. She will not disturb you, but will be there if there are any problems. However I would encourage you not to go out at night but if you do the officer will escort you. "

"So you think I am in danger?"

"Well Miss Taylor, you believe Mr Adams was murdered and, if that is the case, with the questions you have been asking it is possible that Miss Park was attacked in an attempt to stop you. When people realise it was Miss Park who was murdered, and not you, there could be an attempt on your life. Now, please, this is just one possibility and it remains that the death of Mr Adams was an accident and the sad loss of Miss Park was an attempted robbery that went wrong. However, I want to reassure you that I am taking your views seriously and I am doing things."

"Do you know more about Chanie's death?"

"Not really, we have looked at a camera overlooking the piazza but can only see a dark figure walking away but probably male. The autopsy on Miss Park has confirmed she died of stab wounds."

"Was she stabbed once?"

"No, I am not allowed to say precisely but more than once."

"Is it normal for a robber to stab someone more than once?"

"Well, if I am honest, it is not normal for someone to be stabbed at all in Sorrento. It is difficult to understand without knowing the exact circumstances."

"Do you mean whether she put up a fight or not?"

"Possibly."

"Wouldn't she have shouted or cried out? Did anyone hear a noise?"

"We are still making enquiries, but no one has yet reported hearing anything."

"That sounds as if whatever happened did so quickly so that Chanie couldn't shout out. If the attacker tried to rob Chanie first, wouldn't that have given her time to shout out? But if she was silenced first with the first stab, why would he stab her again? What's the point."

"That is a good question Miss Taylor."

"Have you found her purse yet?"

"No and I suspect it has been destroyed."

"Now there is another matter Miss Taylor."

"What's that Ispettore."

"We have issued a statement to the press and it will be in the papers tomorrow. It says that an English woman died as a result of injuries resulting from an attempted robbery. The papers will not mention her name or any details that can link her to you. We have a way of working with the editors and they have all agreed to proceed in this way. It may give us a little more time."

"You know Ispettore, it is so strange being here without her. I can't get out of my head the idea that she will walk through the door."

"I understand Miss Taylor, I do understand."

"How do we move forward?"

"Well, our investigations regarding Miss Park will continue and I shall have to think about the woman with the black hair. I will keep in touch but I must go now."

"Thank you for coming Ispettore."

The Inspector got up from his chair and walked to the door and opened it.

"Ciao Miss Taylor."

"Ciao Ispettore."

Tenika closed the door and returned to the sofa. She knew the Inspector was right to consider all possibilities but, in her view, the evidence was increasingly pointing towards Luke having been murdered. The critical question she asked herself now was whether yesterday's death was a botched attempt at stopping her asking awkward questions. If that was the case then it was quite probable that someone in the extended circle of Luke and his work was responsible. If so, then it was only a matter of time before it became known that it was Chantrea who was murdered and not her. Perhaps this is what the Inspector meant when he said that they may have a little more time.

Tenika sat and reflected a while and then her mobile phone rang.

"Hello."

"Hello Tenika, it's Owen here."

"Ah Owen, I am so sorry about Chanie. I don't know what to say. I'm feeling so guilty that I have let you down by not looking after her."

"Tenika, Tenika stop there. From what I understand Chantrea was out on her own when she was attacked. It has nothing to do with you. It is not your fault. In fact, Var and I have been discussing how awful this must be for you. You two were so close and you are out there on your own."

"Well I feel I have found new friends in the police force here. I seem to be talking to them constantly."

"Has there been any progress on finding out what happened?"

"Not much. We know that Chanie's purse was stolen but it was very dark and the only CCTV pictures show someone, probably male, walking away from the scene but it's so dark there is no detail. The police are still making their enquiries."

"Var and I are getting a flight out tomorrow. We should be in Sorrento about four in the afternoon."

"Where are you staying?"

"We're going to stay at the Vittoria. I think it is very central to Sorrento."

"Yes, it is just off Tasso Square and very close to where we are. How is Var?"

"Well she has gone into emotional control mode. She wants to get out to Italy and bring our daughter back. The Embassy staff have said that there may be a delay whilst the police conduct their investigation but Var wants to get there as soon as possible. She wants to see Chantrea and I want to talk to whoever is in charge of the investigation."

"Ah, that's Inspector Maldini of the Carabinieri."

"Is he any good?"

"Yes, I think he is."

"And I bet you are keeping him on his toes?"

"Well, I am trying to be as helpful as I can."

Tenika thought to herself what would Owen and Var say if they knew she had slapped the Inspector about the head, torn his shirt and been put in a cell. That was something to look forward to.

"Owen, has Var spoken to Ronald?"

"Yes, he can't get away immediately and, given the distance it would take him time to get to Italy anyway. He is probably going to fly straight to the UK and we will meet up when we get Chantrea home. I am sure he is being kept up to date by the Foreign Office and the Embassy in Rome anyway."

"Let me know when you have arrived at the hotel and we can meet up."

"Ok Tenika, stay safe and we'll see you tomorrow."

"Ok, bye."

Tenika reflected upon the conversation she had just had. It is one thing to deal with the thought that a daughter has been killed in a botched mugging but it is something else to be told that you daughter may have been murdered by mistake because she was wearing someone else's clothes. How would Owen and Var react to that? She could hear the Ispettore's words in her ear telling her we didn't know that for certain so we can't say that. But what happens if that postulation becomes a truth? Who is going to tell them and what will they think of her then?

Tenika suddenly realised that this business will become public knowledge back home. All of Chantrea's friends will become aware of what has happened and if it becomes evident that Chantrea was murdered by mistake, what will they think of her. Will she be outcast as the woman who shouldn't be alive, who has taken the life of Chantrea by default. Would she be accused of cheating death at the expense of a beautiful, intelligent and caring woman?

Perhaps if she could get to the bottom of what has happened, it might just throw an understandable explanation of the tragedies that had occurred. It might just make people focus on the bad guys and not just her good fortune.

The evening was beginning to draw in when there was a knock on Tenika's door.

"Who is it?"

"Polizia."

Tenika opened the door. Standing in front of her was a female uniformed police officer. Tenika invited her in.

"Buonasera, Miss Taylor. I am Mariangela Fellini. I will be in the room along the hall."

"Ah, Ispettore Maldini told me you were coming. You speak good English."

"Yes, I took it at school and there are many English people who come to Sorrento so plenty of practice."

"So how does this work?"

"If you stay in your room then I will leave you alone unless you want something. If you go out, I come with you."

"Well I am rather hungry. How do you fancy a walk to the Fauno bar?"

"Ok, let me change. I don't think you want to sit next to a police officer in uniform!"

Mariangela left the room and returned fifteen minutes later. She had been transformed. Her flaxen hair was now flowing and her pale blue eyes stood out. She wore a white shirt that emphasised her golden tanned skin, skinny jeans and a thick cardigan with purple and green colour to it. Her outfit was completed by purple sparkly flat shoes. She carried a large hand bag which she said contained 'necessary equipment'. Tenika was wearing brown soft shoes, similar skinny jeans and a light yellow blouse covered by a tan jacket. The two women seemed to blend together very well.

As they walked the short distance to Fauno bar Tenika noticed that, in flat shoes, Mariangela was about the same height as her. As they approached the Fauno Tenika was immediately spotted by Lucca. He seemed confused as to why Chantrea was missing and although they were shown to a table by a different waiter Lucca came over.

"Where is your friend" he said to Tenika.

"She is not well and so I am her replacement for the night" responded Mariangela giving Tenika no time to come up with a response.

"Ok, well have a good evening."

The waiter looked slightly confused but seemed to accept the version.

"Ciao."

"Grazie Mariangela, I hadn't thought of Lucca."

"No problem."

Tenika felt a little nervous with Mariangela. What had she been told about Chantrea and Luke? Was she there to protect her or watch her. Was Mariangela Inspector Maldini's guard dog to make sure she did not cause any more problems by asking difficult questions of people? Some drinks arrived and Mariangela turned to Tenika.

"You know you are quite famous at the station."

"Why is that?"

Tenika was waiting for the inevitable comment of her slapping Inspector Maldini and ending up in the cell.

"For kicking Constantino. There are a few of us that would have liked to have done that."

Mariangela looked at Tenika and smiled. Tenika smiled back albeit with a sense of embarrassment.

They ordered food and began to ease into a conversation about Sorrento. Mariangela asked a few questions about Tenika's background but nothing intrusive. Slowly Tenika began to relax. Perhaps the person sitting with her was a woman as much as a police officer. There were no questions about Chantrea, well none at first, and Mariangela's manner was friendly and relaxed. Tenika knew the questioning had to change at some point. This was not entirely a social evening. There could be someone in Sorrento wanting to kill her and that was why Mariangela was there. The subject needed to be tackled.

"Can I ask you what the Inspector has said about the death of Chanie?"

"Well as you know the investigation is still progressing, but I understand you think there may be a link between the death of the Englishman and that of your friend. The Ispettore says that you believe your friend's death may have been a mistake because she was wearing your clothes and that you were the intended target."

"Do you think he believes me?"

"I don't know. It is a possibility and that is why I am here for the evenings."

"Why just the evenings?"

"The Ispettore probably thinks that if your idea is correct then you are more at risk at night. Your friend was attacked at night and, if an attack was made on you, it might be done in the same way. So, if I am with you at night it reduces the risk of attack."

"Do you think Sorrento is a safe place?"

"Oh yes, very safe. Muggings on the street are rare here. I cannot remember two deaths within a week of each other that were not traffic related."

Mariangela's comments only provided more reason for Tenika to believe that the deaths were connected and everything now goes back to Luke's death and the mysterious woman with black hair.

"Ispettore Maldini says that your friend's parents are arriving here tomorrow."

"Yes, that's true. How did he know?"

"The Embassy in Rome contacted him because Miss Park's father wants a meeting when they arrive. I think he wants to visit the scene of the attack and have a briefing on what has happened since."

"I know I have to confront the spot too but it's a difficult thought."

"I can understand that. If you want to go this evening or tomorrow, I will go with you."

"Thanks, I don't want to go tonight. Let's see how I feel tomorrow."

"By the way Tenika, can you give me your mobile number in case I need to contact you."

The women exchanged mobile numbers and then took their time to eat their food passing away the time with trivial conversation. When done, they paid the bill and walked slowly back the short distance to the hotel. They made their way up the stairs to the lift and then to the top floor of the building.

"If there is any problem during the night you just come to my room here or ring me. I will also check on you in the morning."

"Ok Mariangela, have a good night. Ciao."

At the same time across town a late night meeting was getting underway.

"Ah, Sovrintendente Mosta, please come in."

"Thank you Sindaco Albero, I am grateful that you could find the time."

"What is it that I can do to help you?"

"I need to talk to you about the two recent deaths in Sorrento involving English people."

"Ah yes, so tragic.   Have you spoken to the British Embassy?"

"Yes, Ispettore Maldini has done so."

"I don't like crime against tourists. Once news is put onto all of the websites it can impact upon people wanting to come here. Robbery frightens people off if they don't think they will be safe."

"Well Alexander, the situation may not be as simple as at first we thought.

"Well Mario, you had better tell me what has changed."

"Well, as you know we believed that the Englishman fell to his death as an accident and we have no desire to change our view. However, it has been suggested to us that his company may have made a donation to your charity and this might have caused some to believe, unreasonably, that the donation had some influence on your brother's company to award the contract. It is therefore possible, and only possible, that some unjustly aggrieved person may then have taken some revenge on the Englishman."

"That is preposterous."

"Alexander, I trust you and your office of Mayor but I need you to help me if my officers are to be sure on these matters. I have to ask you whether the Englishman's company did make a contribution to your Charity?"

"Many people make anonymous donations to my charity. They do not expect to be investigated by the police."

"I am not investigating you Alexander or your donors. I am merely reviewing a theory."

The Mayor got up from his chair and walked to a window and looked out to the lit grounds of his rather large house. He took his time before responding.

"Mario, I am going to answer your question because it is you. I would not do so with anyone else. Do you understand?"

"Of course Alexander."

"I think they made a small donation."

"And Alexander, just how small was it?"

"Mario, you are testing my patience."

The Mayor looked sternly at the Superintendant. He was not happy with the line of questioning.

"Something like ten thousand Euro."

"Did you tell your brother the amount?"

"No, I don't think so. All I remember is that the company made a donation as a contribution to the needy in Sorrento. A good will gesture if you like. They may have told my brother the amount but I did not."

"Who else here would have known about the donation?"

"Only Alexandria Zola, she deals with all the donations directly but she tells no one who they are from."

"Thank you Alexander. The details of the donation will remain silent with me."

"Why are you bothering with theories Mario? The Englishman has been taken back to Britain. The case is closed, isn't it?"

"We are troubled by the murder of the young English woman last night. It is possible the two deaths are linked."

"But Mario, I thought the woman's death was the result of robbery."

The Mayor's voice expressed his frustration.

"Perhaps so, but we think some things are not quite right and my officers want to be sure about these things. You don't want us to be criticised by the British press do you or have politicians from Rome crawling over us?"

The Mayor looked resigned to the way the conversation was going.

"All right, all right do what you must but please be sensitive with your actions. I don't want the good name of Sorrento to be tarnished by unfounded accusations."

"I understand Alexander. We will be very discrete."

The meeting ended and the Superintendent made his way back to the police station. He now knew that a donation of ten thousand Euro was made to the Mayor's fund and he also knew his Inspector needed to know if Alexandria Zola had any connection with others who might have wanted to know about the donation. His meeting with the Mayor was also an indication that the murder of Chantrea was a turning point. Both Inspector Maldini and the Superintendent did not feel comfortable with events even though they did not want to admit it publicly.

DAY NINE

At eight o'clock sharp there was a knock on Tenika's door. She was already up and dressed and another big day lay ahead. She opened the door and found Mariangela standing there in her police uniform.

"Buongiorno Miss Taylor, I hope you slept well."

"Buongiorno, well not too bad thank you. Look, if we are going to spend time together do you think you could call me Tenika?"

"Ok, as you wish. I hope your day goes well with the arrival of Miss Park's parents but if there are any problems contact me at the station. Ok?"

"Yes, thanks. I'm going to breakfast now so I'll come down with you."

The two women got into the lift and if last night they looked like two similar young women out for dinner together, this morning they could not have looked more different. With her uniform on, Mariangela's demeanour had changed. She was more formal and more serious. They emerged from the lift on the first floor. Tenika moved towards the breakfast room and Mariangela towards the reception desk and then the stairs. She turned to Tenika.

"Ciao Tenika."

"Ciao."

Breakfast was her normal mix of cereal, fruit and a croissant washed down with a cappuccino. She didn't have to ask for the cappuccino any more, the elderly female waitress prepared her one as soon as she arrived in the breakfast room. Chantrea's parents would arrive mid-afternoon so there was plenty of time for other tasks. Tenika's mind returned to the woman in her forties with the black hair. Who was she and how would she find out? She thought back to Inspector Maldini's words about considering all possibilities. She thought that after breakfast her first job was to do that, work out what the possibilities were and begin to work her way through them.

Back in her room after breakfast, Tenika sat down on the sofa and began to look at the possibilities. If the woman with black hair was something to do with a competitor to Dynamo, then which one could it be? Could it be as simple as FP Ingegneria? After all, its managing director, Francesco Giardiniere, was very outspoken about the award of the contract. Could she have been used to lure Luke to the cliff edge? Did she work for FP or might she have been brought in by them? Or, as the Inspector mused, was she a prostitute? Did Luke have a weakness in that way? Did he arrange to meet her very late in the evening so that he might not be recognised or seen? But if that was the case, why go to a four star hotel for drinks? It was over the border of Sorrento so did he think that if he met her in the commune of Sant Agnello that it was sufficiently far from Sorrento for no one of consequence to notice? Tenika couldn't accept this version for the simple issue of the alcohol. If Luke was going to go with a prostitute why be so coy about alcohol particularly if it reduced his inhibitions? Tenika wondered if there was a way of checking to see if there was a forty something black haired prostitute working in Sorrento or Sant

Agnello.   She was used to conducting research but not into prostitutes.

Tenika then turned her mind to Luke's support for his sister at her school and the note found on his computer indicating that he intended to make public information about the Headteacher, Suzannah Boswell. Could it possibly be that a Headteacher of an English secondary school could orchestrate the murder of the brother of a teacher because he was going to publish information that might ruin her career? Well, if that was the case, then it would make a fascinating story for the Times Educational Supplement. Sasha did not seem to view this as a possibility. She seemed to see it as over-zealous management, where meeting targets at all costs had become the priority and where staff became the whipping-boys of senior management.   Surely others would have complained as well, Tenika thought. Would a Headteacher wipe out half the staff who blocked or failed to deliver the all important targets? Well there was the case of Harold Shipman.

As Tenika ran over the possibilities, she increasingly believed the answer lay in Sorrento. Somebody in the town, she thought, was pulling the strings. Somebody in the town knew she and Chantrea had been asking questions. Somebody in the town had been sufficiently upset by this to murder Chantrea even if she was mistaken for herself.

Suddenly the phone in the room rang. Tenika picked it up.

"Oh, buongiorno Raf, how are you."

"Buongiorno Tenika. I am well thank you. Tenika, I have heard this morning about the death of another English woman in Sorrento. Is it Chanie?

"Yes Raf it is, but please don't mention this to anyone."

 I am so sorry. Can we talk?"

"Yes, when?"

"I am outside in the car. Can you come now?"

"Yes, I'll just grab my jacket and bag."

Tenika grabbed her jacket and bag and quickly made her way down in the lift and then down the stairs to the road below. Just outside was Raf in his Alfa Romeo car. She got in and he drove off.

"I just have to go via the office and then we can go for a coffee."

"Ok."

A little more than ten minutes later they were at the offices of Dynamo. Raf parked in the staff car park.

"Would you like to come up? I am going to be two minutes."

"Yes, ok."

They got out of the car and walked round to the front of the building. Raf entered a security number and they went through the glass doors and up the stairs into reception. The receptionist smiled at both Raf and Tenika and he beckoned her to follow him through a door into the open plan office area.

"I just need to talk to one of my colleagues for a moment. Please take a seat here. If you would like any water, there is a bottle just over there."

Raf disappeared behind a screen to talk to a male colleague whilst Tenika gazed through the window. It was another fine day. The temperature was expected to be around twenty three degrees celsius and the sky was clear and blue. She wondered how somewhere so beautiful could be so painful at the same time. She asked herself whether she would ever come back to Sorrento or whether the pain would be too great.

Raf returned and smiled. Tenika got up and followed him back to reception. There they came across Maria signing in at reception.

"Buongiorno Maria."

She looked up at Tenika and then to Raf."

"Buongiorno, um Tenika isn't it?"

"Yes, are you here to do more language teaching?"

"Uhm Yes, always more to do."

"Do you only work with people here or elsewhere?"

"No, I work with a few companies here in Sorrento, Morelli, FP, Mondano and the like."

"Well, it's nice to see you again."

"Yes Tenika, we must talk more about life in Britain."

Maria smiled at Tenika and she smiled back. Then she and Raf went down the stairs, out of the glass doors and round to the side of the building where Raf's car was parked.

"I will take you to a coffee place near to where your hotel is so that you can walk back easily."

Raf drove to Piazza Angelina Lauro and parked on the side of the square. They walked over to the Angelina Lauro café and sat at an outside table. It was fairly quiet giving them some privacy. Raf ordered a cappuccino for Tenika and black coffee for himself. Raf sat to the left of Tenika and pulled his seat a little closer. He spoke in hushed tones.

"Tenika, when I heard about the woman being killed I just had this awful feeling that it was connected to the two of you. In fact I was worried that it might have been you. They are saying it was a robbery. What happened?"

"Chanie went out to buy some presents and cakes. It looks as if she got as far as buying the cakes because she was attacked near to the Pizzeria restaurant in Via San Francesca. You know, the small opening by the theatre next to the Basilica and almost opposite the statue."

"Yes, I know it. How did she die?"

"She was stabbed."

"Oh my God, how terrible for her. Were there no witnesses?"

"No, it was very dark, cloudy and no moon. The only camera image shows a dark shadowy figure walking out of the square."

Tenika moved towards Raf and lowered her voice even more.

"Raf, do you remember when you warned Chanie and me about asking awkward questions?"

"Well yes, but ..."

"I think Chanie's death and that of Luke are linked. Chanie was wearing my hat and scarf and I believe she was targeted by someone thinking it was me. In the dark we could look alike wearing the hat and scarf."

"Look, when I said take care of what you say, I meant that Luciano Albero could get very angry make your life difficult but I didn't mean he would kill you. No, I don't believe that. I was also concerned about my own job. I need it and have to remain loyal to the company."

"I believe that Luke's company gave a donation to the Mayor's charity and someone believes this enabled Dynamo to award the contract to Andersons."

"But that would be like a bribe. I know that Italy has its political problems but ...."

"Raf, it doesn't matter whether a bribe was given or not. What matters is what people think did happen and what they think might happen in the future. If a competitor, such as FP, thought that such a payment had been made they might want to stop it happening again by warning off foreign companies and Luke's death might have been the warning. Similarly, if the Mayor or Luciano Albero thought that Chanie and I were going to put the idea of such a payment into the press they might want to stop us to protect their reputation. You could see how pissed off he was with being contacted by the reporter."

"But the Alberos would only need to be concerned if there was evidence of a link between any payment to the Mayor's charity and the decision to give the contract to Luke's company. Even if one was linked to the other, they are too smart for evidence to be left lying around."

"Was there much talk about Chanie and me after the reporter contacted Luciano Albero?"

"He spoke to me about you and he wasn't happy at all. I don't think a lot of people know about you but I guess some do now because Luciano spoke with a number of people in deciding what to do."

They sipped their cappuccinos which brought a temporary halt to the conversation.

"Tell me what you know about Maria."

"Maria Aquila? She has worked with us for about five years or so providing business English lessons to our staff. She helps us to compete in the international field and we need good business English skills. She also helps with checking translations for us."

"Do you know much about her background?"

"No, not really, I think she has lived in Sorrento for about ten years. She worked for other companies and hotels before us. She is a very nice person and very professional in what she does. We like her and I think she likes working with us."

"But she works with other companies as well."

"Yes, she mentioned some in reception but I don't know any more than those she mentioned."

"Is she married or have a partner?"

"I don't think she is married. She does not talk about a husband. As for a partner, I don't really know. She doesn't really talk about those things. I suppose you could say she is a private person but a very nice private person."

As they finished their coffee, Tenika's mind began to focus on the possibility of Maria wittingly or unwittingly passing on information to FP Ingegneria. Could they then have used that information to target Chantrea?

"So what is the next step with Chantrea?"

"Oh, sorry, her parents are arriving today at about three and they will be meeting with the police."

"Well Tenika, if there is more I can do to help please let me know but I don't think Dynamo has anything to do with the deaths of Luke or Chantrea. Luciano Albero can be a bully but I don't think he is a murderer."

"Let's hope so Raf and thank you for calling and taking me out for coffee. I've enjoyed our chat."

"Do you need me to take you to your hotel?"

"No, it's only just round the corner, I can walk."

They got up from their chairs and Raf gave Tenika a kiss on each cheek. They said their goodbyes and Tenika set off for her hotel. As she turned right into Corso Italia, she crossed the road and went into the supermarket. It was lunchtime and bought some soft rolls, ham, cheese and orange juice. As she stood waiting to pay, Tenika thought about Maria. She had black hair and was in her forties. Could she have been the woman with Luke? It was a possibility but it didn't fit with Raf's description of her. Could it be FP Ingegneria that was dealing out retribution and Maria was an unwitting participant in that process? Tenika paid for the items then crossed the road and walked back the short distance to her hotel.

Once back in her room, Tenika looked at the time realising that Var and Owen's plane would be touching down at Naples airport very soon. She probably had two hours to spare at the most before they arrived in Sorrento. A thought occurred to her how she might find out a little more about Maria. Back in London Tenika worked with a woman called Melanie Darvell who had traced her ancestors back to the Hugenots of the seventeenth century. Perhaps she could find something out about Maria's family background.

Tenika called her office on her mobile phone.

"Hello Martin, it's Tenika here. Is Melanie there?"

"Yes, just a moment."

"Hello Melanie Darvelle."

231

"Hi Mel, it's Tenika.

"Hello, how are you? Aren't you in Italy?"

"Yes I am. Mel, I wonder whether you could do me a favour. I want to find out about a woman I have met here called Maria Aquila and I wonder whether you might have a spare moment to apply your genealogical skills to find anything you can about her. She comes from an Italian family that was based in Bournemouth at least ten years ago."

"Hmm I suppose I can. I am a bit tied up at the moment but I will have a go when I get home. Is that ok?"

"Yes, but asap would be really helpful. If you find anything can you text or ring me on my mobile?"

"Sure, can you spell the last name for me?"

"Yes, it's A-Q-U-I-L-A."

"Ok, got that. I'll see what I come up with."

"Thanks Mel, you're a star."

Tenika was feeling tired. She hadn't slept well the previous night and the emotional strain was taking its toll. She decided to take a nap before Var and Owen's arrival. She set her alarm for three thirty, closed the shutters to the glass doors and settled down on her bed. It didn't take long before she was fast asleep. Shortly before three thirty, her mobile phone rang and Tenika woke with a start and grabbed her phone.

"Hello."

"Tenika, it's Var. We're here."

"Sorry Var, I've been having a nap. Where's here?"

"At the Vittoria hotel."

"Great, I'm looking forward to seeing you."

"Inspector Maldini is coming to collect us at four thirty to go to the scene and talk through things. I want you to come with us, if you want to."

"Yes Var, I do."

"Well when you're ready come over to the hotel. We are in room 314."

"Ok Var, I'll be over soon."

As Tenika began preparations to walk to the Vittoria hotel, she felt herself becoming emotional again. She wondered how Var would be, emotional or controlled and how would she cope with standing at the spot where Chantrea lost her life? She pulled herself together. This was no time for self indulgent sentiment, it was Var and Owen who needed support now.

Tenika walked the very short distance from her hotel to the Vittoria. All she had to do was turn right out of her hotel and walk less than one hundred metres to the hotel's entrance on Corso Italia. The Vittoria was a four star hotel and rather grand. It took a prime position overlooking the Marina Piccola. It was rather different to the Palazzo Abagnale with its contemporary feel. The Vittoria had a feel of a hotel exuding a style that had been there for over one hundred years catering for the needs of the weary, yet reasonably well off, traveller.

Tenika arrived at the door of room 314, took a deep breath and knocked. The door opened and Owen stood tall looking at her. He was about the same height as her with a heavy build and thinning grey hair. His round face looked a little pale and he didn't look as if he had slept for some time. She stepped in and he hugged her firmly. Over his shoulder she could see Var looking rather gaunt and dark round the eyes. She was shorter and with a much more slender frame. Her face gave nothing away other than solemnity and dignity. Tenika released herself from Owen's embrace and moved towards Var. Tenika could feel the emotion rising in her and as the two women embraced felt tears reaching her eyes. They held each other for some time then Tenika and Var kissed each other and sat down on the bed holding hands.

"Tenika, I am so happy to see you and to know that you are safe."

"I'm so pleased that you and Owen are here but I don't know what I can say that is of any use. I've lost my best friend but you have lost your only daughter."

"She is with many other members of my family that I have lost over the years. She is safe now and surrounded by other loved ones."

Tenika was so impressed by the way Var could rationalise and accept Chantrea's death as passing into a new state of being, joining those ancestors long gone before. She looked up at Owen whose face bore the pain of someone with a much greater struggle in coming to terms with the loss of Chantrea.

"We had some tea sent up and there's lots here, would you like a cup?"

"Hmm yes thanks."

Var got up and attended to Tenika's drink. She gave Tenika the tea and sat down on the bed again.

"The Inspector is coming at 4.30 pm. What is he like? Owen hopes he is competent."

"I think he is competent and a decent man too. He tries to think of all the angles but he is careful with his language though. He speaks good English so there is no problem there."

"They are all careful with their language. You should talk to them at the Embassy, never a straight answer" commented Owen.

"Does Inspector Maldini know I will be here?"

"Yes, Owen told them that we wanted you at the meeting. He was very firm with them. By the way, we have some flowers down at reception we are going to leave at the scene. Owen and I have already written and card but I got one for you if you wish."

"Oh yes, I'd love to."

Var handed over a small card for Tenika to write something on whilst she drank her tea. Owen and Var continued to unpack and prepare for the arrival of Inspector Maldini. Not much was said. They were all conscious of what was to come and small talk had fizzled out. Tenika thought hard about what to write.

"Always loved you & will never leave you."

She put the card into the small envelope and finished her tea. The room was quiet when the inevitable knock on the door arrived and Owen again opened the door.

Inspector Maldini stood in the doorway. He was wearing a dark suit and looked rather formal. His face displayed compassion and his voice was soft and caring.

"You must be Mr Park, I am Inspector Maldini."

"Please call me Owen. Let me introduce you to my wife, Var."

The Inspector moved forward and took Var's hand.

"Let me say to you both that I am so sad for your loss. It is a terrible thing that has happened."

"Thank you Inspector" said Var.

"And you know Tenika. I understand she has been helping you?"

"Yes Owen, I am very acquainted with Miss Taylor. She has been ... uhm ... very energetic with her assistance and we have been grateful for that."

Inspector Maldini looked at Tenika who responded with a rather sheepish look of embarrassment.

"Mr and Mrs Park, can I also introduce you to one of my officers who is working on the case. Her name is Mariangela Fellini and she also knows Miss Taylor."

On cue, Mariangela appeared in the doorway in her uniform. She too looked sombre.

"Hello Mr and Mrs Park. I too am very sorry for your loss."

Mariangela moved forward and shook hands with Owen and Var. Tenika caught her eye with a wry smile. The Inspector has brought his dog handler she thought.

"Ok, now we have all met each other let me say what is going to happen. Firstly, we are going to the hospital to see Chantrea and then we will go to the scene. The hospital has just called me to say they are prepared so we can go when you are ready."

"I think we are ready so let's do it" remarked Owen.

They all left the room and made their way into a lift and down to the reception area. Owen went up to the receptionist who picked up a bunch of flowers and handed them to him. The reception staff had been advised on what was happening and they looked serious and respectful. The group made their way through the large doors to the driveway beyond.

"Mr and Mrs Park, would you come with me in this car and Miss Taylor if you would go with the officer in the other car."

The Inspector held the car door open for Var whilst Tenika got into a police car driven by Mariangela.

"How are you Tenika?"

"I'm ok, feeling a little sad and apprehensive. Has the Ispettore brought you along to keep me under control?"

Mariangela's face remained serious at this quip.

"No, I am here to protect you."

"What do you mean?"

"Later Tenika, not now. Let us pay our respects to your friend."

The two cars left the Grand Hotel Vittoria turning right across Tasso Square and up along Corso Italia until they reached the hospital. Inspector Maldini led the group through the main entrance where they were met by a hospital manager who greeted Var and Owen and then led them to a lift where they went down to the basement of the hospital. They were then led to a room with double doors. The manager asked the group to remain outside the room whilst he went inside. The group was quiet. Tenika looked at Var and thought how elegant she looked in a well cut black and white dress that showed off her slim physique. Owen, on the other hand looked very ashen and near to tears. Inspector Maldini and Mariangela Fellini stood to one side of the others and were respectful and sombre in their mood.

The manager came out of the room and beckoned Var and Owen to enter. As they did, Chantrea came into view lying on a table draped with a bed sheet underneath her body and one on top of her. As before, the sheets were perfectly folded, care had clearly been taken to present Chantrea as best as possible. Her hair had again been combed and her face was clean and the mark on one side of her face, caused by her fall to the ground, had been masked by the use of make-up.

Owen moved forward with Var to his left with Tenika to his right. Owen began to shake as he got closer and Tenika put her arm round his waist to support him. Var looked down on her daughter with a great calmness but her face showing the sadness she felt. Owen was struggling to accept what confronted him. Tears ran down his face as Tenika held him firmly. Behind them stood the Inspector, Officer Fellini and a nurse. They just looked on saying nothing.

Var turned to Owen and Tenika.

"She looks so peaceful and without pain."

"She looks beautiful" uttered Owen in broken voice.

Var turned to the nurse.

"Can we sit with her for a while?"

"Si" came the reply.

There were already two chairs in the room and the nurse went off to find another one. Inspector Maldini announced he and Mariangela would step outside and leave them alone with Chantrea for a few minutes. The three of them sat close together. Owen holding Var's right hand and Tenika holding firmly onto Owen's right. Little was said as they sat there. There wasn't much each could say that would make the others feel any better. Merely being there with Chantrea made them more at ease with themselves.

Although not Chantrea's biological father, he had married Var when Chantrea was seven years old and had treated her as his own daughter from that day. Chantrea's relationship with her natural father had, on the other hand, been rather cool. Living in New Zealand had not helped but, even so, Ronald had struggled to be a close father. When Chantrea was sixteen she decided to change her name to Park because she wanted to make a clear statement to Owen about where her feelings lay. He had been overwhelmed by this gesture and from that moment he was her father and she his daughter.

After sitting with Chantrea for fifteen minutes Owen said they would have to rejoin the Inspector to move on to their next appointment. Var got up and spoke to Chantrea in Khmer and Owen kissed her on the forehead and told Chantrea that he would be back to take her home. Tenika stroked Chantrea's cheek and also kissed her. She reminded Chantrea that she had said she would return and would see her again soon.

They walked slowly towards the door. Var went up to the nurse.

"Thank you for being so respectful to my daughter."

"No problem" replied the nurse.

They went through the door and found the Inspector and Mariangela outside. The manager had disappeared.

"If you are ready we will go to the scene?"

"Yes, let's do that" replied Owen.

The Inspector led the way back to the main entrance of the hospital and on to the cars. The journey to Via San Francesco only took five minutes. The cars parked on the far side of the square and immediately Tenika could see across the square an area cordoned off by police tape. Another surge of emotion swept through her. She got out of the car and walked behind Owen and

Var, who was carrying the flowers, as they crossed the square via the statue of San Antonio Abbatte. The Inspector led the way and Officer Fellini walked at Tenika's side.

It was late in the afternoon and the shadows were gathering. Tenika could see that to the side of the restaurant they had visited was an area under an archway leading to the theatre entrance that had been cordoned off. They walked up to the tape and they could see coloured marks on the floor placed there by the police to indicate how they found the scene but the paving had been cleaned. There was no blood to be seen.

"Where was she found?" enquired Owen.

"My officers found her in the doorway here."

"Was she on the floor?"

"Yes."

"I can see how at night this area would be very dark."

"True, and on the night there was no moonlight either."

"Did anyone in the restaurant see anything?"

"Unfortunately not. Your daughter went into the restaurant to buy some cakes but the diners were not seated in the conservatory area here, they were in the far side of the restaurant and little can be seen from that side."

Owen looked at Var with the flowers and turned to the Inspector.

"Can we place the flowers on the spot?"

"Yes, but my officer will do it for you."

Tenika moved forward and got her card from her handbag and placed it in the middle of the flowers. Var had placed her and Owen's card just inside the cellophane wrapping. It read '*Until we meet again*'. Mariangela Fellini took the flowers, ducked under the tape and placed them on the spot where Chantrea died. Owen again had tears running down his face and Tenika was fighting the emotion surging in side of her. She stood between Owen and Var and placed one arm round each. Var stood staring at the spot with an emotionless face. She had seen many tragic events in the past and had learned to control her emotions.

"Are there any cameras here?" asked Owen.

"Yes, there is one on the building behind us but all that it shows is a shadowy figure walking from the square. I'm afraid it does not give enough detail to be helpful other than the movement suggests it is a man. Look, when you are ready we will go back to the hotel and we can talk more there in private."

Owen nodded but kept his eyes on the flowers that so visibly marked the spot of his daughter's death. Tenika hugged Var who looked into Tenika's eyes.

"In my life I have lost so many people I love. I can only believe that I will meet them all again one day."

They had taken in as much as they wanted to see and began to walk slowly back to the cars. No one spoke, they held their own thoughts as they reflected on the scene and its consequences. The cars drove slowly back to the hotel and they walked thoughtfully in through the main entrance. They were welcomed by the hotel manager who shook hands with Var and Owen. He led them off through a doorway and Owen looked at Inspector Maldini quizzically.

"I have asked the hotel for a room in which we can talk and have coffee."

Owen nodded in acknowledgement and they found themselves led to a function room. There was tea, coffee and soft drinks available in the room. The hotel manager turned to the group.

"You will be private here. There is no one else in this part of the building. If you need anything at all please use the telephone on the wall."

Inspector Maldini thanked the manager and suggested they all got a drink. Var and Owen had tea, Tenika had coffee with milk whilst the Inspector and Officer Fellini had black coffee. They all sat down round a square table.

"Mr and Mrs Park, I want to tell you that we are treating the murder of your daughter with the highest priority. I have a number of officers working on the case and hopeful we will catch the person responsible. I would like to say something to you confidentially if you are agreeable?"

"Of course Inspector, go on."

"Ok, so what I say now does not go out of this room. You must tell no one. I am telling you these things because I want to be as open as I can. So, we think your daughter's death may be linked to another case that Miss Taylor has been helping us with."

Tenika looked across to Mariangela who looked back at her without any expression on her face. This is not what Tenika expected to hear. Where had the Inspector's caution gone and what about all of the possibilities?

"I don't have all of the answers yet and I will need your patience and trust to continue with our investigations."

"Will you keep us informed of progress?"

"If you are agreeable to confidentiality, then yes. I also need to inform you that your daughter's death is in the papers although little detail has been given. We may choose not to give much detail to the press and may even give the impression that we have few leads. We don't want to give all of our information to the person responsible. Do you understand?"

"Yes, Inspector that sounds sensible. Thank you for bringing us into your confidence."

Owen continued with his questions.

"And what happens now to Chantrea and her belongings?"

"Your daughter's body will remain at the hospital. Her belongings are at the police station and are being treated as evidence. The body and belongings will be released when we have reached a satisfactory conclusion to the case. I am going to give you my card and you can ring me at any time. I apologise in advance if I am not available but you will be able to leave a message and I will get back to you."

Var turned to Owen.

"I am feeling tired, do you mind if I go up to the room."

"Of course not, I'll come with you."

They all got up from their chairs and Var looked at the Inspector.

"Thank you for what you have done today and all that you have done so far. I have seen terrible things in my life, I know what people can do to each other. I want you to keep Tenika safe. I know what she can be like so please look after her."

"I will keep her safe, please don't worry. In fact I would like to talk to her now for a few minutes."

"Thank you Inspector."

Var and Owen shook hands with the Inspector and Officer Fellini and left the room. The Inspector beckoned Tenika to sit down again.

"Thank you for not telling them of the trouble I have given you."

"Uhm no, no Miss Taylor, I think I may need to apologise to you."

"Why?"

"Because I now believe that Mr Adams was murdered as you have been saying all along."

Tenika sat up and looked at the Inspector and Mariangela. She looked a little surprised.

"What's changed your mind?"

"I asked the Hotel Alpha for their camera recording of the evening when Mr Adams was there with the woman with black hair. The recording shows Mr Adams going to the toilet and whilst he is away the woman puts something in his drink. She thinks no one is looking because it is late and there are few people around but she forgot the camera behind her."

"So she spiked his drink?"

"It looks that way. It would only have needed 25 grammes of pure alcohol, which is tasteless, to give the reading in the pathology report. This is not very much and Mr Adams had a large natural orange juice so it is quite possible he would have not tasted anything added."

"And you say the camera was behind her so it does not show her face?"

"No, I am afraid not."

"There is something else."

"What is it?"

"The barman contacted me with information about the woman. He did not think much of it but thought he would tell me anyway. He said he had been trying to remember her ordering the drinks and thinking about her accent. He says he couldn't place the accent, there was something different about it."

"Ispettore, there is a woman who provides business English lessons at Dynamo who has black hair and I think is in her forties.

246

Her name is Maria Aquila. She says she was brought up in England and moved to Italy many years ago. She speaks very good Italian but has a subtle English accent in the background. I saw her briefly recently and she told me that FP Ingegneria is, or was, also one of her clients. It is quite possible that she found out about the donation to the Mayor's fund, perhaps by overhearing conversation, and unwittingly or knowingly passed the information on to those at FP provoking a response."

"Mmm let us take this slowly Miss Taylor. Did you see Maria Aquila before or after the death of Miss Park. The last time was after. It was this morning. Raf contacted me because he had heard of the death of a woman and thought it might be me. He collected me to have coffee but we stopped off at his office for a couple of minutes and I saw here there."

"Let us suppose for a moment that you are right in that this Maria Aquila somehow passed on information about the donation resulting in the same woman being involved in his death at Sant Agnello. Let us also suppose that the death of Miss Park was linked to that of Mr Adams because the same people wanted to kill you because you were asking too many questions and mistakenly attacked Miss Park because she was wearing your scarf and hat. The fact that Maria Aquila knows you are alive may find its way to those who killed Miss Park by exactly the same route as that information that led to the death of Mr Adams."

"Oh my God, yes you are right."

"But, Miss Taylor, this assumes your assumptions are correct. Ok, it seems it is time I met Maria Aquila. Are you going to see Mr and Mrs Park now?"

"Yes, for a short while and then go back to the hotel."

"Ok, Officer Fellini will stay here with you and make sure you get back to your hotel safely."

They all got up and made their way back to reception. The Inspector waved goodbye as he went through the main doors and Tenika and Officer Fellini took the lift to the third floor and room 314. Tenika knocked on the door and Owen opened it and Tenika walked in. Owen could see Officer Fellini in the hallway and beckoned her in.

"It's ok, I can stay here outside. I don't want to intrude."

Tenika returned to the doorway.

"Are you sure?"

"Yes."

The conversation between the three of them was convivial albeit lacking in humour. Var had a habit of holding or touching people's hand when making a point to them, and quickly she was holding Tenika's hand warmly. She wanted to return to the Inspector's comment that Chantrea's death may be linked to another case.

"What did the Inspector mean about a link with another case?"

Tenika suspected the Inspector has not mentioned the detail of the Luke's death so as not to concern Var and Owen any more than was necessary. What was she to do? Tell Var all of the details or hold back? If she told Var the truth would Var be overly concerned about Tenika's safety? Perhaps a tactic of some detail, if not all, might be best for now.

"He meant a case in which an English chap was injured in the nearby commune of Sant Agnello. It's possible some sort of targeting of English people is happening but the Inspector doesn't want visitors to worry that they are in danger."

"And how are you helping him?"

"Chantrea and I met the chap who was injured in Sant Agnello at a restaurant one lunchtime. He was with a work colleague. Chanie and I had helped the Inspector with details of the meeting and whether others were there and so on. We have sort of suggested lines of enquiry."

"Mmm that sounds like you. You will be careful, won't you?"

"Of course, don't worry."

A natural lull occurred in the conversation and Tenika decided it was time to give privacy back to Var and Owen. Tenika kissed Var and Owen as she bid her farewell. Owen opened the door.

"Just one moment Tenika. I have something for you from Sokhong."

Var handed over a small envelope to Tenika.

"Please don't open it now. Wait until you get back to your hotel."

Tenika put the envelope in her bag and said goodbye to Var and Owen. She and Officer Fellini got into the lift and made their way back to the car.

"Var is a very special woman."

"Yes, and Chanie was every bit as beautiful as her."

The journey to Palazzo Abagnale was less than one minute and luckily there was a space outside the Armani shop where the officer could park. They made their way up to Tenika's room and the officer said she would leave Tenika alone in her room for now as she had to telephone the police station from her bedroom. Tenika shut the door behind her the room seemed strangely silent and empty. She sat on the bed and pulled out the small envelope from Sokhong, Var's older sister. In it was a small card with a picture of Angor Wat, the temple complex and symbol of Cambodia, in the top right hand corner. In the centre of the card were a few words in handwriting.

> *"I am still holding your hand*
> *and will never let go."*

Tenika felt tears well up in her. Sokhong so understood the darker side of human nature and the need for social support and mental strength to get through dark days. The symbolism of Sokhong's card was powerful. It dispelled the guilt Tenika felt over Chantrea's death and gave her a renewed determination to see this business through whatever might come her way. If Sokhong could stand up to, and survive, the terrors of Pol Pot then she could stand up to the menace at large in Sorrento. She put the card back into her hand bag and her fingers found the knife she had bought from the shop. Just insurance she thought.

Later that afternoon Maria Aquila arrived at the police station having voluntarily come to see Inspector Maldini following a call from his office to Dynamo who then contacted her. She found herself in the same interview room as that used by Tenika in her now infamous face slapping, shirt tearing incident.

"Thank you Miss Aquila for coming to see me today, I will try not to detain you too long."

"That is quite alright Ispettore, how can I help you."

"I am interested to know a little about your work. Can you tell me what you do."

Maria seemed a little puzzled by the question but answered anyway."

"I provide lessons in business English to business people in Sorrento, Sant Agnello and other places. They are usually people who work in the international field and need good technical language for their work. It is usually done on a one to one basis but sometimes it is done in small groups."

"And does this instruction take place at the executive's place of work?"

"Yes, usually."

"How long does the instruction last for?"

"Well it depends on the starting point of the executive. It is usually some weeks but can be some months with an individual. Sometimes it is dependent upon a specific project and the language needed to perhaps win a contract or deliver it with partners."

"So with such businesses you must find out quite a bit about what they do?"

"Yes, I suppose I do, but it is confidential. I don't tell anyone outside a business what I learn within it."

"But sometimes, perhaps there is talk in a company about competitors, their strengths and weaknesses, what they do and how they do it?"

"Of course, but it is not for me to pass such judgements. My job is to help people express their technical ideas in good English. When such talk goes on I just keep quiet."

"Can I ask Ispettore, what is this all about?"

"I am sorry, we are investigating the possible leak of sensitive commercial information and I am talking to people, like yourself, who come into contact with business people at their premises to see what your experience is of hearing about information from other businesses. For example, in your travels between businesses have you heard anything about donations to the Mayor's charity fund?"

"Uhm no not at all, if you mean specific donations, facts and figures and the like, then I've heard nothing. I have heard rumblings about not knowing the facts and figures, how the fund seems to be rather secret. I have also heard occasional rumblings about the Alberos and whether there is any commercial advantage gained by Dynamo from having the Mayor as Luciano Albero's brother."

"Can I ask where you have heard this?"

"FP, of course, but then it has been in the papers and other places. I can't recall."

"Given your experience of both FP and Dynamo, do you think there is any advantage gained by Dynamo from the brotherly relationship?"

"I don't really know. I have not heard anything specific and Luciano Albero seems to be someone who makes up his own mind about things. I can't say that anything specific stands out from either business which suggests one has lost or one has gained from the relationship."

"Miss Aquila, this is a very sensitive conversation and I would be grateful if you would not mention it to anyone at all."

"Of course Ispettore."

"In which case, thank you for coming in today. Could you just write down your address and contact number in case I need to ask you for more help?"

"Yes Inspector, I am happy to help at any time."

With the address and telephone number written down, the Inspector escorted Maria back to reception where he thanked her once again. As he walked back to his office, Inspector Maldini reflected upon his interview with Maria. Her body language didn't suggest she was lying. Her answers seemed natural and honest. She didn't seem anxious or nervous. In fact there was nothing in the interview which suggested she knew anything about the donation to the Mayor's fund nor was part of discussions about competitors. To check, however, Inspector Maldini felt he should speak with FP and Dynamo to see what they thought of Maria. Although the afternoon was drawing on, Inspector Maldini telephoned Dynamo and was put through to Luciano Albero.

"Ah Signor Albero?"

"Si."

"This is Inspector Maldini from the Caribinieri. I need to come and see you immediately. Can you see me in about twenty minutes?"

"Yes, if you wish."

"Thank you. I will see you soon."

Inspector Maldini then made a similar call to Francesco Giardiniere at FP Ingegneria and a meeting was arranged for two hours later. The Inspector was keen to compare the impressions of Maria Aquila, her version of whether she had access to detailed information about each company and whether she took part in discussions or kept quiet as she said. Pietro Maldini arrived at Dynamo and was shown to Luciano Albero's office.

"Buongiorno Signor Albero."

"Buon pomeriggio Ispettore, please take a seat. How can I help you?"

"I want to begin by saying that I do not believe your brother, the Mayor, or you are corrupt or have done anything wrong. You are not under suspicion of doing anything. I need your help however in understanding whether things have happened that you might not be aware of."

"I don't quite understand Inspector, but I will help if I can."

"Ok, did you know that Anderson's had made a donation to the Mayor's charity?"

"Yes, I did."

"And would others here have known of the donation?"

"Those people involved with the negotiations with Andersons discussed various options of financial support to Sorrento. They wanted to show their commitment to the commune. The Mayor's fund was an obvious option."

"Was it a condition of the contract?"

"I thought you might ask this. No, not at all. It was they who raised the issue. I think they wanted to show it was not just about money for them. They wanted a relationship with Sorrento."

"And you liked that?"

"Of course, but we are hard headed Inspector. We wanted the right company for the job not one that would simply pay a lot of money to my brother's fund. Do you think I am foolish?"

"No Luciano, I don't. How did the arrangement with the Ambasciatori come about?"

"We knew there would be quite a few visits and they asked if we could handle the arrangements this end. They didn't like having a long distance relationship with a hotel or hotels. We were quite happy with this and we built the cost into the figures. The Ambasciatori was also happy because we know them."

"The rooms you booked were always Premier rooms?"

"Yes, why not? A happy worker is a good worker."

"So who would have been involved in these discussions with Andersons?"

"Myself, Silvano Maggio our technical director and Rafael Bellomi who led on the delivery of the contract."

"Are these things talked about in the company, over lunch, coffee?"

"No, I don't think so. The implementation of the contract, yes of course but I don't think either Silvano or Rafael would discuss the contractual conversations. I don't like that and they know it. It is not good for our commercial intelligence to become public knowledge and I have to be firm on that. I think it is also fair to say that the staff know I don't like discussion about my brother. They are entitled to their views, as anyone is, but they can express them outside in the bar."

"So someone like Maria Aquila, who works with you on developing business English would not know about these discussions?"

"No, why should she? She will know about the implementation side of things but should know nothing about the contractual discussions. I would be very disappointed if Silvano or Rafael mentioned these things in her presence. Anyway, I find her very professional. She works with other companies including our competitor FP but she is discrete. She says nothing here about the other companies she works with and I am confident she says nothing about us."

"Well look Luciano, I think you have answered my questions. Thank you again and I hope I haven't troubled you."

"No, of course not Ispettore, I will get someone to show you out."

As the Inspector drove across Sorrento to FP Ingegneria he reflected upon the conversation with Luciano Albero. His answers seemed to fit in with those of Maria Aquila and Signor Albero is quite a formidable man. If anyone broke his rules on discussing contractual matters they were liable to lose their jobs. Wouldn't that cast a shadow over the possibility of informal talk over coffee or lunch? He wondered what response he would get from Signor Francesco Giardiniere at FP. When the Inspector arrived, he was shown quickly to the office of Francesco Giardiniere. It was plain to see that the company offices were not stylish and well kept as those of Dynamo. Was this a sign of lack of profitability and more reason for feeling aggrieved if potential work went overseas?

"Buonasera Signor Giardiniere."

"Buonasera Ispettore."

If Luciano Albero showed the signs of a fifty something man who indulged a passion for food, Francesco Giardiniere was rather different. Standing just under two metres tall be was slim and with thinning hair that seemed to have its own intentions of how it would sit on his head. He did not have the intensity or physical presence of Luciano Albero. In fact, he seemed much gentler in his mannerisms.

"Signor Giardiniere, you have been very vocal in the past about Dynamo and the award of a contract to a British company, Andersons."

"Yes, I have."

"Could you tell me why?"

"It's very simple. These are tough economic times and we think that Italian work should go to Italian companies if they have the skills to do it. I don't have a problem in bringing in overseas companies if the local ones can't do the job but we thought we could do the job and we thought there were probably others that could do the job."

"Were there any other reasons?"

"You mean the Alberos? Everyone knows brothers will help each other."

"What do you mean by that?"

"We all know that the British firm makes a donation to the Mayor's fund and next minute the British firm gets the contract with Dynamo."

"Do you have any evidence of that?"

"There was lots of talk about it in the press at the time."

"Did anyone tell you directly that's what had happened?"

"No, but we all know what was going on."

"Come now Signor Giardiniere, isn't the real position that Maria Aquila who works with you and Dynamo let it slip in a meeting, over lunch or coffee? Isn't that true?"

"I don't know who you have been talking to but Maria doesn't say anything about her other clients. In fact she told me off one day when I made a joke about the Alberos in front of her. She said she didn't like it because it might be seen as a compromising situation for her. I had to apologise to her. Ah well, there you go."

"I assume you have heard about the death of Mr Adams who was working with Dynamo on the contract you have complained about?"

"Yes, I have. He fell to his death didn't he? It's very tragic for his family."

"There is a view Signor Giardiniere that says you were so upset about the contract going to the British company that you wanted to make a point to the Alberos by killing Mr Adams. What do you say to that?"

"I say you are off your head. Look, I was angry about the situation and I said things to the press but I would not kill anyone. That's absurd."

Signor Giardiniere's manner was changing and the Inspector was watching carefully.

"Are you sure you did not employ the services of someone to push him off the cliff?"

"No! No! We are an old Sorrento business and have prided ourselves on being honest. You can ask anyone who knows me. This is a ridiculous idea."

"How are profits in the company?"

"They are down as they are with so many companies in Italy and across Europe. That is why I think we must work together and protect ourselves a little to maintain employment. You know, I have people here who have worked for me for years and others who depend on their income here to maintain their lives. I will fight to survive, but do you really think I would put it all at risk by having an Englishman pushed off a cliff?"

Signor Giardiniere was close to tears and the Inspector knew it was time to pull back.

"I am sorry if I have upset you Signor Giardiniere, but a policeman sometimes must ask difficult questions. I am grateful to you for answering mine."

"I do understand what you say and I am sure a policeman's job is a difficult one but I am shocked at your suggestion."

"I will leave you now. Thank you for giving me your time."

The two men stood up and shook hands and Signor Giardiniere showed the Inspector the way out. As they reached the outer door the Inspector turned to Francesco Gardiniere.

"Signor, I believe what you have told me and I must ask you a favour. I would like you not to tell anyone of this discussion. If you think of any more you wish to say please let me or my

Sovrintendente know. It would help me a lot if you could do this for me now."

"I do not know what is going on in your head Ispettore, but I am an honourable man and I will do as you ask. I hope you will explain all of this to me at some point."

"Thank you, I am very grateful and yes I will."

The Inspector left the building reflecting on what he had heard and seen. He felt he had been up a false road. There was no evidence in front of him that Maria Aquila had acted in an unprofessional way or that she had passed information to FP. Indeed, the reaction of Francesco Giardiniere to the questions made the Inspector believe he was telling the truth. Giardiniere had let off steam to the press as his own company profits were coming under pressure but he had not murdered Luke Adams.

Across town, Tenika was back at her hotel when she receives a call on her mobile from Melanie Darvell who had been looking at the background of Maria Aquila.

"Hi Mel, how have you got on?"

"You are moving in strange circles that's all I can say."

"What do you mean?"

"I can find an Aquila family in Bournemouth. They run an Italian restaurant called Aquila on Holdenhurst Road. I guess you know that aquila is Italian for eagle. Now you said that Maria was in her forties, so I looked at birth records that might apply and found a Maria Aquila born between January and March 1970 in

Marylebone in London. I would need the birth certificate to be more precise on the date."

"Ah, so do you think that is her?"

"Well, the problem is that a Maria Aquila died in Marylebone between April and June 1971 aged just 1. Now the probability is that this is the same person."

"So, hang on, that's a child called Maria Aquila who has died at the age of 1?"

"Yes, that's right. I can't find any other birth record of a Maria Aquila born in the years to give someone an age in their late 30s through to 50."

"What does that mean?"

"Well your Maria Aquila might have been born abroad and is registered in another country so there would be no record in the UK. However, I can't find any trace of a Maria Aquila on the electoral roll and I have been back fifteen years. The other thought is that Maria Aquila might not be the real name of your person. Using the name of a dead child is a neat way to conceal identity because if someone does a quick check on birth, they will find one. It's only if a further check on death is done that would reveal a corresponding death."

"Oh I see, so why did you do a check on deaths then?"

"Because I know you, and I doubted if this was a straight forward query!"

"Right, can you do me another quick check?"

"Go on, I might not be able to do it until tomorrow because I have to go out this evening."

"Ok, it's on another woman called Suzannah Boswell and she is headteacher of Hollingsworth High school in Kent. See what you come up with."

"Ok, will do. Must dash now. See you."

"Bye Mel."

Tenika sat down and looked at her scribbled note. So, If Maria Aquila was a false name, then who is she and why did she change her name? Why create such an elaborate smokescreen? She thought back to the comments from Raf that she was a private individual who gave little away about her background. This sounded like the time for another conversation with Inspector Maldini. Tenika took his card from her handbag and picked up her mobile phone. Then she thought about Mariangela and whether the right thing was to advise her of what she was about to do. Tenika went along the corridor and knocked on Mariangela's door. The door opened and Mariangela smiled.

"Hi Tenika, is there a problem?"

"Hi, not exactly, Can I come in?"

"Sure."

"My friend in London did some checks on Maria Aquila and couldn't find a birth record for her other than for a child who was born in 1970 and died in 1971. Now Maria could have been born in another country and registered there or Maria Aquila is not her real name. It could be being used to cover up who she really is. I feel I

263

need to talk to Ispettore Maldini but didn't want to call him without letting you know."

"Thank you that was probably a good idea. He is probably at home now, so let me ring him then he will know we are working together."

Mariangela took out her mobile phone and rang the Inspector.

"Ah Ispettore, I am with Miss Taylor and she has information she wishes to give to you. She did not want to disturb you so late but I told her you would want to know."

"Thank you Mariangela, pass her on to me."

"Buona sera Ispettore."

"Buona sera Miss Taylor. I have news for you also. I have met and spoken with Maria Aquila, Luciano Albero from Dynamo and Francesco Giardiniere from FP. There is no evidence of Maria passing on information about the donation to FP. Her version of events is corroborated by both Signor Albero and Signor Giardiniere. They both say she is very professional and never talks about other clients. I also asked Signor Giardiniere about the death of Mr Adams. He insisted he had nothing to do with it and I believe what he has said to me. So, Miss Taylor, I don't believe that Maria Aquila passed information on to FP, nor do I believe that Signor Giardiniere was involved in the death of Mr Adams. Perhaps she is the wrong woman with black hair. Oh, and I asked one of my officers to speak with some street ladies and they have confirmed they don't know any prostitute in Sorrento or Sant Agnello who fits the description of the woman with black hair. So Miss Taylor, what is your news?"

"I asked a friend in London to do some checks on Maria Aquila. You will recall she said her family came from Bournemouth. Well my friend did find a family running a restaurant called Aquila in Bournemouth. However, and probably more importantly, she could not find a birth record for Maria other than that of a child born in 1970 who died in 1971. I am sure you will know Ispettore the use of a dead child's name is a common way of concealing an identity."

"Yes Miss Taylor I do know that and I also know that Maria Aquila could have been born in another country and be registered there. What I do believe is that there is no link between Maria Aquila, FP and the death of Mr Adams."

"Are there any checks you can do Ispettore, that will not take much time, just to check her out?"

The Inspector could hear the urgency in Tenika's voice and sensed she was not going to let the matter drop unless he did something. Ok, I will see what I can do. I need to bring this conversation about Maria Aquila to an end.

"Grazie Ispettore."

"I must go now. Ciao."

The Inspector pressed his end call button and walked across his lounge to his jacket. He took out his wallet and searched for a card. He found what he was looking for and rang the number. It was answered by a woman with a very formal British accent.

"Buona sera, Georgina James."

"Good evening Georgina, it is Pietro Maldini here from the Sorrento Carabinieri."

"Hello Pietro, how nice to hear from you so soon after that last matter."

"Georgina, I am sorry to call so late, but I wonder whether the Embassy could do me a favour. Are you alone?"

"Let me just walk into another room, we have some business people here for dinner .... there you are all alone."

"We have a woman in Sorrento who I would like to know a little more about. Her name is Maria Aquila and there is a belief that this is not her real name. She has told people she comes from Bournemouth but there is some doubt about that too. Is there any quick check that you can do to see if there is any concern about this woman?"

"For you Pietro we are always willing to help. I will get someone onto it in the morning and will let you know as soon as we have anything for you."

"Thank you Georgina, you are so kind."

"Not at all. Have a good evening Pietro."

"And you too."

Back at Palazzo Abagnale, Tenika was sitting on Mariangela's bed looking rather down.

"Not good news from the Ispettore?"

"No, it looks like FP is not responsible for the death of Luke Adams and Maria is not in league with FP passing information about the donation by Andersons to the mayor's charity. It's a bit of a dead end but something is not right about Maria Aquila."

"Are you seeing Var and Owen this evening?"

"No, I've told them to spend time together. I will see them tomorrow."

"Come on, let's go and get some dinner somewhere."

DAY TEN

Tenika rose early. She found it difficult to sleep without Chantrea with her in the room. The routines and fabric of life had changed and she found it difficult to adjust. There was an underlying imbalance in her life now and it troubled her. At eight o'clock sharp there was a knock on the door as Officer Mariangela Fellini checked that Tenika was ok before she went off to the police station. As the Officer went off to work, Tenika went down for breakfast pondering what the day would bring. She was due to see Var and Owen later in the day but her mind was still focused on Maria Aquila and the apparent false name. She hoped the Inspector had been able to do some checks and that this conundrum would be resolved soon.

With only three days left before her flight back to Gatwick, Tenika began to feel a sense of impending failure to resolving what happened to Luke and Chantrea. When she returned to her room after breakfast, Tenika sat on the bed slightly at a loss of what to do next. Suddenly the phone in her room sprang into life.

"Buongiorno."

"Buongiorno Tenika, it's Maria here, Maria Aquila."

"Maria, what a surprise."

"Tenika, I am sorry for such an early call but I wanted to catch you before you planned your day. I don't get much opportunity to talk with people from Britain nowadays and less so with women like yourself. So, I wondered whether you might like to come for lunch today?"

""Maria, that's very kind of you to think of me. Yes, I would love to. Where shall we go and what time?"

"Would you like to come to my place at about one o'clock? I'll cook us something."

"Yes, that's fine. What is the address?"

"Angelo Abitazione. It is a house on the Via Nastro Verde just past the Hotel Aminta on the left hand side. There is a big white gate but you can push it open easily."

"Ok, that sounds fine. I look forward to seeing you at one."

"Good, Ciao Tenika."

"Ciao."

Tenika put the phone down and reflected upon what had just happened. She could not believe her luck. Perhaps now she would be able to get to the bottom of whom Maria Aquila really is, always assuming that Maria was willing to tell. Tenika felt more positive. This was a step forward she thought. Her day was looking up.

No sooner had Tenika sat back down on the bed than her mobile phone began to ring. This was beginning to feel like London busses she thought. Tenika moved round the bed to her mobile phone sitting on the bedside table.

"Hello."

"Hi Tenika it's Mel."

"Oh thanks for getting back to me so soon."

"No problem, when I got back last night I couldn't sleep so I did a little digging for you. Your Suzannah Bosworth was born between April and May 1979 and her maiden name is Watson. Her husband is called Gerald. Interestingly, she has a twin brother named James so I assume they are not identical twins. Not much at the moment but I will let you know if I find more."

"Ok Mel, thanks. Bye."

"Bye."

Tenika looked down at the note she had written, now sitting on her bedside table, with the details provided by Mel. She thought there wasn't much to go on and was unsure the information would take her forward. However, at that moment it didn't matter because she was looking forward to lunch with Maria and the opportunities that seemed to present.

All of a sudden there was a knock on the door. Tenika opened it and was surprised to See Var standing there.

"I thought you might like to look at the shops with me."

"Of course Var, what have you done with Owen?"

"He is talking to various people about arrangements to get Chantrea home when the police release her body. Thankfully Chantrea gave Owen details of the holiday insurance and he has contacted them and I think they have appointed a repatriation company to deal with matters."

Var went into Tenika's room whilst she collected her things and then they went down in the lift to reception where they were greeted and asked where they might be going. Tenika told the receptionist that they were off to the shops and she would be back in a couple of hours. As they went through the outside door onto Corso Italia Tenika whispered

"I think the Inspector has asked them to keep an eye on me and try to find out where I go during the day."

"He's just doing his job Tenika and I did ask him to keep you safe."

"Yes, you did and I am very touched by that."

The women walked down the short distance to Tasso Square and then in to Via San Cesareo. Although still quite early in the day, the narrow road was already filling with tourists and locals. The locals tended to walk faster because they knew what they wanted to buy whilst the tourists tended to walk slower because many were not buying at all, just looking and taking in the atmosphere. There were individuals taking pictures and others with expensive looking video cameras. Tenika and Var could hear many languages being spoken, some they could recognise and some they could not. English was often heard and occasionally Japanese tourists wearing white face masks would pass them by.

Var and Tenika took a slow walk down the old narrow street stopping at many shops to look and take in the variety of products on offer. They chatted about designs, colours, prices, the noises and smells. Although neither woman demonstrated a particularly happy disposition, for both the time was a welcome partial release from the tragedy they both suffered from. It was something else to think about for the moment although both knew that the consequences of Chantrea's death would soon crush in on them again.

As they began to wind their way back towards Tasso Square Var asked Tenika if the investigation had got any further. Tenika told Var about her conversation with the Inspector that seemed to rule out Maria from passing on information about the donation to the Mayor's charity fund and also rule out FP from being involved in Luke's death. Tenika also told her about the information provided by Mel seeming to indicate that Maria Aquila was using a false name for some reason. Tenika confided in Var that the options and time were perhaps running out to get to the bottom of the affair. Var's response was that the most important issue was for Tenika to remain safe. She said that enough tragedy had occurred and Var didn't want any more. At that moment Tenika's mobile phone rang.

"Buongiorno."

"Buongiorno Miss Taylor, it's Ispettore Maldini here."

"Oh, hello."

"Miss Taylor, after we spoke yesterday I contacted the British Embassy in Rome to ask them if it was possible to find anything out about Maria Aquila. They have rung me back this morning. Now what I am about to say is confidential. Is that ok?"

"Yes, of course."

"All I can say is that she has had a change of name and that this is known to the British authorities. However, I am not able to tell you why she changed her name but I can say that it was for reasons that are legal. She has no criminal background. Now I am telling you these things because I know you feel she is involved in these matters in some way. However, I cannot find any evidence of involvement and she doesn't appear to have done anything wrong in Britain or Italy. It may be she is not the woman with black hair. We may have to accept that."

"I hear what you are saying Ispettore. Look, I am due to fly home in three days so I shall be out of your hair soon."

"You are not a problem to me Miss Taylor but I don't want you to do something you, and I, will regret later. We must be cautious."

"Ok Ispettore, thank you for taking the time to ring me."

"No problem Miss Taylor. Ciao."

Tenika didn't tell the Inspector about her lunch appointment with Maria. She felt she would have had a lecture about what she could and should not do. Anyway, if Maria was so innocent, then it would be lunch and a chat and no more. The Inspector's words did pose her a problem, however, in that she had agreed to the confidentiality of Maria's change in name. Would she feel obliged not to mention the subject to be faithful to her word? Would it arise naturally? Was there some other way of getting to the question without raising it directly? The thoughts consumed her as she and Var walked slowly back towards the Vittoria hotel.

Var and Tenika parted company at the entrance to the grounds of the Vittoria and Tenika walked the short distance back to Palazzo Abagnale. Once back in her room there was a need to prepare for her lunch with Maria. Tenika sat on the sofa thinking about whether she needed tactics or just let the conversation run but be ready if an opening arose regarding her change of name. She knew she had to be careful, it would not look good if Maria became aware that Tenika had done background research on her. The suspicion and doubt would then be returned upon her.

Tenika thought about where Maria lived and, from her walk through the olive groves the other day, knew roughly where it was. Perhaps on another day when she had not spent two hours wandering around shops, she might walk to Maria's house. On this occasion, however, Tenika decided it was worth investing in what might be ten to fifteen Euros on a taxi. Tenika refreshed herself and changed into a sleeveless brown dress with brown and white diagonal stripes across it. The day was warm and she didn't feel she needed a shrug or jacket to go with it.

Tenika walked from the hotel down to Tasso Square and across the road to the taxi rank. She asked the first driver how much he would charge and he said fifteen Euros. She put her hand on his arm and looked him in the eyes and asked if he could do it for twelve. He melted in her gaze and agreed twelve Euros. The taxi drove along Corso Italia past the Cathedral, the hospital and then the Capodimonte hotel as the road began a steep climb up the hillside. After about a kilometre the town faded out and the scenery was dominated by the sea on the right hand side and steep green hillside on the left. The road forked and the taxi took a left fork so that the sea became hidden by the hillside. The road climbed relentlessly with regular tight hairpin bends which the taxi took at quite a speed. The bends were so tight that it was impossible to see what was coming in the opposite direction. Tenika's mind was screaming 'slow down' but the taxi seemed to accelerate into the bends as if the hillside was challenging the taxi driver to compete with it. As the taxi twisted and turned through the bends, intermittently Tenika could see the town way below and the sea stretching out to Vesuvius and Naples. There were some large houses built into the hillside and occasional hotels. The Hotel Aminta came into view and Tenika knew they were almost there. She alerted the driver to this and about four hundred metres past the Aminta she saw a property on the left come into view. It had a large white gate and, as the taxi slowed down, she could see the name of Angelo Abitazione, Angel House, on the wall by the side of the gate. Tenika put her hand into her bag to take out her purse and realised she had left her mobile phone in the bedroom. Did this increase the risk to an unacceptable level she wondered? She decided she had come this far and there was no point in turning back. She paid the taxi driver who gave Tenika his card and suggested she call him when she wanted to return. She thanked him, got out of the taxi and pushed at the white gate. It opened easily as Maria had said it would.

The property was single story and rectangular in shape. It had white walls and a terracotta coloured roof. It had seen better days and the garden was laid to lawn albeit that it had suffered from the hot Sorrento summer. Tenika walked up the driveway passed a black Fiat Punto car to the brown wooden front door. She knocked hard on the door and, after a few seconds, it was opened by Maria. She was wearing black trousers and a grey short sleeved top. Her black hair was tied back and she had gone to some lengths to use make-up to maximise her looks. Even Tenika thought that Maria looked very attractive.

"Hello Tenika, thank you for coming."

"Ciao Maria, thanks for inviting me."

"Do come in and make yourself at home."

Tenika entered the house and was struck by it's simple but quality decor. The main living area was open plan with double doors leading onto a large patio area at the back. There was an open fire place and on each side of it were two cream coloured sofas facing each other. Behind the sofas was a large dining table with six chairs and beyond that was a large kitchen area.

"Have you modernised the house?"

"Yes, it was a bit dilapidated when I bought it. It was a stone house with some plastering her and there and what I did was to go back to the stone and decide what to expose and what to cover up. I had new floor tiles laid across the entire floor area of the house, then had the ceilings and windows painted. Once that was done it was a case of finding furniture. I've been here ten years so it hasn't been a rush. There's loads to do outside but the ground is so hard and I am not much of a gardener."

"I think it's really nice and what is so important is that you have been able to stamp your own personality on it."

"Look Tenika, I think I should say how sorry I am that your friend has died. It must have come as a terrible shock."

"Yes, it has. I've been in a bit of a daze to be honest and I haven't slept much since."

"Do the police know what happened?"

"Well her purse was stolen so they think it was a robbery that went wrong."

"It's awful and so unlike Sorrento."

"Yes, and when you take into account the death of Luke Adams, whom you knew at Dynamo, it's been quite an awful couple of weeks."

"I knew him a little from my work there but it is so awful to think of him somehow falling to his death. It's not the first time a British traveller to Sorrento has gone over the cliff but it is rare. Right let me get on with lunch and you take a seat on a sofa."

Tenika sat down and thought that actually Maria seems like a very nice person. The house seemed very normal although she noticed that the photos on display seemed to be Sorrento based along with some holiday photographs. She couldn't see any that shouted as being family photos.

"Would you like a glass of wine or fruit juice or coffee?"

"Fruit juice please."

"Is orange ok? You've noticed that Sorrento is covered with orange trees?"

"Yes, I love the way Corso Italia is lined with orange trees from Tasso Square up and beyond the station."

"Yes, it is very nice."

Maria brought Tenika her drink.

"I am doing some crab pasta with a salad and bread. How does that sound?"

"Fabulous."

"Ok, I am ready. Tenika, could you sit here? You will get a good view of the bay and a little of the communes across the Piano di Sorrento."

Tenika sat down at the table with her back to the kitchen but the view out of the window was wonderful. The hillside fell away so steeply that it revealed the plateau on which Sorrento and its neighbours resided.

"This is a lovely place."

"I was very lucky. It was in such a poor state that it couldn't be rented and needed someone to do it up. I came on the scene at just the right moment. I saw it and bought it. So Tenika, where do you live in the UK?"

"I live in Wimbledon, South London. I have a small two bed flat."

"Ah, how is London nowadays?"

"More people, more cars and more traffic jams."

"What about you Maria. What are your origins?"

"Well I was born to an Italian family who came to Britain in the sixties. They lived in London originally and I was born there. Later we moved to Bournemouth where they still run a restaurant."

"Ah so that's where you get your cooking talent from."

"Well I wouldn't go that far."

What is the restaurant called?"

"Aquila. Not very original I know."

Tenika reminded herself that everything Maria had said could be true albeit that having said she was born in London, the probability of it being true was declining. She knew she needed to be careful in what she said."

"So what brought you to Sorrento?"

"I was fed up with life in Bournemouth. I was single and wanted to do more with my life. I wanted to live here and try to create a different life and I think I have done that. The climate here is fabulous, the pace of life is good and the people really great."

"Your Italian is very good."

"Thanks Tenika, I have tried to adopt an Italian accent but it is not easy when you're not born here. I must say that your's isn't bad either."

"I started it at school and took it through to University where I did it as a minority subject and acquired an Italian boyfriend but, yeh, it's not bad. My accent screams British speaker though."

"So Maria, are you still single? Do you have a partner? Don't answer that if it's too private."

"No it's ok. I have had one or two relationships since I've been here but they haven't come to much. I suppose I may have to accept being forever single. Not that I mind, I am very happy in my own company and this is a wonderful place to grow old."

The more they talked, the more Tenika felt comfortable with Maria even though she came with doubts and suspicions.

"So Tenika, how did you meet Luke?"

"Chanie and I met him at Emilia's trattoria at Marina Grande. We were sitting next to each other and got chatting."

"Did you feel attracted to him?"

"I don't know. He was very charming and we talked well together. He seemed very genuine. I was quite upset to hear he had died."

"And you have been trying to find out what happened to him?"

"Well sort of, but the police have decided it was an accident so the case is closed."

"You don't agree with them?"

"Well some aspects of it don't feel right."

"I heard Luciano Albero was not happy about being questioned by a reporter. He thought you had prompted the reporter with your questions. He was very angry."

"I didn't set out to do that but I was just trying to find out what might have happened."

"You seem a very determined woman Tenika."

"My mother always said that women had to be twice as good as men to get on. I'm a bit competitive I suppose. I want to sort things out better than others. Some people tell me I can be a bit like a dog with a bone, never letting go until the job is done."

"That is an admirable quality Tenika."

"Thank you."

Maria cleared the plates from the table and went into the kitchen. Tenika was feeling rather apprehensive with the line of questioning from Maria. Was Maria checking her out now? Was she fishing to see what Tenika Knew? This was not the time to mention anything about a woman with black hair. Maria spoke to Tenika from the kitchen.

"And what about your friend, are you determined to find out what happened to her?"

Tenika took a slow intake of breath. The question sounded dangerous. Tenika decided to play safe with the answer.

"Her parents would like to know but the police are handling the case. There isn't much I can do."

"Would you like some melon?"

"Yes thanks Maria that would be nice."

"How does the bay look at the moment?"

"It looks beautiful."

Suddenly the back of Tenika's head exploded in pain and her face thumped hard into the table surface. Although it only took seconds to lose consciousness, in Tenika's head they went very slowly. Her eyes were staring across the table and she couldn't move her body. Slowly, and without any control, she began to slide from being slumped on the table to crumpling on the floor. She ended on her back and darkness enveloped her."

When her senses returned, she found herself with hands and feet tied and with tape across her mouth and round her head. She wasn't wearing any shoes. Pain was throbbing through her head and she could see blood on her arm and shoulder from her wound. She was no longer in the house. It seemed to be some sort of large shed or a barn. There wasn't much in it but it was sturdy and the door was shut. She was also tied to a strong vertical beam such that her movement was very restricted.

Now she knew her suspicions about Maria were correct although still didn't know what the motivation was for this mayhem. Her head was in a lot of pain and she found it difficult to think clearly. She regretted not telling the Inspector that she was meeting Maria for lunch but knew that at some point later in the day Officer Fellini would come knocking at her hotel door. Tenika kept telling herself to stay alive. She reminded herself over and over again that Var and Sokhong did it on the Cambodian farms and so must she.

At six o'clock Officer Fellini knocked on Tenika's hotel room door but there was no answer. She went down to reception and enquired if they had seen her. She was told Tenika left before one o'clock and had looked very smart in her dress with the diagonal stripes. Officer Fellini assumed this was an indication that Tenika had gone to a specific meeting such as lunch with Var and Own and was not yet back. She thought no more of it assuming that Tenika would return in due course.

At eight o'clock, and with no sign of Tenika, Officer Fellini rang Var and Owen's room at the Vittora.

"Buonasera Owen."

"Buonasera. Who is that?"

"It is Officer Fellini. Have you or your wife seen Tenika today?"

"Yes, Var went shopping with her for a couple of hours this morning. We had thought she would drop in on us this afternoon but she hasn't."

"Could you tell me what Tenika was wearing this morning?"

"Just a moment .... apparently jeans and light yellow shirt. Why do you ask? Is there a problem?"

"No, I am sure there is none. Did she say anything to your wife about meeting anyone this afternoon?"

"Uhm I'll ask .... no, she didn't."

"Ok, if she does come to you would you ask her to ring me straight away?"

"Of course we will."

"Thank you so much Mr Park. Goodbye."

Owen put the phone down and looked at Var. They tried not be anxious, after all Tenika is nearly thirty and can look after herself. They came to the view that she had been distracted somewhere and would be back later that evening. Owen agreed to ring Tenika at her hotel later that evening just to make sure.

Officer Fellini now phoned Tenika on her mobile and gained no answer. She now decided it was time to alert Inspector Maldini to the fact that Tenika had not yet returned to her hotel. He also rang Tenika's mobile but gained no answer. He wanted more time to elapse before beginning a missing person alert although was concerned if Tenika has initiated some action of her own without informing him or Officer Fellini. He asked the officer to wait until ten o'clock and if she had not returned by then to ring him again.

At ten o'clock Officer Fellini, still in her uniform, knocked on Tenika's hotel door room but gained no response. She then rang Owen and Var at the Vittoria to check she was not there either. Owen was now becoming concerned that Tenika had gone missing but Officer Fellini assured him that there was no evidence of that yet and that she was just being cautious. He asked her to keep him informed and if she appeared to ring him no matter what the time was. She assured him she would and the call ended. Officer Fellini then rang Inspector Maldini to confirm Tenika had not returned. He said he would come to the hotel and arrived fifteen minutes later. He went straight to reception and asked for a card to open Tenika's room and, armed with it, went up the lift to the top floor where he found Officer Fellini.

"Buonasera Officer Fellini."

"Buonasera Ispettore."

"I see Miss Taylor is giving us more problems. Reception has given me a card to open her room. Let's see what it tells us but be careful it might be a crime scene."

284

The inspector opened the door, lent in and placed the card into the electrical junction and turned on the light. The room was tidy and had no immediate evidence suggesting Tenika had been abducted following a struggle.

"Ok, the room seems in order, let's take a look."

Inspector Maldini and Officer Fellini entered the room and looked to see if there was any indication of where Tenika might be. There was no evidence of Tenika leaving the room in a rush. Items in the room were in an ordered way suggesting she had deliberately left the room after tidying it. He looked at a bedside table and picked up a piece of paper with writing on it. He studied it and looked puzzled for some seconds.

"Officer Fellini, I need to go back to the police station immediately. You are off duty now and don't need to come with me."

"Have you found something?"

"Yes, I think I know who Miss Taylor is with and, more importantly, why she is with that person."

"Is she in danger?"

"Yes, I think she is but I must go back to the station first."

"With your permission, I would like to come with you and help. I feel I am involved now with Tenika and I would like to see this through."

"Ok, but we must go."

The Inspector and Officer Fellini quickly returned to the car parked outside the hotel and drove quickly the short distance to the police station.

"Can you tell me who she is with?" queries Officer Fellini.

"Well, let's get back to the station first, then I need to check something. When we arrive can you arrange some back-up for us at an address that I will get at the station."

As they arrived at the station, the Inspector walked quickly to his office whilst Officer Fellini went to the operations room to have two officers assigned to support herself and the Inspector. The operations officer send a radio message to a police car containing two officers already out in Sorrento to wait for instructions on where to meet the Inspector.

Inspector Maldini looked into his desk drawer and pulled out a pad. On it was an address. He tore the sheet from the pad and walked quickly to the operations room to collect Officer Fellini. He entered the room and spoke to the operations officer.

"Ok, have we back-up?"

"Yes Sir, all arranged."

"Good, tell them to go to number 15, Vista Collina, Via San Lucia. Tell them to wait for me and to park out of sight. Oh and no sirens, tell them to approach quietly. Right, come on Fellini."

The Inspector and Officer Fellini walked quickly to the car and then sped through the dark streets of Sorrento to the block of flats on Via San Lucia, which was on the eastern outskirts of Sorrento. They arrived within ten minutes and found the back-up police car already there. The Inspector beckoned to the two officers in the police car to join him. They gathered together outside the block of flats and the Inspector told the three officers to go quietly with him to the flat in question. He didn't want the occupants to know they were approaching.

The entrance door to the building was protected by a key pad and the Inspector pressed the button for flat 1. A male voice answered the call.

"Buonasera, I am Inspector Maldini from the Carabinieri and I need to enter the building. Could you open the front door for me? Please come and check my identity if you wish."

The door buzzed and Inspector Maldini pushed it open. All four officers quietly ascended the stairs to the third floor where they found flat 15. The Inspector knocked loudly on the door. Seconds later it was opened by an elderly woman of about sixty years of age.

"Buonasera, I am Inspector Maldini from the police, is Maria Aquila in this flat?"

The elderly woman looked quizzically at the Inspector.

"No, I have never heard of such a person."

"What is your name?"

"Donatella Rosucci."

"May we come in please?"

"If you wish."

All four officers entered the flat. They found the woman's husband there but no one else. The officers looked in all the rooms and checked for signs of a younger woman's presence but none was found. Donatella and her husband looked confused and a little worried about what was happening around them. The Inspector began to realise he had been duped.

"It looks as if I must apologise to you Signora Rosucci. I have been given a false address for the person I am looking for."

"Are we in danger?"

"No, I don't think you are at all. Again, I apologise."

The officers withdrew from the flat and looked to the Inspector for what to do next.

"Ok, you two can carry on with your duties whilst Fellini and I will return to the station."

They walked down the stairs and out of the front door. The two back-up officers returned to their car and drove off. Inspector Maldini and Officer Maldini sat in their car and the Inspector pulled out his mobile phone.

"Buonasera Soprintendende, it's Pietro here."

"Buonasera Pietro, what is the problem?"

"I believe Maria Aquila has kidnapped Miss Taylor or worse. I feel we must inform airports and all borders just in case."

"Are you sure Pietro?"

"Yes, I am."

"Ok, leave it to me I will get on to it straight away."

"Ciao."

The Inspector returned to his piece of paper with writing on it. This time he called the telephone number although he suspected what the outcome would be? His suspicions were confirmed, the number was not working. The Inspector started the engine of the car and began to drive quickly back to the police station.

"This is not a good evening. Miss Taylor's instincts were right, things were not as they seemed and I did not consider all possibilities. A lesson for you Fellini, don't discount anything however improbable. What is worse, is that I gave my word to Mrs Park that I would keep Miss Taylor safe and I may have failed in that too."

When they arrived back at the station, the Inspector and Officer Fellini made straight for the Inspector's office. Within minutes they were joined by Superintendent Mosta.

"Ah Ispettore and Officer Fellini, I have actioned the ports and airports alert for Maria Aquila. If she is still in Italy she will not get out of it through a port or airport. Why do you think Maria Aquila has taken Miss Taylor?"

"Because Soprintendende, I believe she murdered, or had murdered, Luke Adams then tried to Murder Miss Taylor but Miss Park was killed in error and now has taken Miss Taylor to complete the job."

"So how do we move forward?"

"We have to find a correct address for Maria Aquila. It looks as if she has been living behind a smokescreen of false information about her address. The phone number she has given me does not work. It is also late and we might not be able to move forward much until the morning. I am going to have Officer Fellini check the mobile number she gave me to see if it is a real number or one that has been suspended. If it was real there may be an address attached to it."

"Ok Ispettore, keep me informed of progress."

"Si Sovrintendende."

As the Superintendent left the office, the Inspector wrote the mobile number onto a piece of paper and handed it to Officer Fellini. She, in turn, left the office to conduct her investigation. The Inspector leant back on his chair and closed his eyes. He thought about Luke's death at the foot of the cliff and the savagery of Chantrea's murder. He did not feel good about this situation. He just hoped that Tenika's tenacity and determination was keeping her alive. It was after midnight now, what more could he do? How did Dynamo contact her, he wondered. The Inspector reached into his jacket pocked for his wallet and pulled out a card. He looked hard at the card and then picked up his mobile and dialled the number. It rang for some time and then was answered by a tired sounding voice.

"Si."

"Buonasera Signor Albero. It is inspector Maldini here. I am very sorry for troubling you at this late hour but I need your help in an urgent matter."

"What can I do for you Ispettore."

"I need the telephone number of your brother, Luciano. I must contact him tonight."

"I think he keeps his mobile with him at all times, including by his bed. I will give you that one."

The Inspector made a note of the number and thanked the Mayor for his help. He then dialled the number and hoped that it would be answered. Disappointingly it wasn't and the Inspector was directed to the answering service. The Inspector ended the call and rang again. He hoped the nuisance factor would bring a response. This time the call was answered. It was a rather irritated voice of Luciano Albero.

"Buonasera, who is this?"

"Buonasera Signor Albero. It is inspector Maldini here. I am very sorry for troubling you but your brother the Mayor gave me your number as I need your help in an urgent matter."

"At this time of night Ispettore?"

"Yes, I am sorry, but it is very urgent."

"What is it then? What do you want?"

"I need to know how you contact Maria Aquila, the telephone number or the address you use."

"What is it about this woman that you are so interested in and why can't it wait till the morning?"

"I cannot say Signor Albero other than it is of great importance."

"Well I don't have the answer here, I need to talk to our personnel people."

"What about the individuals she has been helping with English. Would they have her mobile number?"

"Possibly Ispettore, ok, I will see what I can do."

"Please ring me back on this number as soon as you can."

"You had better have a good reason Ispettore because I am about to disturb people's sleep."

"I understand Signor Albero, and yes there is a good reason."

"Ok, I will ring you back as soon as I can."

"Grazie Luciano."

The Inspector put his phone down and realised that unless Luciano Albero could come up with an address or telephone number tonight, there was probably little more that could be done before morning. The Inspector was staring at the wall fearful that by the morning he would have a third murder on his hands when Officer Fellini came back into the room.

"Have you got anything?"

"Yes, but not much. The number was live until first thing this morning. It is a pay as you go phone so it was not linked to a contract giving any address."

"Hmmm it seems Signora Aquila is one step ahead of us."

"Can you get me some coffee?"

"Of course Ispettore."

Officer Fellini went off for coffee and the Inspector got up from his chair and began to pace across the room. He was deep in thought. The evidence was beginning to suggest an elaborate process of concealment of identity. Maria Aquila did not want people to be able to track her down or know her origins. The information from the British Embassy allied to that from Tenika's room identified those origins and the probable motivation for what had happened. However, the Inspector found it astonishing how such motivations had created planned murders of at least two people and a conscious attempt to prevent him from finding her. He felt disappointed with himself that his original thinking had been swayed by the lack of evidence and a desire on all parts to file the death of Luke Adams under 'accident'. Of course he had never met Luke Adams as Tenika and Chantrea had. Would it have made a difference? Would he have seen whatever it was she had? This case was providing Inspector Maldini with the classic conflict for police officers, whether to follow the evidence or instinct – particularly when one does not match the other.

Officer Fellini returned with the coffee and they both sat down. A few sips into the coffee and Inspector Maldini's mobile phone rang.

"Buonasera."

"Buonasera Ispettore, it is Luciano Albero here. I have a number for you. It is the one we use to contact Maria. However, I have not been able to find an address. I think it will have to wait until first thing in the morning."

293

"Ok Luciano, let me have the number."

The inspector wrote the number down and compared it with that given to him by Maria.

"Luciano thank you very much for doing this for me. If you can check an address first thing in the morning I would be so grateful."

"As you wish Ispettore. Buonanotte."

"Buonanotte Luciano."

The Inspector looked again at the number given to him by Luciano Albero and that by Maria Aquila. He looked up at Officer Fellini.

"These numbers are the same."

"And what do you think to that Ispettore?"

"Well, we don't have another number to check that might lead us to an address. There may be something symbolic in Maria closing down her phone used for work. On the one hand she may know we can't track her on that number and she could have another pay as you go phone. On the other hand she may be closing down one side of her life here, as if to say, the murders have been committed, I am going to be sought for them so it is time to move on."

"You mean rather like some suicides who sort out their affairs before killing themselves?"

"Well in this case I think she may be offering herself up for someone else. Look there is little we can do now. Let's begin again at eight o'clock at the Vittoria. I think I have to talk to Owen and Var Park."

Across Sorrento, in a very dark barn, Tenika sat tied and gagged. Her head still throbbed and she felt dizzy at regular intervals. The door to the barn opened and in stepped Maria carrying a large shoulder bag. Her manner had changed. The charming woman had gone replaced by a surly person talking to herself. Maria took a torch out of her bag, turned it on and placed in on a ledge so that it shone in Tenika's face. With the light shining in her eyes, Tenika couldn't see much but could make out Maria pacing up and down the barn talking to herself quietly and gesticulating. She then came over to Tenika.

"Are you awake?"

Tenika made no movement or sound. Maria slapped her hard across the face and Tenika cried out in pain. Maria grabbed Tenika by her hair and pulled her head upright. She looked into Tenika's glazed eyes.

"Ah so you are awake in there."

Tenika didn't look at Maria preferring to gaze past her face. She groaned with the pain and at times fought to take in the air she needed. The tape across her mouth prevented any intake of air through her mouth. Maria snarled at Tenika.

"You stupid cow, why couldn't you leave this bone alone? He was nothing to you, just a casual lunch encounter. If only you had just walked away you and your friend would be still together now. If only you knew what you have done .... if only you knew."

Maria roughly pushed Tenika's head to one side catching a glancing blow in the wooden upright. Tenika winced with the pain it caused. Maria sat on a barrel across the barn from her and to the right of the torch.

"Do you know what love is? Real love that is? Have you ever had a longing for someone so great that you carry a pain inside you all the time? Have you ever cared for someone such that you'll do anything for them? I've loved someone all my life. I've cared for them, watched over them, admired them and protected them and would have carried on doing just that if you had not walked into that restaurant and sat next to that man.

Do you have a sister Tenika? I do and she is the most wonderful person in the world. She is strong, intelligent and beautiful. I suppose some people see you that way. I wanted to be the best sister in the world to her but I couldn't be. You see I wasn't born that way. I spent my childhood looking at my sister, and the world she lived in, through a barricade of clothing, expectations, attitudes and people peering at me in a strange way. That barricade was impenetrable for a young child growing up. It was only later that I found a way through and could become the sister that I always wanted to be. And if that wasn't hard enough, once I could become the sister I wanted to be, I found I was the subject of more stares and judgements. So you see Tenika, that's why I came here. I could start again. I could begin a new life as a sister and a woman. Oh Tenika, I have had such a good past ten years."

Tenika tried to grasp what was going on. The use of the torch made Tenika wonder whether she was in an out-building on the same site as Maria's house or whether she had been taken to a different location having no electricity. What was Maria meaning about a barricade? Tenika felt weak. She needed a drink and felt hungry. She was also anxious about where this was all leading to. Maria was talking more calmly now and that made Tenika feel a little safer but the instability of the Maria sitting in front of her still made Tenika feel tense and frightened. If only she could talk to Maria perhaps she could talk her into being stable and reasonable.

"Do you know what has been so upsetting Tenika? It's been watching people snipe at my sister when all she does is try to better herself and those around her. Those people like Sasha and Luke Adams who try to destroy the work she's been doing for all those years. It's been so painful, Tenika, so painful. I had to do something to help her, to protect her. Do you understand Tenika? I couldn't let anyone bring her down. I had to make sure she could carry on her work. Do you know Tenika, she would ring me in tears to tell me about the sniping and gossiping behind her back. They just wouldn't listen to her. If they had listened and done what they were told, well there wouldn't have been a need, would there?

Tenika was trying to put the pieces together. It sounded as if Maria was talking about Suzannah Boswell, the Head teacher at Sasha's school but the information from Mel was that Suzannah had a twin brother. In her pained and confused state, a penny slowly dropped. It all began to make bizarre sense.

"If you had a sister and loved her as I love mine, you would have done the same. I know you would. It was fate. She was telling me about this man who was threatening to expose her, give lurid stories to the press, and ruin her reputation. She was beside herself not knowing what to do and I so wanted to help her. And then, this man, like an act of heavenly intervention walked into Dynamo one day. Well Tenika, I couldn't believe it. I just couldn't believe it. It was as if God had come to my rescue and delivered

297

him up to me. Well, Tenika, it was then a question of how and when?"

Tenika listened to the beginning of what seemed to be a confession. She desperately needed to get the tape from her mouth not just because it would help her breath better, but also because she could join in the conversation and have some impact upon it and Maria's state of mind. Tenika began to display the signs of choking and struggling for breath. Her body flopped to one side as she appeared to struggle for breath. Maria got up and came over to her and grabbed Tenika by her hair.

"You're not going to choke to death on me just yet."

Maria forced her finger tips under the tape and pulled it down until it was off from Tenika's top lip and beneath her bottom lip. She could breath normally again and took deep breaths to steady herself. Maria went back into the light took something from the bag and came back to Tenika.

"Now look what I found in your bag, a lovely new knife."

Maria held the knife to Tenika's chest.

"Now let's be clear, if you try to shout or cry out, I will kill you. Now you know I will because you have seen my work, haven't you. Do you understand me?"

Maria dug the knife into Tenika's chest covered merely by her thin dress. Tenika winced as the knife dug into her skin drawing blood. Tenika nodded her agreement. She could feel her heart racing, her head throbbing and a wave of dizziness engulfing her. Suddenly she felt sick and turned her head a little as she vomited to her right side. Whilst some of the vomit landed on the ground next to her, a good deal found its way onto her right arm and down her right hand side. Vomit dribbled from Tenika's mouth and the stench and taste made her retch time and again. Tenika wanted to be consumed by something or someone that would take her to a better place. Her body shuddered and waves of pain swept through her. Somehow, she kept in mind the thought of Sokhong holding her hand. Like a flickering light at the back of her mind, Tenika fought to see Sokhong's hand in hers even though she was coughing, grunting and fighting for breath at the same time. She wanted to cry but refused to allow herself to. Tenika didn't mind the other undignified noises she was making, but she was not going to cry.

Tenika heard noises as Maria moved about the barn. She went out of the door and returned a few minutes later. Tenika could see little with the light in her eyes and, to be honest, felt so wretched that she couldn't really care less what Maria was doing. She sensed Maria coming close again.

"You disgusting bitch."

There was a brief sound of a bucket swinging on the handle and then Tenika was hit by a wall of water. She was left gasping for breath yet again and now her head and torso were soaked. The water had cleaned her face and arm and seemed to have washed some of the vomit from being by her side. There was still a smell but Tenika felt a little better albeit she now sat in water.

"Thank you" whispered Tenika.

"You smell no better than an animal."

"So you killed Luke because he was going to expose Suzannah Boswell?"

299

Tenika's voice was weak and broken but, in the stillness of the night, it was clear enough for Maria to hear.

"Yes, there was no other option. I couldn't let him do that."

"How did you do it?"

"Well the first job was to get to know him slowly. I saw him briefly when he came to Dynamo, just to talk to but enough to get his trust and interest. I always had an idea of him going over the cliff. It just needed some careful planning. There are always people in the transgender community who need money to hide their past along with hangers on, the pushers and pimps. I found a man who would do most things for money and who would be my key agent in getting rid of Luke bloody Adams. So on the night in question, I spoke to him at Dynamo and put on this great act of being in pain, no one to listen to me, having to hold everything in and so on. He was very kind and wanted to help if possible and so we arranged to meet that evening. I told him I had things to prepare for my work with other clients and that I could only meet him very late in the evening. He was fine about it and so we met at the Hotel Alpha."

"How did you get the alcohol into him?" Tenika whispered.

"Well I bought the drinks, he was charming and we talked. At a point in the evening he went to the men's room and I slipped some odour and taste free alcohol into his drink. He had fresh orange juice so I knew he wouldn't taste it. It wasn't very much, just enough to be recognised in his body afterwards."

"So how did you get him over the edge?"

Tenika lifted up her head. The light was still in her eyes and bothering her but she wanted to hear the answers.

"You know Tenika that took some planning and a little help. The key to it all was the twenty second delay on the cameras at the Hotel Corallo and the fact that the screens were visible in reception. You know it took me some time to find that hotel but when I did and with its location I just knew the job could be done with a little help from a friend. So, when Luke Adams and I left the Hotel Alpha we walked back towards the sea and stopped off at the bar next to the Corallo. It had closed for the night and deserted. The side of the bar facing the sea was in shadow caused by the light coming from the hotel Corallo. At the same time my friend went into the hotel to talk to the receptionist about the hotel, you know facilities, cost and so on. He kept an eye on the screens. I took Luke round to the corner of the bar where I knew he could be seen by the camera and asked him to stand there whilst I took a picture using my mobile phone. Of course, I was out of sight of the cameras. As soon as my friend saw Luke on the screen he pressed his send button and my phone vibrated. I knew I had twenty seconds to complete the task. You know Luke was a bit of a puppy, ask him to do something and he obliged. I asked him to look out to sea and he did. I slipped my shoes off, walked up behind him, grabbed his legs and .... well goodbye problem. I quickly moved backwards into the darkness and I knew the camera would show him gone. I went home very happy that night Tenika. I knew that I had protected my sister, kept her secure. I thought she could get on with her work without the threats of people like him."

Tenika looked past the torch light into the darkness. She couldn't really see much of Maria. The coldness of Maria's

301

description made Tenika fear for her life. Surely Maria was not going to let her go after confessing? Wasn't she a problem now too? Tenika tried to make sense of what she was hearing. That Maria had started off in life as Suzannah Boswell's twin brother but wanted to be a girl and play the role of Suzannah's sister was clear now. It seemed also that Maria had been through a transgender procedure. What was so confusing and frightening was the fixation on her sister, a need to do anything to help or protect her but in ways that seemed to have no moral boundary. What kind of psychosis was this, how far did her delusions go and what more would those delusions cause Maria to do? Tenika still had a throbbing pain in her head and felt so uncomfortable tied up and wet through. She still had a vomit taste in her mouth and her body was aching from her limbs being tied and sitting in the same position for some hours.

"So why did you kill Chanie?"

"Well that was your fault. You decided to poke your nose into my business. You kept asking questions and when the reporter spoke to Luciano Albero and he went mad I knew things might all go wrong. I asked Rafael about you and he said you were a strong woman who was determined to find out what had happened to Luke Adams. I knew then you were a threat to my sister and to me. You had to be stopped. It really was as simple as that.

"But you killed her and not me."

"Ah yes, well that's what happens when you delegate, sometimes mistakes are made. I am not sure how the stupid fool mistook her for you but she was part of this conspiracy against me so she got what she deserved."

Tenika's face broke into something of a smile.

"She was wearing my hat and scarf."

"Well there you are then. It was your fault. Oh, and do you want to know something Tenika?"

Maria's figure came closer to Tenika out of the darkness. Maria bent down, her face a short distance from that of Tenika.

"When your friend died she squealed like a pig and her last breath was to call for you. Yes, can you think of that she called Teeeee, Teeeeee. Now how does that make you feel? Hmm? Guilty?"

Tenika could feel Maria's breath on her face and although her own heart was pounding she felt strangely calm even with these words thrust into her face. She had a firm grip on Sokhong's hand now and knew she had to stay as calm as possible if she was ever going to see Sokhong again. Perhaps there would be a moment when her raging anger at the death of her dearest friend might be of use but it was not now.

"So what happens now?"

"Well Tenika, you've ruined it all. If you had not got involved I could have got on with my life .... but not now. Perhaps this is how it was meant to be, my sacrifice for the benefit of my sister. It's time for you to sleep Tenika, we have a long journey ahead of us tomorrow."

Maria came out of the darkness and pulled the tape back up over Tenika's mouth. Maria pressed it hard against her skin so that Tenika would not be able to speak or shout. A throaty groan was about the best she could do. Not that Tenika was in the mood for shouting or screaming. She felt tired and sleepy. She wanted the throbbing in her head to go away. She closed her eyes and saw Sokhong's hand clearly in her mind. She focused on it as long as she could until sleep overcame her.

DAY ELEVEN

Both Inspector Maldini and Officer Fellini were in the police station early. Overnight, Inspector Maldini had checks undertaken on a possible ownership of a car and utilities in Maria's name.

"Buongiorno Ispettore. Have we any news?"

"Ah, buongiorno Officer Fellini. Yes, we have an address for Maria Aquila from the electricity company. It is Angelo Abitazione on Via Nastro Verde. You are coming with me and there is a second car with armed officers coming as well. I have also asked for a forensic officer to go over to the Palazzo Abagnale to take finger prints from Miss Taylor's room and then join us and we are just waiting for that individual to arrive. I have briefed the officers and I think we are ready to go."

Inspector Maldini and Officer Fellini made their way to the car park where the forensic officer had just driven in. Inspector Maldini spoke to the forensic officer and then the three cars drove together along Corso Italia, past the hospital and hotel Capodimonte then working their way up the hillside until they reached the one story house on Via Nastro Verde. The white gate pushed open easily and the police officers entered the grounds. Inspector Maldini instructed the two accompanying officers to go round to the back of the property. There was no car to be seen and no sound came from the house. Inspector Maldini and Officer Fellini approached the front. The Inspector knocked hard on the front door. There was no sound and no response.

"Ok Fellini, you stay here whilst I go round the back. No heroics ok?"

Officer Fellini nodded as the Inspector left her to go round to the back of the property. Once there he ordered one of the smaller of the officers to go the front of the house and, with the second officer, inspected the rear door. It looked older and weaker than the front door. The Inspector asked the officer if he thought he could open the door with force. The officer nodded to him. With two lunges of a very large booted foot, the lock and door frame gave way. Then using his shoulder the door was pushed open. The Inspector went slowly into the house looking around him as he went. He made his way to the front door and opened it for Officer Fellini and her colleague.

"Ok, I want us to look round the house for any sign of Miss Taylor. Remember, this may be a crime scene so go slowly and take care. Look for any signs of her being here including signs of a struggle."

The house was clean and ordered. The items used for the lunch had been cleared away. There were no obvious signs that two people had been there for lunch the previous day. In fact there were no obvious signs that two people had been in the property at all. An inspection of the main bedroom revealed that clothing had not been removed to any extent and both a large and small suitcase was found. A jewellery box was found as was Maria's passport in a bedside table drawer.

"What do you think Ispettore?" queried Officer Fellini.

"I am not sure. The evidence is that Maria Aquila has not fled. The house looks like it should be if someone was out at work.

There is food in the house and her belongings seem to be all in place. But ...."

The Inspector shook his head and returned to the open plan dining area. He asked the two other officers to look around the grounds to see if there was anything of note including freshly dug ground. The Inspector stared at the floor.

"You know Fellini, I was once told that clues are often found on the floor because it is hard to clean floors of all evidence."

"What do you think that is?"

Officer Fellini pointed towards a mark in the grouting between the marble tiles near to the dining table. The Inspector got down on his knees to look closely.

"Hmmm I am not sure Fellini but let's get the foresnsic officer in to take a sample and we can try to find out."

The female forensic officer was about mid-thirties, dark haired and bespectacled. She had worked with the Inspector before and knew what he might want. She came in and knelt down by the tile.

"I guess Ispettore you want to know if this is dried blood and, if so, whose it is. I've taken finger prints from Miss Taylor's room along with hair from a brush and clothing. I know there were two women in the room but we can obtain Miss Park's finger prints and her DNA from the hospital. I'll take this sample and then look for finger prints in all the usual suspect places."

"Grazie Manuela, I need the results quickly."

"You always do Ispettore."

Suddenly there was a shout from outside the house. One of the officers was calling the Inspector. He went outside to an officer standing by a refuse bin.

"Ispettore, I took a look in the bin and found this at the bottom of the bin under all the other rubbish."

At the feet of the officer was a black plastic bag which the officer had opened. Inside were food scraps, packaging and bits of a broken plate.

"Have you touched this at all?"

"No Sir."

The Inspector went back into the house and brought Manuela out to look at the plate.

"Can you take a quick look at the broken plate in the bag and tell me if you think there is anything of assistance there."

Manuela got down onto her knees and looked into the plastic bag at the broken plate. She used a magnifying glass to scan the visible surface.

"I can't be certain without taking the bits back to the lab, but one of the broken edges seems to have a couple of hairs and what might be flakes of skin and blood."

The Inspector looked at Manuela. He looked pale and worried.

"Manuela, I really need the results quickly."

"I understand Ispettore, I really do."

At that moment the Inspector's mobile phone went off. He turned away from Manuela for a moment.

"Buongiorno."

"Buongiorno Ispettore."

"Ah, Sovrintendente, how can I help you?"

"Pietro, we have had Owen Park on the phone to us. He knows Miss Taylor did not come back to the hotel last night and wants to know what is happening. Can you speak with him? By the way, how are you getting on? What did you find at Maria Aquila's house?"

"Yes, I will speak with him. They are not at the house. It has been cleaned but we might have found samples of blood on the floor and on a broken plate hidden in the waste bin. The forensic officer is taking samples now but I need the result of a DNA match with Miss Taylor as soon as possible."

"Your voice tells me you think the samples might be of Miss Taylor."

"Yes Sovrintendente, your assumption is correct. I am going to seal this property off in case it is a crime scene. Could you send another officer over to the property as I want to keep the armed officers with me."

"Of course Pietro."

"Grazie Sovrintendente, I will complete the tasks here and then head back to the station."

"Ok, ciao."

Inspector Maldini called the officers together and instructed the two male officers to wait until the forensic officer's work was completed and then to seal off the property with tape. They were then to return to the station but only when a relief officer arrived who was to remain stationed at the property to ensure nobody came onto it.

"Officer Fellini, we will go back to the station but I think we have a detour on the way."

They got into the Inspector's car and began the journey back into Sorrento town.

"You are not happy with what you found at the house, Ispettore?"

"I am not sure. If it is blood on the floor and the broken plate, then the question is who does it belong to? If it is Miss Taylor's then things are not looking good."

"Where are we going first?"

"To the Vittoria to see Var and Owen Park. They know Miss Taylor is missing.

In the hills above Sorrento the early morning sun began to send shafts of light into the barn. It was a structure used by workmen on the hillside probably in the olive gathering season yet to come. It was reasonably well built although of some age. It was very simple inside. It contained little by way of large machinery or equipment, nor any kind of sophisticated effects that would make the barn habitable. There was a table and some chairs at one end, a makeshift food and drink preparation area containing a camping stove, kettle and cups. The other end, where Tenika was tied to a vertical beam, was largely empty save for netting, barrels and some tools and wood.

As Tenika stirred from her night of broken sleep, pain shot through her body. Her head still ached but she now had pains shooting through her from sitting in such a confined way for hours. Every limb ached and a pain ran all the way up her back. Tenika's face was sore from where Maria had struck her the night before and as she looked at Maria, who was sitting two metres away drinking from a mug, she noticed a ring on Maria's right hand that had probably caused unseen damage.

Tenika took in the details of the barn, or large shed as she thought. She could see the kettle and stove which didn't seem to fit in with the rest of the dilapidated structure. As Tenika looked around she could see her shoes about two metres away. They looked as if they had been thrown from where she was sitting. Was the kettle and stove evidence of some sort of pre-prepared plan? If so, what came next? What did Maria mean when she said they were going on a journey? Tenika looked up towards Maria just as she did the same to her. Their eyes met and Maria smiled.

"Well I see you are awake. I hope you slept well. This is a big day for us. The day we go on a long journey."

Tenika tried to talk through the tape across her mouth but nothing came out other than a garbled noise. Maria picked up Tenika's knife, got up and came towards her. She held the knife at Tenika's throat and Tenika could feel its point pressing into her skin.

311

"Do you remember our agreement last night?" Maria asked.

Tenika nodded.

"Good, but just remember what happens to those who get in my way."

Maria stared into Tenika's eyes who decided to take a submissive stance. Tenika looked down trying hard not to pose any threat to Maria. Fingers again pulled the tape down from Tenika's mouth such that she could breathe easier and speak.

Maria stood up and looked down at Tenika.

"Would you like a drink?"

"Yes please" responded Tenika in a weak voice

Maria walked over to the table on which stood the camping stove, and poured some water into a mug. She walked slowly back and knelt down beside Tenika.

"This is your one chance to get a drink Tenika so don't waste it."

Tenika was in no mood to be awkward. There wasn't much she could do anyway. Maria held the mug to Tenika's lips and poured the water into her mouth. She repeated the action a number of times until the mug was empty. Maria got up and walked back to the table.

"Thank you" whispered Tenika.

"That's ok, I need you in good order for our journey."

"Where are we going?"

"More of that later Tenika, I have to make preparations first."

In Sorrento town centre, Inspector Maldini had arrived at the Vittoria hotel. He and Officer Fellini made their way to Owen and Var Park's room. The Inspector suggested to Officer Fellini that he did the talking as this was likely to be a difficult meeting. He knocked on the door and swiftly it was opened by Var.

"Oh Inspector, thank you for coming, please come in."

"Thank you Mrs Park, and good morning to you Mr Park."

Owen took a couple of steps towards the Inspector. He looked very serious.

"Do you have any idea where Tenika is? She has not answered her mobile or room telephone. I've been over to her hotel in case she was ill and they wouldn't open the door for me. All they kept saying was that they didn't know where she was and I should call the police."

"I don't know exactly where Miss Taylor is, however I believe she is with a woman called Maria Aquila."

"Who is Maria Aquila and what do you mean you believe she is with her?"

There was impatience in Owen's voice. The strain of losing his daughter and possibly losing someone who had become rather like a second daughter was showing through.

"I believe Maria Aquila is involved in the death of Luke Adams and ....."

"Yes, and?" demanded Owen.

The Inspector looked at both Var and Owen and the words left his mouth.

"And the death of your daughter."

There was no flicker of emotion on the face of Var but Owen was visibly shaken.

"What do you mean, the death of Chantrea?" asked Owen.

"I no longer believe that your daughter's death was as a result of a street robbery. I believe your daughter was killed by mistake. Someone wanted to attack Miss Taylor but mistook your daughter for her."

"How could that happen, they clearly look different."

When your daughter went out that night, she wore Miss Taylor's scarf and hat. I believe that in the darkness of the street the assailant used the scarf and hat as an indicator of who was wearing the items."

"So you think Chantrea was murdered."

"I am sorry Mr Park but yes I do."

"So, this Maria woman is she responsible for all of this?"

"I don't know if Maria Aquila actually killed your daughter or organised it. However I believe she is responsible for your daughter's death."

"I fear this is going to be a rather stupid question but have you checked at this woman's house?"

"Yes Mr Park, I have and neither Miss Taylor nor Maria Aquila are there.

"So let me get this straight, you think this Maria Aquila wanted to kill, or have killed, Tenika but murdered our daughter by mistake and now has taken Tenika .... why to finish the job?"

"I don't know the precise purpose of Maria Aquila in holding Miss Taylor if that is what has happened."

"For Christ's sake you gave your word to Var that you would look after Tenika."

This was the statement that the Inspector expected at some point in the conversation. It came with the venom and sharpness he expected and deserved. Inspector Maldini looked at both Owen and Var.

"I know what I said and you are right to criticise me if you wish. I will find Miss Taylor. I will do this."

Owen was clearly emotional. Anger was burning through him as was the pain resulting from confronting the possible loss of Tenika. Var had stood still with virtually no emotion on her face for the whole time. Now, she moved forward and took the Inspector's hands into hers.

"Owen is very upset Inspector, he means no criticism of you. Thank you for telling us what the situation is but we must let you get on to do your job. Please do your very best to find Tenika before she runs out of diamonds in her hem."

Var gazed into the eyes of the Inspector and he felt the warmth in her hands.

"I will Mrs Park."

Inspector Maldini felt extremely emotional as he looked into Var's eyes. He released Var's hands, turned and left the room with Officer Fellini. They made their way back to their car and returned to the police station.

Mariangela Fellini could see the emotion in the Inspector's face. She had rarely seen him like this and knew he felt they were on the edge of a disaster. She thought how this was an awful part of the job, telling people their children were dead and, worse, murdered. She also thought what an exceptional woman Var was, to be able to see beyond personal pain and encourage collective optimism. She thought that if Chantrea had acquired such qualities from her mother then she had been a remarkable woman too.

"What is our next move Ispettore?"

"Well Fellini I want you to get the details of Maria Aquila's black Fiat Punto out to all officers just in case it has been left in open view. It would be very helpful to find the car. I am going to talk to the Sovrintendente, we may need the help of helicopters to scour the rural areas. However, most importantly we need the results from forensics. I want you also to get a check done on the mobile number given to me by Maria Aquila I want to know who she has called and who has called her for the past month."

Back at the barn, Tenika's stiffness was beginning to ease a little as she gently moved her body one way and then another. Her wrists and shoulders were sore from her hands being tied tightly behind her back and then to the vertical beam. Her knees ached from the contorted position in which she had been sitting and still the pain in her head persisted. At least most of the water had dried from her body although the ground on which she sat remained wet. Tenika looked across to Maria who was sitting at the table writing in what looked like a note book.

"Tell me about your sister. Is she older or younger than you?

Maria looked up at Tenika, got up, walked over to the barrel and sat down.

"Suzannah and I are twins. Not identical though. When I was very young I thought she was an angel. She looked after me, played with me and I thought she was just beautiful. I wanted to do all the things she did and just as well and at the start that's what I did. I loved to dress up in her clothes because I wanted to be her. We were so close. She was always very clever, she knew what she wanted and I just wanted to help her. In fact my mother began to call me Suzannah's little helper and I rather liked that. She had lovely brown eyes and light brown hair with a touch of ginger to it. I've got similar hair although mine is coloured now. Things began to change when we went to school. I began to realise that other children were looking at me differently than they did with my sister. Other girls didn't talk to me in the same way. I began to get shunted to the sidelines of activity. I remember one time describing myself as Suzannah's sister and other children laughing at me, telling me I was daft. I tried to convince them but they just laughed even more."

"That must have been painful" whispered Tenika.

"Yes it was, but of course the problem was that for the first time I was being confronted with being a boy when I was consumed with being a girl just like my sister. I wanted to do everything she did, I wanted to be right by her side as if we were one and the same person. I know non-identical twins are not meant to be like that but for me it was an overwhelming urge. I was as much a girl then as I am now."

"How did you cope?"

"Not very well at first, I was frustrated and angry. As I got older I realised I was wearing a boy's body which prevented me doing what I longed to do. I took my frustrations out on my horrible body. I made it quite clear it was not wanted but I also developed my intention to protect Suzannah from those other greedy children who wanted to spend too much time with her and steal her attentions. I would help Suzannah in all sorts of ways and she would hug me and tell me she loved me. I can tell you Tenika that every time Suzannah told me she loved me I had a sensation that ran through my body."

"Did you feel others were a threat to your relationship with your sister?"

"Yes, of course, they were trying to get in between Suzannah and me. They were trying to harm her."

"In what way?"

318

"They wanted her to do things without me. They wanted her to change her thoughts and ideas. They wanted her to treat me like a boy."

"And as Suzannah got older, did she have boyfriends?"

"Are you doing this deliberately? Trying to irritate me? Yes, there were boys who wanted to come in between Suzannah and me but I was able to persuade them to have other ideas. She was mine and I wasn't going to let some filthy minded boy get his hands on her."

"It must have been hard being a teenager in a boy's body."

"You don't know the half of it Tenika. I hated it, was disgusted by it but I had to learn to live with it and cope with other boys. Luckily my dad is tall and so both Suzannah and me are above average height. That gave me an advantage with other boys. I had to be strong or I would get the same ridiculing that I had when I was a child. They learned not to mess with me Tenika I can tell you."

There was something in Maria's voice that indicated this was the period when the vicious and sadistic side of violence was developed and, worse, that the growing adolescent boy enjoyed the power it gave him.

"So do you have many friends Maria?"

"No, I don't need friends. I have Suzannah."

"But she has a family of her own."

"She has to go through the charade of having a family in order to have children. It doesn't matter though, I love her and she loves me. That's all there is to it."

"Back at your home, I noticed there were no photos of Suzannah."

"Have you any idea of the problems of changing from a man to a woman, the questions, justifications, medical examinations, surgery, judgements, people's looks and society's prejudice. When I came to Sorrento I needed to begin again as Maria Aquila, a new identity and a new life. I purged myself of all the photos of my old life to avoid questions. I didn't want anyone to know that my sister's brother had gone through a realignment operation. I didn't want the local press coverage, the mutterings of old fashioned conservatives or the religious brigade. As far as the local people were concerned, her brother went to work abroad and that's the end to it. I needed to make sure there was no connection with my past on show, so no pictures."

Tenika closed her eyes and rested her head back on the vertical beam. Her head hurt as she did so and her face showed a grimace of pain. What kind of monster was sitting in front of her? Was she like this from birth? Did the genes get screwed up somewhere along the line? Tenika did feel that Maria had gone through much in her life and a lot of it was not very nice but that couldn't justify the horrendous violence perpetrated on Luke and Chantrea. Maria was one screwed up person, she thought, highly unstable and programmed to deal with threats to her and her sister. So what was in store for Tenika? She didn't think she would be released and allowed to tell the tale so would she share the same fate as Luke and Chantrea? What was all this about a journey? Did that give the glimpse of some time to find some way out of the situation? Would she have to be released from the beam to go on the journey and would that moment be her one and only moment to get away? If so, what could she do? Tenika began to think of possible actions she might take given her hands and feet were tied. Maria, meanwhile, got up from the barrel and returned to the table to continue with her writing.

The morning was progressing and Inspector Maldini was growing further impatient with the forensics team. He needed the answers to his questions. Superintendent Mosta had given permission for two helicopters to be used in the search for the Fiat Punto in rural areas but this, by his own admission, was like trying to find a needle in a haystack. The Inspector's mobile phone rang and he reached for it.

"Buongiorno."

"Buongiorno Ispettore, it's Manuela here."

"Ah Manuela, what have you found?"

"Well, there are no finger prints in the house that match any at the Palazzo Abagnale hotel room. In fact I would say that the obvious places for prints have been wiped recently. However, the stain on the grout between the tiles by the dining table did have blood in it. I don't know whose yet because the DNA result is not back, however the broken plate in the bag also had blood on it and the scraps of hair attached to the plate match hair I found on a brush at the hotel room. Ispettore, I need the DNA result to be certain but my instincts tell me that the broken plate was used to hit Miss Taylor and she has sustained an injury to her head."

"Grazie Manuela, please let me know as soon as you get the DNA result."

"Ok, ciao."

The Inspector stared down at his desk reflecting on what Manuela had said. Was she still alive and if so where was she? Was she now dead and where might the body be? If Tenika was dead and her body dumped somewhere, where was Maria Aquila? Given the registration number of her Fiat Punto had been widely circulated, the Inspector was confident it would be spotted if it was being driven. Perhaps she had changed cars? Perhaps she was in a hire car or a car lent to her! If Tenika was alive and with Maria, where were they and how much time did he have before the inevitable ending? The Inspector knew there were too many questions and not enough answers.

In the barn, Tenika was watching Maria writing in a note pad.

"What are you writing?"

Maria stopped and looked across at Tenika.

"A letter to Suzannah."

"What's the letter about?"

Maria took a long look at Tenika.

"I am explaining things to her, telling her why things have got fucked up and why I won't be around to help her in the future."

Tenika thought about what Maria had just said.

"What do you mean by that?" Tenika asked as softly as she could.

Maria did not look at Tenika but just sat at the table writing and talking.

"You've ruined everything Tenika. Things would have worked out if you had just not got involved, but now .... "

Maria sighed heavily.

"Now they will know you are missing and if Inspector Maldini is any good he will put two and two together eventually. I gave him my mobile number and whilst it does not work now he will be able to check my incoming and outgoing calls. Eventually he will stumble upon my friend who helped me with Luke Adams and your friend. So you see the game is up Tenika. It is just a matter of time. That is why we must go on a journey.

"What kind of journey?" asked Tenika.

"One which will enable my sister to live her life without any embarrassment or questioning about what has happened here."

"I don't understand what you mean."

"Do you think it would help my sister's career to have me in prison every day for the rest of her life? How would that help her? There would be constant reminders always being thrown at her by the jealous and hypocritical complainants. No, I have to solve the problem, I have to protect her and that can only be done by us going on a long journey."

For Tenika, the meaning of the long journey was beginning to emerge. She had one critical question. Would Maria answer it?

"Have you been writing a goodbye letter to Suzannah?"

"Yes, I have done what I was put on this earth to do. My time is up."

Tenika now realised the full meaning of the journey. Maria was going to commit suicide and kill her at the same time. How was she going to do it and when? There seemed to be some sort of plan about how the journey would be approached. That gave Tenika an idea that she had some time left before the journey began, but how much time and what could she do tied to a post?

Maria stood up and walked across to the barn door, opened it and went out. A few minutes later came back in with a bag and she took it over to the table. There was enough sunlight coming through the wooden frame of the barn to light the barn very well. From the bag, Maria took out a mirror and propped it up on the table. She then took out a hair brush and began to brush her hair. She looked across to Tenika.

"Well you don't think I am going on the journey looking a mess do you?"

This was both bizarre and terrifying at the same time. What else did she have in her bag? What kind of ritual was being played out here? How long would it take? Tenika watched Maria complete the task of brushing her hair and then she began to clean her face and put make-up on.

When this task was completed, Maria took a dress from the bag. It was long and white and she took care with it, handling it carefully so that it would not be creased. Tenika watched her take off her shoes, slip out of her jeans and remove her top and then carefully put the dress on. When done, Maria looked at herself in the mirror as if to check everything looked well on her. Then when Maria seemed happy with the resultant look, she turned to Tenika.

"It's time for the journey Tenika."

Tenika watched as Maria picked up her knife and walk slowly towards her.

"Are you going to leave me looking like this?" Tenika said softly.

"What do you mean?" responded Maria.

"I look a mess. Don't you want Suzannah to be proud of you? What would she think when she is told you took me on the journey looking like a dog? Wouldn't she be proud if you had prepared me with care too? You wouldn't want people to laugh at her because I went on the journey in a filthy, smelly state, would you?"

"But you have no travelling clothes Tenika."

"No, but I have my dignity. Let me get cleaned up at least."

Maria stopped to think. She seemed to be trying to work out what the consequences might be of Tenika's suggestion.

"Perhaps she would be proud if I helped you on your way."

Maria turned to Tenika and her voice became cold and forceful.

"But remember Tenika, one false move or one sound and I will kill you where you stand."

Tenika looked down at the knife in Maria's hand and then up to her face. It was calm and with a wry smile to it. She wondered if she had looked much the same as she took Luke's legs up and over the railings to his death on the rocks below. She accepted that Maria would strike her with the knife with no compassion at all. It was just a job that needed doing, rather like putting the rubbish out.

"Don't worry I am not going to try anything."

Maria bent down in front of Tenika and looked her in the eyes.

"Then let's be clear. I will release you and you will go over to the table, clean your disgusting face, brush your filthy hair and then Tenika you will be on your way."

Maria put the knife into her left hand and began to stand up but then swung her right hand hard into Tenika's face. There was a tremendous crack as Maria's palm smashed into Tenika's cheek. It forced a cry from Tenika as the pain bolted through her body. Blood began to run down her face from a cut caused by a ring on one of Maria's fingers. Tenika could feel her body shake with pain and shock and her feelings of fear were rising by the moment. She closed her eyes and let out groans of pain whilst behind her eyes she was fighting to refocus on Sokhong's hand. Maria bent down again, grabbed Tenika by the hair and pulled her face up. Tenika let out another groan of pain.

"And that was just a reminder for you to do as you are told or you will die here like the dog you are."

Maria cut the tape holding Tenika to the post, stood up and took a couple of steps back.

"Ok, get up."

Getting up was easier said than done. It wasn't just that Tenika's hands were tied behind her or that her feet were tied at the ankles, it was also the stiffness and pain she felt throughout her body as she moved. Her first attempts to get up failed miserably, she couldn't get her balance nor find the strength to raise herself. She began to use the post as a support moving her legs until her feet were underneath her body then raising herself slowly whilst using the post to stop herself from falling over. Finally she was upright with the post at her back. Her joints ached, her face was sore and her head still had a continuous pain. It was the headache from hell. She looked up at Maria who still stood near to her with the knife pointing in her direction.

"Ok, move slowly towards the table."

All that Tenika could do was a sort of shuffle given her feet were tied. It took quite a time to move the ten metres or so to the table. She felt dizzy as she moved and at times had to stop to compose herself and then move forward again. Maria told Tenika to sit down on the chair which she did and then was able to see herself in the mirror. She looked horrendous. Her hair was matted with blood down the right side of her head. Tenika could see that the blood had run down her neck onto her shoulder and arm. Her left eye was only about half as open as her right due to the blows received from Maria. She was cut under her left eye and blood was seeping down her face. There was still evidence of the vomit from the night before on her neck and clothing. This was the worst she had ever looked or felt in her life. Maria told her to put her arms out in front of her and, as she did so, Maria moved to the left of Tenika and cut the tape holding her hands together. Maria moved quickly back behind Tenika and pushed the knife through the dress and into her skin. Tenika felt the blade point puncture her skin and the pain was excruciating. She gritted her teeth, closed her eyes and grimaced as more pain shot through her body.

"Don't get any clever ideas Tenika. Use the water in the kettle and the cloth in front of you to clean yourself."

Tenika welcomed the opportunity to clean herself and took her time to do so. If she was to meet her death here, she wanted to make herself look as dignified as she could. She cleaned her hands, neck and face. Her hands were trembling as she did so. She then began to wipe blood from her hair but found the pain in her head too much to put any pressure on the scalp. She did as much as she could and then picked up the hair brush and began to gently brush her hair. Her hair was knotted and Tenika was only able to take a few knots out but at least one side looked reasonable. When she tried to brush the other side, however, the pain was sharp and she pulled away.

"Shall I help you Tenika? Give me the brush."

Tenika complied and as Maria pushed the brush into her hair a stinging sharp pain exploded in Tenika's head. She let out a gasp of pain as Maria went for a second stroke with the brush.

"Come on Tenika, let's not be a baby now. This will only take a moment or two."

More brush strokes followed and the intensity of the pain increased. Tenika felt dizzy and nauseous. The brush strokes stopped and Tenika was left with a stinging pain on the side of her head.

"There you look very nice now. My sister will be proud of how I helped you. Now stand up and turn round."

Tenika stood slowly. She still found it difficult to move due to the pain in her joints and her feet being tied. She moved aside from the chair, turned and faced Maria. Tenika had her hands by her side as she stood to her full height and looked Maria fully in the eyes.

"If you are going to send me on my journey, then do it now."

"Tenika it will be my pleasure and then I will be able to follow you."

Maria pulled her arm back ready to release a long and strong lunge with the knife into Tenika's stomach. Through Tenika's eyes time seemed to slow down dramatically. She stood perfectly still as she watched the knife in Maria's hand move back and then begin its movement towards her. Maria's body began to move forward with her arm movement. The knife would be plunged into Tenika with the full force of Maria's body behind it. The knife moved inexorably towards Tenika's body and yet she stood perfectly still not moving at all. Maria's face showed the expectation of success to come. She was focussed on the knife entering Tenika's body and nothing else mattered.

At the final moment Tenika bent her knees and moved her hips and felt a searing pain rip through the side of her body. The force of Maria's thrust brought her into Tenika's arms. Suddenly the anger held inside Tenika could be let out. This was her moment, the difference between life and death. She pushed back on Maria letting rip with a sound that echoed a primal scream from deep within backed by every cell of her body. The balance of the women changed and now it was Tenika moving forward. She pushed Maria off her feet and the pair fell into the side of the barn hitting benching, buckets, wooden posts and the like. Tenika cried out in pain as she crashed into various hard items but kept a firm hold on Maria.

Both women were hurt by the fall exhaling grunts and cries of pain and both took seconds to regain their senses. Suddenly both women were aware of the knife in Maria's hand. Tenika was lying across Maria and lunged at her hand grabbing her by the wrist. Both women were twisting their bodies trying to gain purchase and advantage over the other. Both were grunting under the pressure of holding firm on the knife. Whoever lost the will now would die and they both knew it. Maria managed to move her head towards Tenika's arm and plunged her teeth into Tenika's flesh. Tenika screamed with pain but refused to let go of Maria's wrist. Blood began to pour out of the wound and Tenika began to punch Maria in the head then grab her by the hair in an attempt to get her to release her bite. Tenika pulled a handful of hair from Maria's head and Maria screamed and released her bite. The surge in adrenalin that rushed through Maria's body enabled her to force Tenika off of her and roll Tenika onto her back.

Maria was snarling as she fought to move the knife back towards Tenika's body. Tenika had a firm grip on Maria's wrist but Maria now had the advantage of being on top and able to use her body weight to press down with the knife. Maria's head came closer to Tenika's and her face had a look of fearful determination to complete the job. Tenika launched her head into Maria's face who cried out but seemed to stop her movement which only gave Tenika the opportunity to do exactly the same again. The balance shifted as Tenika was able to push Maria back. Blood was now streaming from Maria's broken nose and she now had difficulty in breathing. Tenika twisted her body, pushed Maria back and slammed Maria's knife wielding hand into the corner of the table, then again and again. Tenika tore the knife from Maria's hand and threw it across the barn.

Maria's body was caught in an awkward position and she struggled to move. Tenika put her hand out for something, anything, and her fingers found a heavy wooden stake. It was Tenika who was now filled with adrenalin and a desire to live. She struck at Maria who put up her hand to protect herself. Maria cried out in pain, but Tenika struck again and again until she could not resist with her hands. Tenika struck Maria full in the face with the stake and then struck her again screaming 'bitch' at Maria with each strike.

Maria's body became limp with unconsciousness and Tenika rolled off her and the full impact of the effort and injuries released dreadful pain throughout her body. She propped herself up against the table and gasped for air, her chest heaving with the effort and her throat issuing guttural noises. She stared down at Maria half expecting her to make another effort to kill her but Maria's body didn't move. Tenika looked across the floor to where she had thrown the knife and could see it lying almost against the far wall. She forced herself up and shuffled across the floor to it, sat down on the floor before grasping the knife and cutting the tape binding her ankles. Fear returned to Tenika as she thought Maria might regain consciousness. She remembered the netting that had lain on the floor near to the post against which she had been tied. Tenika went over to it and cut at it with the knife to create some strands of net that could be used to return the favour to Maria.

Tenika approached Maria cautiously, she wasn't sure if she was still unconscious or waiting her turn to take the moment. Tenika also had the knife in her hand although wasn't sure if she would plunge it into Maria if she was attacked by her. In the event, Maria didn't regain consciousness and Tenika quickly tied Maria's hands and feet as best she could. As she completed tying Maria's hands, Tenika bent down and looked into Maria's bloodied face. She was panting and growled at Maria as much as her body would allow.

"That'll teach you to try and fuck with me."

Only then when Maria's hands were tied did Tenika begin to relax and her rate and depth of breathing reduce. Tenika sat down again and watched Maria and as she did so she felt a stinging pain in her side. She looked down to see the side of her dress was red with blood from the knife wound when Maria lunged at her. She placed her hand over her dress on the wound and pressed hard. The barn was silent and she could hear the faint sound of a helicopter somewhere in the sky outside. Thoughts of escape then began to fill her mind. Tenika looked across the barn to her shoes, got up and walked slowly to them. She put them on and moved to the barn door. Tenika opened it and saw nothing but olive trees. The barn was on the side of a hill overlooking Sorrento. As Tenika looked round she could see the Fiat Punto parked under trees some fifty metres away. She could also see a track leading away from the barn and Tenika began to walk along it as quickly as she could. Her movements were painful and awkward given she had high heels on her shoes. She still had a throbbing headache, her side stung and her joints pained her. She walked for some minutes before she began to see a property ahead. She made for it walking as quickly as she could across the rough ground. The track brought her onto a road and she could see there were three houses near to each other. One had a car outside and she made for that. Tenika approached the front door and banged hard on it. She waited for what seemed ages before the door opened and a rather startled woman looked at her. She reduced the door opening so that just her face could be seen.

"Buongiorno, I have been attacked and I need help from the police. Can you help me?"

Tenika's voice was thin and broken.

"Wait there."

The woman closed the door and Tenika stood there feeling more emotional by the second. Her thoughts kept returning to Maria who she thought would awaken any moment and come looking for her. The door opened again and an elderly man standing nearly two metres tall confronted her. He looked Tenika up and down and then spoke in English.

"What has happened to you?"

"I have been attacked and need the police. Can you call them please? My name is Tenika ...."

Tenika began to feel faint as the exertion overcame her. She felt herself about to fall and put her hand out towards the man. He stepped forward and caught her as she toppled forward. The man shouted for his wife and she came to the door and helped him carry Tenika inside. They could see she had a head injury and the blood on her dress suggested more injury. They could also see the marks to her face and blood running down her arm from the bite. The gentleman pointed towards the tape still wrapped round one ankle and the many marks and scratches on her hands, arms and knees along with her torn tights.

"God, this woman has been in a battle" the man said to his wife.

The woman quickly found some cotton towels and placed them under Tenika as she was laid on a long sofa. The elderly man went to his phone and called the police.

"Buongiorno, I need the police and an ambulance. A young black woman has just come to my door. She says she has been attacked and she is in a very bad way. She has a serious head injury and she has blood all over her. Oh, she seems to be English. Our address? Yes, it is Tramonto Casa on Via Talagnano, just south of Sorrento. Ok?"

The man came back to his wife and Tenika.

"They are on their way."

A few minutes later the phone rang in Inspector Maldini's office.

"Si."

"Ispettore, a report has come in of an English woman with a head injury turning up at a house on Via Talagnano. A car and an ambulance are on their way."

"What house?"

"Tramonto Casa."

334

"Grazie, tell the car attending to wait for my arrival."

The Inspector stood up quickly and opened his door. He shouted loudly for Officer Fellini and made his way towards the entrance to the car park. Mariangela Fellini caught up with him as he approached the outside door.

"Has something happened Ispettore?"

"A report has come in of an English woman turning up at a house on Via Talagnano."

"Is she ok?"

"I don't know but she has injuries. An ambulance is on its way."

The two officers ran to the car and sped away along Corso Italia towards the hill overlooking Sorrento and the thousands of acres of olive trees that cover it. About fifteen minutes later they were at the three isolated properties high up on the hill overlooking Sorrento. A police car and ambulance were already at one of the properties. Inspector Maldini and Officer Fellini got out of the car and rushed into the house where they found Tenika being attended to by the paramedics. The Inspector was shaken by the sight of Tenika. She had regained consciousness and looked up at him. She gave him a brief smile. Officer Fellini went round to the back of the sofa and Tenika held up her left hand which Mariangela grasped with a smile.

"It's good to have you back Tenika."

The Inspector beckoned to one of the paramedics to move away from Tenika and talk to him.

"How is she?"

"She has a nasty head injury and a knife wound to her side along with all the normal injuries you would expect from someone in a fight and she has a nasty bite on her arm but otherwise not too bad. We will put a neck brace on her and get her off to the hospital."

"Ok, I need to talk to her, it is very important."

"Please keep it calm and I don't want her to move her head."

"Ok."

The Inspector moved to a point where Tenika could see him without moving her head.

"Miss Taylor, I need to ask you some questions."

"Yes, Ispettore."

"Where is Maria Aquila?"

Tenika's eyes opened widely as if suddenly she remembered how she got to this point.

"The barn, the barn."

"What barn?"

"A track along the road, in amongst the olive trees, a barn."

The elderly gentleman house owner who was in the corner watching events took a step forward.

" I think I know what she is referring to."

The Inspector looked across to him.

"There is a track off the road about one hundred metres away. It leads into the olive groves and there is an old shed about three hundred metres in."

"You own this house?"

"Yes, I am Gennaro Fontana and this is my wife Sophia."

"Ok, show us the track, now."

The gentleman walked out of the room towards the front door and the Inspector beckoned to the two male officers to accompany him. He looked up at Officer Fellini and told her to stay with Tenika.

"Will the track take a car?"

"Oh yes."

"Right, let's take the marked police car."

The two uniformed officers got into the front of the car whilst Inspector Maldini and Gennaro got into the back. Gennaro pointed the way to the track and then headed into the olive grove. The track was uneven and bumpy but soon the barn came into view and as they got closer so did the Fiat Punto. Inspector Maldini turned to Gennaro.

"Please stay in the car."

Then the three officers got out of the car and Inspector Maldini ordered one officer to go round to the back of the barn just in case there was another exit. The Inspector approached the entrance with caution. He took hold of the door handle and pulled it open sharply and stood away from the entrance out of view. The Inspector then shouted loudly.

"This is Inspector Maldini. I know you are in there Maria. It is all over, you must come with me now."

The officer with Inspector Maldini, took out his pistol and prepared to enter the barn. The Inspector nodded and the officer quickly entered the barn.

"Ispettore, quickly."

Inspector Maldini walked into the barn to find Maria on the floor semi-conscious and tied with the strands of netting. He went over to her and saw her bloody face then turned to the armed officer.

"It's ok put your weapon away. Go back to the car and call in for another ambulance. I also want a full forensics team out here. Oh, and tell Franco to come in here."

"Miss Aquila, an ambulance will be here soon and you will be taken to hospital. You will be ok there."

Maria who was lying on her side, looked up at the Inspector. She was still having difficulty breathing and her spirit seemed to have ebbed away.

"I don't want to be ok, I want to die. Why didn't she finish me off?"

"I don't know Miss Aquila, perhaps Miss Taylor has more compassion than you."

Officer Franco entered the barn and came over to the Inspector and Maria.

"I want you to stay here with her until the ambulance arrives. Don't touch anything."

"Of course Ispettore."

The Inspector looked around the barn. He could see the evidence of a struggle with broken items lying on the floor, others strewn around and the tell-tale signs of blood. He walked over to the upright beam where he could see signs of tape still attached to it, the vomit and water. He began to feel that Tenika had been lucky to survive. The Inspector walked out of the barn and telephoned Superintendent Mosta. The short call was followed by one to the Vittoria hotel.

"Buongiorno Owen."

"Buongiorno Inspector."

"Owen, I want you to know that I have found Miss Taylor. She is alive and on her way to hospital for a check up."

"Has she been injured at all?"

"I am not sure yet but I will let you know later."

"Ok, thanks for telephoning us and you will let us know more in due course? We would like to see her as soon as possible."

"Yes, don't worry as soon as the examination is complete and she can see visitors I will let you know."

"Thank you."

As the Inspector put away his phone, he could hear the sirens of more police and ambulance vehicles arriving. An ambulance came into view and slowly drove up the track to the barn. The paramedics got out of the vehicle and walked up to the Inspector.

"We have a woman in here who is tied up and injured. However this is a crime scene and she has committed crimes so I don't want anything disturbed is that clear? I will need to talk to her before you do anything ok?"

The paramedics nodded and followed the Inspector into the barn where Officer Franco was standing over Maria. Inspector Maldini bent down to talk to Maria.

"Maria the paramedics are here to tend to you and take you to hospital. If you agree for them to tend to you and remain calm they will free your hands and feet. Are you agreeable to that?"

"Maria nodded in a rather resigned way."

Inspector Maldini stood up and looked to the paramedics.

"Ok, you can do your work and untie her but take care she might try anything. I think she is a suicide risk so take care with your equipment."

He then turned to Officer Franco.

"Stay here and watch carefully, she might try something. If she does, handcuff her straight away. Ok? Don't mess about."

As the Inspector walked out of the barn a forensics team arrived as did a further police car with two officers. Inspector Maldini briefed the forensics team to do a thorough search of the barn and of the Fiat car. He instructed the two officers to tape off the whole area and arrange for a transporter to take the Fiat back to the police workshop. He then began the walk back to the house where Tenika had been attended to by the paramedics. By the time he arrived back, the ambulance had gone and Officer Fellini had gone with it. Inspector Maldini knocked on the door and Gennaro opened it.

"Buongiorno, is my officer still with you?"

"No Ispettore, they weren't happy with the head injury so have taken the woman to hospital. Your officer has gone with them."

"Ok grazie. I will have to send someone round later to take a formal statement from you."

"As you wish Ispettore."

The Inspector returned to his car and drove over to the hospital. He parked and made his way to the reception area.

"Buongiorno, I am Inspector Maldini from the Carabinieri. You have recently received a female patient with a head wound and one of my officers is with her. I need to find out how she is."

"Just one moment Ispettore."

The receptionist made a short telephone call to find out where Tenika was now.

"She is in X-ray now but someone is coming for you."

"Grazie."

The Inspector waited a few minutes before a nurse arrived to take him off to see a doctor. They walked to a lift and went up one floor before walking along a long corridor to a waiting room. The Inspector was ushered in where he found Officer Fellini.

"Buon pomeriggio Officer Fellini. How is she?"

"They haven't said anything yet but they were concerned about her head wound. She has had an X-ray and someone is due to come to tell us the outcome."

The Inspector sat down but within moments a male doctor came into the room.

"Buongiorno, please stay seated, I will bring a chair over."

"I am Inspector Maldini and this is Officer Fellini, how is Miss Taylor?"

"She has suffered a slight depressed fracture to her skull, a knife wound to her side, quite a large laceration to her arm from a bite wound and lost quite a bit of blood. Other than those injuries, there are quite a few minor cuts and bruises. She has a cut on her face and will have a bruised eye in due course but these are not too serious."

"What about the fracture to her skull?"

"I think she has been very lucky Inspector. The skull fracture is only slightly depressed and we don't think it will need surgery. We have stitched her up and normally such a fracture will heal itself and the bone knits itself together again. Your officer told us she may have been hit by a plate. Well she was lucky because the plate broke and it was the plate breaking that absorbed some of the force. It was that which saved her a much more serious outcome. She may have a headache for a bit and we would want to keep an eye on her for a while just to make sure there is no internal bleeding. The signs are good however. The knife wound has given her quite a big cut but it's a flesh wound so painful but not life threatening. Again, she has been very lucky in that respect. We are now in the process of cleaning and stitching her side, arm and the cut on her face, giving her some blood, some sedative and antibiotics for the bite. When these tasks are done I will let you know and you can see her but she may be very sleepy for a while."

"Grazie dottore. Are you able to say anything about Maria Aquila who also came in today with Miss Taylor but in a different ambulance?"

"Yes, she has also had an X-ray and has suffered a broken nose and a broken cheek bone on the left hand side of her face and a broken arm. She has gone to surgery to put these things right. I understand there is a risk she might wish to take her own life?"

"Si dottore."

"Then I will ensure all the normal precautions are taken."

"Grazi, I will arrange for an officer to stand guard when she is out of theatre. I may want to handcuff her good hand to the bed

343

so that she cannot do any more harm. I want her also in a separate room."

"As you wish and I will advise the staff."

The doctor shook hands with the Inspector and left the room. The Inspector turned to Officer Fellini.

"You can go back to the station now. Call for a car to pick you up, I will hang on here for a while. Could you check on progress at the barn. Try to get the forensic report hurried up if you can. I am assuming Miss Taylor was transported in the Fiat from Maria Aquila's house to the barn but I want the evidence for it. Check also that the transporter is at the barn as well. Oh, and can you drop in on Sovrintendente Mosta just to bring him up to date? I will ring the station to have another officer sent here to look over Maria Aquila."

"And Ispettore will you let me know later how Tenika is?"

"Sure, I will do that."

Officer Fellini moved to the door of the waiting room and turned to the Inspector.

"I like her Ispettore. I want her to be well."

"I know Mariangela, I like her as well."

Inspector Maldini took out his phone and rang the station. He asked for another officer to come to the hospital. He was determined not to lose Maria Aquila again. The Inspector settled in his seat thinking about whether there was anything else he could have done to identify Maria Aquila as the culprit earlier and

344

save Tenika from her beating. He closed his eyes and rested for a while. About half an hour later the door opened and the doctor had returned. Inspector Maldini stood up quickly.

"Ok Ispettore, all is done you can see her now."

The doctor led Inspector Maldini along the corridor and then turned right into a ward area.

"We have put her into a separate room."

The doctor opened the door to see Tenika lying asleep in a bed. Her head was bandaged and her face looked swollen from the blows she had taken but, at the same time, she looked peaceful. She was attached to a saline drip along with a heart and respiratory monitor.

"As I said earlier Inspector, we have given her a sedative to help her relax for a while. She needs time to recover."

"Do you mind if I sit with her?"

"No, of course not Ispettore. Would you like me to have someone get you a coffee?"

"Well only if it is no trouble to you."

"No, it is no trouble at all."

The Inspector sat to the side of Tenika and looked at her. He admired her tenacity and courage to protect her friends and seek out the truth. He gazed at her battered swollen face and time drifted by. Fifteen minutes or so later an officer opened the door.

"Ah, Ispettore, I have come to look after the other woman."

"Good, but you must keep a close eye on her because she may wish to take her own life. One arm is broken, so I want you to handcuff her good arm to the bed. Is that clear? She is dangerous and I want no chances taken. You must stay in her room, watch her all the time."

"I understand Ispettore."

The two men went out of the room and along the corridor to the ward desk. A nurse smiled at them.

"This officer is to stay with Maria Aquila when she comes from the theatre. He must stay by her side all the time with no exceptions. She may be dangerous and I don't want any risk of further injury to her or to any of you. I have told my officer to handcuff her good hand to the bed. It is my decision and it must be done."

The nurse looked a little shocked at the severity of the action but agreed it could be done.

"The dottore has said she might try to take her life."

"Yes that is correct. Please be vigilant with anything that could be used. Now the officer will remain here until she returns from the operating theatre."

"Si Ispettore, I understand. We will take care in our handling of her."

The Inspector turned and returned to Tenika's room. She was still asleep and lay on the bed without any movement. The Inspector returned to the seat and gazed at Tenika when his mobile phone went off. He quickly answered it in a hushed tone.

"Buongiorno."

"Ah Ispettore, it's Sovrintendente Mosta here.   Officer Fellini has been into see me and thank you for asking her to do so. I understand you are staying at the hospital for a while so I will look after things here. I think I should advise the British Embassy as well given we have two British women in hospital there. I will try to keep the press at bay although information might get out from the hospital. I think I will ring the Chief Executive at the hospital and see what can be done and I might talk with the editors again."

"Grazie Sovrintendente, I am so grateful to you."

"No Pietro, thank you for pushing the Mayor and me on the business of Luke Adams. It would have been easy not to do so but if you had taken that course of action perhaps Miss Taylor would be dead now.

"Grazie, I will see you later."

"Ok, ciao."

The Inspector put his phone away and settled in to his seat. Every fifteen minutes a nurse came in to check on Tenika. After an hour, the nurse said it would then be every half hour. At the end of the second hour, the Inspector began to wonder how long he could remain there. He looked down at his watch and when he looked up again he saw that Tenika's eyes were open. Pietro Maldini felt quite emotional to see Tenika return to consciousness.

"Hello Inspector, have I caused you more difficulty?"

Tenika's voice was thin displaying her weakness.   Pietro Maldini smiled.

"No, not at all. I am just so happy, well we are all so happy, to see you are well.

"What about Maria?"

"She is here too but under guard."

"She murdered Luke and Chanie and she wanted to kill herself and me."

I know but you are safe now. I have spoken to Owen and Var. They know you are safe although I didn't tell them about your injuries. They would like to see you."

"I would like that if you would let them."

"You are weak and need rest, perhaps tomorrow morning might be best. I think Mariangela Fellini would like to sit with you if you are agreeable?"

"Yes I would like that."

"Ok, leave it to me."

The Inspector got up and left the room. He took out his phone and rang the police station where he was put through to Officer Fellini. She was keen to return to the hospital and informed the Inspector that the forensics team had found a letter written in a note book that he should see. It had been checked for fingerprints and only those of Maria Aquila were on it. The booklet had been sent over to the police station and it was in the Inspector's office. He thanked Officer Fellini and said he would wait until she arrived which she did within fifteen minutes. As Mariangela Fellini entered Tenika's room she greeted her with a broad smile. Mariangela came round the bed and took Tenika's hand into hers.

"It's so good to see you are awake."

"Thanks, but I must look an awful mess" whispered Tenika.

"Well, yes you do actually."

With that comment, all three smiled at each other and Inspector Maldini left the room to return to the police station. On his return he went straight to his office to look at the notebook and its contents. The notebook appeared to be new. Its condition was good and there was nothing in it other than a letter to Maria's sister, Suzannah. It was clearly written as a last letter to Suzannah. It assumed that Maria would have been successful in taking her own life and set out what Maria had done to protect Suzannah. The letter was a confession of crime and a statement of love at the same time. The long letter retraced Maria's life from an early age setting out events along the way that demonstrated her devotion and love for her sister. Indeed, the letter seemed to be saying that everything Maria had ever done was for Suzannah. The idolisation of her sister along with a psychotic disorder which caused her to see so many people as threats to her sister, allied to Maria's internal conflict with her sexuality meant that she had grown up to be a very dysfunctional person and a very dangerous one as well.

This was not the first suicide note that the Inspector had ever read. There was a part of him that often felt a pang of sadness for someone that feels a need to destroy themselves for whatever reason. In this case his feelings were tempered by the cruelty and wickedness she had inflicted on others without remorse. Even to the end, Maria's letter referred to the solution of a final problem, her own death. Perhaps this is the key quality of a martyr who is prepared, perhaps happily, to sacrifice their own life for those of others, that they see themselves as a low value object to be used within the solution of a technical operation rather than a valued person to be preserved and revered. It was clear from the letter that Maria saw her function in life to support her sister and do whatever was needed to give the assistance she thought was needed for what she saw as threats or problems. She dismissed her own existence as unimportant in the struggle to be close to the heart of her sister.

The Inspector's eye caught upon a section of the letter:

'Darling Suzi, I hope you will be proud of me for what I have done for you. I so want you to be successful in all you do and I am as proud of you today as I have always been. But Suzi, the world is not perfect and my plans have been messed up by a problem here that I am solving today. I can't allow my lack of forethought to be used against you. I couldn't bear the thought of others using my failure to protect you properly as a stick to beat you with. I can't allow the police, who won't understand the reasons for what I have done, to begin a process that will lead to a continuous and lifelong process of attention for you. That's why I realise my job is done, there is no more I can do and whilst it will tear my heart apart to leave you, I know that will be the most precious solution I can give to you.......'

The Inspector was respectful of the love Maria had for her sister but saddened also by the way the mind can become so corrupted that the world inhabited by Maria, and others like her, has no accommodation of the moral and social boundaries of the population that surrounds them. Yet it had been Maria who had been subject to discrimination and abuse by the very same population over her sexuality causing her to live a life separated from daily contact with the very person who was the core passion of her life.

The passage from Maria's letter reminded him that there were police procedures that needed attending to including a formal interview with Maria and charges for two murders and one grotesque assault. Those procedures were perhaps for tomorrow but before then he had to arrange relief officers to guard Maria overnight.

Back at the hospital, Tenika was comforted by the presence of Mariangela Fellini being with her. Mariangela was still in her uniform and Tenika somehow felt safe as a consequence. It was also good to have a friendly face to talk to, not that her voice could cope with too much talking. As the evening wore on Tenika became more tired and sleepy. She finally fell into a deep sleep and Mariangela settled into her chair for the night. She had lost Tenika once and didn't intend to do so again.

DAY TWELVE

Tenika opened her eyes at about six thirty in the morning. She was lying on the right hand side of her face, the side without the cut from being hit by Maria, and could see the door to the room and the cream coloured walls. She turned her face the other way and found Mariangela Fellini curled up asleep on a chair just over a metre away. To the left of her was a bedside cabinet and on it was a plastic cup with water. She had been taken off the drip late the previous evening so she could now move a little easier so twisted her body to reach the cup. A sharp pain dug into her right hand side from the knife wound and Tenika let out a groan. The noise awoke Mariangela who quickly moved from her chair to reach the cup and give it to Tenika. As she did so, she also expressed some discomfort arising from stiffness after hours curled up on the chair.

"Thanks. We're a bit of a pair this morning" whispered Tenika.

Mariangela smiled and pulled her chair a little closer. She took hold of Tenika's hand.

"How are you feeling this morning?"

"Not too bad, my side hurts a bit but my face isn't stinging any more and my head feels a lot better. Have you been here all night?"

"Yes."

"Grazie Mariangela, I really appreciate it. How long can you stay?"

"Well I am sure someone will replace me. I can ring the station to find out. Then I will need to go back to the hotel to clean up and change. I shall contact the Ispettore later to find out what he wants me to do then."

"What do you think will happen today?"

"Well Maria Aquila has not been cautioned or formally arrested yet because her condition did not allow her to understand what was doing on. I am sure the Ispettore will want to do this as soon as she is fit enough and perhaps that will happen today. There will also be a need to take a formal statement from you and I am sure also Owen and Var Park will want to see you at some time."

"So, quite a lot needs to be done then."

"Yes, and the procedure must be done right or a judge will throw it out."

"It will be good to see Var and Own again and I must get to see Sokhong soon as well."

"Who is Sokhong?"

"She is Var's sister and she sent me a note from Britain which Var gave to me when she arrived here. It's message was very important to me getting through the night with Maria and I need to thank her."

"You are lucky to have such loving people around you."

"Yes Mariangela I am and shall have to try to focus on what I've got rather than what I've lost."

"What about you Mariangela, who do you have to look after you?"

"Oh, I have my parents who live in Napoli and a brother who works in Rome."

"And a man to look after you?"

Mariangela laughed loudly.

"No, there is not much time for men being a busy police officer. I would like to become a detective but the hours are crazy. The Ispettore has worked almost non-stop trying to find you."

"I've been a lot of trouble to him, haven't I?"

"Not really, we wouldn't have caught Maria had it not been for you."

At that moment a nurse walked into the room to check on Tenika and Mariangela took the opportunity to phone the police station. The nurse checked Tenika's temperature and looked at her dressings on her wounds for signs of blood. She asked if Tenika had pain and needed more pain killer. Tenika thought about her painful side and dull headache and asked for more and the nurse said she would arrange it.

"What did they say?"

"They are going to send someone over now so that I can be relieved."

"Mariangela, I've just thought that I am due to fly home tomorrow. Do you think I will?"

"I am not sure given your condition. Who are you flying with?"

"British Airways."

"Has anyone told them about Chanie?"

"No, I don't think anyone has. Perhaps Owen might have."

"Would you like me to deal with it?"

"Yes, if you would."

"Ok, where are your travel papers?"

"They are in the safe and the number is 7956."

"Ok, when I go back to the hotel, I will ring Owen and, if necessary, give the airline a call."

"Thanks Mariangela. I feel a bit useless here."

"It won't be for long, I am sure of that."

A few minutes later another police officer arrived to relieve Mariangela. This time it was a tall young man, Officer Tortelli.

"Ok, it's time for me to go. I hope to see you later."

"Ciao Mariangela, thanks for everything."

Mariangela left the room and Tenika's attention turned to the young officer. He looked rather nervous.

"Buongiorno Officer Tortelli."

"Buongiorno Miss Taylor."

"Are you feeling alright? You look a little nervous."

"Yes, I am fine. I have heard a lot about you."

"What do you mean?"

"Well, er... how you persuaded the Ispettore to take more interest in the case."

Tenika smiled broadly.

"You mean how I hit him?"

The officer shrugged his shoulders and smiled.

"Well don't worry Officer Tortelli I am in no state to be able to hit you."

"Do you know anything about the situation regarding Maria Aquila?"

"No, other than another officer also has arrived to guard her. Her good hand is handcuffed to the bed. That's all I know."

Tenika nodded at the officer and she gestured for him to sit down. He did so and pulled out his mobile phone. Tenika felt very hungry and hoped breakfast would come soon.

Back at the police station, Inspector Maldini had arrived for an early meeting with Superintendent Mosta. They too had Maria Aquila on their minds along with the question of how to proceed. The letter written by Maria in her note book provided all the evidence needed to know that Maria had murdered Luke and arranged the death of Chantrea. They agreed that they could do little until the hospital said she was able to be interviewed in which case it would be done formally in the hospital and then she would be charged. The police had also obtained details of all the people on Maria's mobile phone contact list. They were all being interviewed and the Inspector was confident that soon they would find the person Maria had colluded with in both deaths. However, they could formally interview Tenika if she was fit enough and the Inspector felt that so long as her head wound did not prove too painful this would be possible.

They decided the Inspector should go to the hospital to see how Tenika and Maria were both doing. He could then decide if Maria or Tenika could be formally interviewed and when Var and Owen could visit Tenika. There was also a need to ensure legal representation was available to each woman should they ask for it and the Inspector agreed to notify the duty solicitor.

About an hour later the Inspector arrived at the hospital and made his way to see Tenika. As he entered the room Officer Tortelli stood up and the breakfast things were being cleared away. Tenika was sitting up in bed and she looked a lot better after a night's rest.

"Good morning Miss Taylor, how do you feel today?"

"Buongiorno Ispettore, a little better thanks."

"Miss Taylor we need to take a detailed statement from you about what happened yesterday. Do you feel up to making one?"

"Well, I guess it's better to get it out of the way and most things are still fresh in my head although some of it might be a bit fuzzy."

"That's ok, we can go slowly, but first I want to look in on Maria Aquila so I will return in a while."

The Inspector went off to see Maria. She was still handcuffed to the bed but awake and looking pensive.

"How long do I have to remain handcuffed like this?"

"Miss Aquila, we believe you may try to take your life or injure others here. So until we feel otherwise, you will remain handcuffed and have an officer remain in your room at all times. We will need to formally interview you when the doctor says you are fit enough and when that happens you will be entitled to legal representation. Do you have your own lawyer?"

"No."

"In which case I will ask the duty solicitor to visit you and provide you with advice. By the way, we have been in touch with the British Embassy in Rome and I believe they are contacting your sister in Kent."

Suddenly Maria's eyes flashed at the Inspector and her voice became firm and urgent.

"You have no need to do that. She is such a busy woman, I don't want her troubled by this. Can't you just let her have the notebook?"

"I am sorry Miss Aquila, the notebook is evidence and so cannot be shown to anyone at the moment and, as for contacting your sister, I'm afraid it's just procedure. Now I am going to see your doctor to find out if we can interview you or not. I will return in due course."

The Inspector left the room with Maria staring at the far wall of the room and looking very unhappy. He soon tracked down a doctor who was able to confirm that within the confines of Maria's broken arm, broken nose and fractured cheek which provided her with some pain, she was able to be interviewed. However, the doctor asked that if the interview was going to be prolonged she be interviewed in forty five minute sessions with half an hour respite in between. This the Inspector agreed to and he returned to Maria's room.

"I have spoken to the doctor and he agrees that you are fit enough to be interviewed. As a consequence, I intend to begin interviewing you later this afternoon when there will be a legal representative present for you and we will also have a recording machine set up."

Maria didn't look at the Inspector, instead she stared straight ahead at the wall.

"You have my words written in the booklet. There is nothing more I have to say."

"We shall see later today Miss Aquila."

The Inspector nodded at the officer present and then left the room. He walked the short distance between Maria's room and that of Tenika.

"Hello again Miss Taylor, I think we will take your statement soon but I am going to ask Officer Fellini to join us because her English is better than that of Officer Tortelli and I am going to ask her to write the statement down in Italian based upon what you tell us. Is that ok? You will be able to check it at the end. Now you are entitled to have a legal representative here and an interpreter if you wish."

"I am happy for Officer Fellini to write my words down and I don't think I need either a legal representative or an interpreter but thank you for offering."

"Ok Miss Taylor, I am going to contact Officer Fellini now and then ring the Vittoria hotel to inform Mr and Mrs Park that they can visit you in about three hours."

Inspector Maldini stepped out of the room to make the phone calls and Tenika reflected upon the thought of seeing Var and Owen soon. She was eager to see them but hoped their own sadness was not weighing down too heavily on them. After a few minutes the Inspector returned and about five minutes later so did Officer Fellini. The Inspector released Officer Tortelli from his duty and he returned to the police station. Officer Fellini smiled at Tenika and she returned the compliment.

"I have spoken to Owen and British Airways and alerted them to the problem. I also found your travel insurance documents with Columbus and I have contacted them also about you and made the link to Chanie's case. They have opened a case file for you and are going to see if they can link your return to that of Chanie. They said they would inform the repatriation company to ensure they were aware of your situation. I also asked them to record my conversation with them just in case of any problems later. They will wait for you to speak to them about what help they can give although Mr Park will keep in touch with Columbus to monitor the situation. I have also spoken to the hotel and they are going to assign your room to you for another day, if needed, without charge."

"Grazie Mariangela, that's really helpful."

The room was prepared for the interview with Officer Fellini sitting at a small desk by the side of Tenika's bed and Inspector Maldini on the other side.

"Ok, so we will do this in English and Italian and you can answer or ask me to explain a question in either language. Is that ok? However Officer Fellini will write your words down in Italian so that it can be used later in court."

"That's fine Ispettore, let's do it."

So the interview began with Tenika telling the Inspector about the telephone invitation to lunch two days previously. It moved on to the lunch itself and the conversation they had. Then to the excruciating pain from being hit on the head, waking in the dark barn and all that followed. The Inspector was slow and methodical in his process wanting to get each action in the order it occurred. He allowed Tenika to think about actions and get them right as far as she could remember and Officer Fellini was scrupulous in wanting to get Tenika's words absolutely accurate in the statement. Occasionally she stopped Tenika and checked the wording she had down making adjustments to get the precision of Tenika's account right. When it came to the battle at the end in the barn, Tenika admitted that her head was fuzzy and she couldn't remember all the actions precisely. All she could remember was that she was fighting to stay alive. She described picking up the heavy wooden stake and hitting Maria two or three times with it. She remembered hitting Maria's arm and then her face. It was a blur and she was awash with the emotion of fear. She admitted that at that moment she did not think about whether Maria would live or not, just that she wanted to survive and would have done anything to do so.

Tenika's account was shocking to both the Inspector and Office Fellini and at times they all just sat in silence as the facts of the account settled into their minds. It was an account of depravity executed with a cold and calculated savagery. It took more than two hours to make the statement and all three of them were relieved when it was done.

"Well after that I think we could all do with a coffee. I will go and get some coffee if you Miss Taylor would read through the statement and sign it if you are happy with it as an accurate record. Officer Fellini will help with any words you don't understand although I know your Italian is very good."

Tenika was rather tired and her headache was becoming worse but she wanted to get the job done and begin to move on. She took the bundle of papers and began to work her way through them. After a few minutes the Inspector returned with a tray of coffees for them all. Tenika thanked him and carried on reading the papers. It took quite a time and needed occasional references back to Officer Fellini but, with sips from her coffee, in the end Tenika was happy with the statement and she signed it. She handed the papers back to Officer Fellini and lay back on her pillows with a sense of relief. She closed her eyes and took some deep breaths. A nurse came in to check on her and asked how her pain was. Tenika mentioned her growing headache and the nurse went off to get more pain relief. Officer Fellini handed the statement papers to Inspector Maldini who checked each page had been signed and then got up and went out of the room. Tenika looked across to Officer Fellini.

"I know I am in here for good reasons but I would like to get out and get the sun whilst it is still there."

"Yes, whilst it is still warm for you British for us Italians it is getting cool now."

The door opened and Inspector Maldini stepped in.

"Miss Taylor, there are some visitors for you."

He stepped back and into the room came Var and Owen. The Inspector beckoned to Officer Fellini who left the room and stood guard outside. Var was carrying a bunch of flowers and smiled broadly at Tenika. She sat one side of Tenika whilst Owen sat on her other side. Var placed the flowers on the bed and grasped Tenika's hand.

"It's so good to see you" said Var softly.

Owen's relief was clear in his voice.

"Yes, you had us, well me, worried for a while. Var was always certain you would surface in one piece."

"Chantrea was taken by surprise and I knew that you would be prepared for anything. I just knew you were strong enough."

Tenika was feeling very emotional with the show of warmth. She took a deep breath and ordered Owen to press a red button by the side of her bed. Within moments a nurse came into the room. Tenika picked up the flowers and asked firmly, but politely, for them to be put into a vase. She handed the flowers to the nurse who nodded rather than choosing to argue.

"I can see you're getting stronger" said Owen with a grin.

Tenika leant across and put her right hand onto Owen's and looked at them both.

"So how have you two been?"

"Well, we've been worrying about you for a start" said Owen.

"We have been fine. We have spent quite a bit of time at some of the churches, just sitting and thinking of Chantrea and you. We have lit quite a few candles for you both."

Var's words were soft which she delivered with a hint of a smile. She squeezed Tenika's hand and looked deeply into her eyes.

"We will all get through this you know. Chantrea is still with us and we will always be with her, all four of us."

Suddenly the grief from losing Chantrea returned to Tenika overwhelming the relief of still being alive. This was probably a turning point in her life even though she wouldn't know for some time in which direction she would head. Tears rolled down her face and she clasped the hands of Var and Owen very tightly.

Inspector Maldini went back to the police station to prepare for the interview with Maria Aquila. He again read through Maria's letter in the notebook along with Tenika's statement. He wasn't sure if Maria was going to give a full confession or say nothing. He needed to be on top of the facts so that, if necessary, he could present an overwhelming case that Maria could not deny. He felt the letter in the note book would be enough to convict Maria but preferred her to explain and acknowledge the deaths of Luke and Chantrea as well as the barbaric treatment of Tenika. There was also outstanding the matter of Maria's accomplice. Would she identify him or her? The Inspector was confident of finding the individual via Maria's phone records and, hopefully, recognition by staff at the hotel Corallo but wanted a name from Maria if at all possible. This was one aspiration he was not fully confident of achieving in the interview.

The Inspector sent one of the administrative staff to the hospital to set up the recording equipment and test it and he made sure that legal representation for Maria would be present at the interview. He arranged for detective Roberto Bariti to sit in with him on the interview and spent time briefing him on the case and his approach to the interview. By mid-afternoon all was prepared and it was time for the Inspector and detective Bariti to leave for the hospital.

When they arrived they made their way to the ward and asked for a doctor to attend. A female doctor arrived soon after and the Inspector asked her to check that Maria was still fit to be interviewed. He did not want anything to go wrong and certainly no legal challenge that Maria's condition had deteriorated during the day rendering the interview inadmissible in court. The doctor spent some time with Maria checking her physical condition and talking briefly with her. She then returned to the Inspector and confirmed that Maria was fit for interview but reminded him of the forty five minute limit to each session of interview. The Inspector acknowledged the limit and, with detective Bariti, entered Maria's room.

Lorenzo Mancini, the legal representative was already present and sitting at Maria's side. Also in the room was the officer responsible for guarding Maria. The Inspector turned on the tape recording machine and began his introductory remarks. He introduced himself and those others who were in the room, gave the date and commencement time of the interview. He explained the purpose of the interview which was to ask questions of Maria about the deaths of Luke Adams and Chantrea Park along with the attempted murder of Tenika Taylor. Lorenzo Mancini then intervened to ask for the handcuffs to be removed so as to aid the positive nature of the interview. Given there were three police officers in the room, he argued, there was little chance of Maria being able to do anything and she had assured him she would not do anything silly whilst being interviewed. The Inspector agreed and asked the guarding officer to remove the handcuffs. Now, they were ready to proceed.

"Look, I am very sorry but I need to go to the toilet. I am anxious and it makes me want to go."

Inspector Maldini was not impressed by this request. He looked across at the legal representative who suggested Maria's request was accepted as it would enable the interview to then proceed without interruption. The Inspector did not want any reason for the interview to be challenged in court and so, reluctantly, agreed. The Inspector got up and pressed the red button by Maria's bed and within moments a nurse arrived. The Inspector turned to her.

"I am sorry but would you please take Miss Aquila to the toilet. Please stay with her the entire time and my officer here will accompany you to and from the door to the toilet. The nurse helped Maria out of bed and she held onto the arm of the nurse as they walked slowly out of the room followed by the police officer. The Inspector turned to detective Bariti and raised his eyebrows but said nothing.

The toilet was some way down the corridor and walking slowly took Maria some time to get there. She entered with the nurse and the officer waited outside. Although only a few minutes the time seemed to go by very slowly. Then she appeared through the door of the toilet and began the slow walk back. As they reached an intersection with another corridor Maria pointed and said 'look'. Both the nurse and the officer looked down the corridor but saw nothing. This momentary diversion of attention gave Maria her chance. She slipped her arm from that of the nurse, turned and began to run back down the corridor. Maria's action gave her a momentary start on the officer who turned to pursue her just a metre or two behind.

"Stop" he shouted and began to give chase.

Then he made a fatal mistake that will haunt him forever. He slowed in his pursuit of Maria because he could see the corridor led nowhere other than the toilet.

"You can't get away, don't be stupid."

Maria continued to run towards the end of the corridor. She ran past the toilet and threw herself at the window at the end of the corridor. There was a huge crash as the window gave way and Maria's body went through it. Glass splinters fell to the floor and there was a silence for a moment and then a thud as Maria's body hit the ground below.

"Oh my God" said the officer as both he and the nurse turned and ran back. The officer ran towards the room whilst the nurse ran back to the nurse's station to call for an emergency team. Inspector Maldini heard the crash and came out of the room to find the office running towards him.

"Where is she?"

"She's gone through the window to the ground below."

The officer was in shock and showing signs of panic. Maldini turned to detective Bariti and told him to get hold of the officer and sit him down. The Inspector ran down the corridor to the broken window and looked out. He could see Maria lying on a concrete pathway about six meters below. Even from his vantage point he could see a lot of blood on the pathway. There was a doctor at her side and other medical staff were running towards her. They gathered round and began tending to her. Another member of staff brought a trolley along and they quickly picked her up and pushed off towards the emergency department.

Inspector Maldini walked quickly back to the room to find a bemused legal representative.

"I am sorry signor Mancini the interview will not take place. Your client has thrown herself out of a window. If you will excuse me there are things I must do."

The Inspector walked out of the room and pulled his mobile phone out. He called Officer Fellini and told her to keep everyone in the room and walked down the stairs towards the emergency department. As he arrived there was much activity going on and he kept out of the way as medical staff tended to Maria. Twenty minutes passed before a young male doctor came to see him. He shook his head.

"Are you the policeman?"

"Yes, Ispettore Maldini."

"I am sorry but the woman is dead. She had many injuries but the main one was a massive blow to the head. I am sure there will be an autopsy done on her. Do you want to see her?"

"No, no thank you."

The Inspector turned and walked slowly back towards Tenika's room. On the way he pulled his mobile out again and rang the Superintendent.

"Ah Sovrintendente, it's Pietro Maldini here."

"How are you getting on with the interview?"

"There's been a problem. Before we began the interview she requested to go to the toilet and on her way back to the room she got away from the officer and nurse and threw herself through a window and fell to the ground below. She is dead."

There was a silence at the other end.

"Mmmm well Ispettore that will save us some time and cost and give certainty that she will not harm anyone else in the future. I will contact the Embassy but you might like to know that earlier the Embassy called to say Miss Aquila's sister, Suzannah Boswell, is flying out tonight. I will see her and break the news if you wish."

"No, I will do it. At least we have the letter in the notebook. I will be back at the station soon."

"Ok, ciao."

The Inspector continued to walk back to Tenika's room reflecting upon the traumatic last two days. He felt drained and wasn't looking forward to meeting Suzannah Boswell. Perhaps if she had a different management style, he thought, would all of this never have happened? He reached the room and walked in. Officer Fellini was now inside the room and everyone's eyes turned and focused on him. Owen got up.

"What's been going on Inspector?"

"There has been an incident and Miss Aquila is dead."

"How?"

"She has fallen through a window to the ground below."

They all looked shocked at the news. Tenika's voice cut through the silence.

"Was it an accident?"

The Inspector looked at Tenika and she could see from his drawn face how he was affected by the event. His eyes looked down for a few seconds.

"No, it wasn't an accident. Miss Aquila was in control of her actions."

"So she has done what she said she would do."

"Yes Miss Taylor, it would seem to be that way."

"What will happen now about Chantrea's body? Will it be released?" asked Owen.

"Well I must go back to the station and make a report. I will also talk to my Sovrintendente but I think with the evidence we have it is likely that Miss Park's body will be released tomorrow. I will try to call you this evening or in the morning to confirm."

"Ispettore, I don't want to stay here any more. I want to return to the hotel."

Tenika's voice was strong and the Inspector knew from the tone that Tenika had made her mind up.

"Let me talk to the doctor."

The Inspector left the room and they all looked at each other with some shock on their faces. Nobody said anything for some time, then Var looked at Tenika.

"I feel a little sorry for her. She must have been in a desperate place to want to kill herself. It's a shame her mental health problems couldn't have been helped sometime in the past and perhaps we would all not be sitting here."

Tenika smiled at Var. She had such a warm heart and positive frame of mind. Perhaps her own experiences in Cambodia had brought her to a place where she didn't want any more unnecessary death around her. Tenika looked at Owen whose eyes were focused on the floor. She knew he probably would have liked Maria to spend the rest of her life in prison and was unlikely to hold Var's compassionate view of Maria.

A few minutes later, the Inspector returned and looked at them all.

"I have spoken to the doctor. She is not keen on Miss Taylor leaving just yet but I have agreed that Officer Fellini will be based at the Palazzo Abagnale to keep watch on her and that Miss Taylor will restrict her movements over the next couple of days. On that basis the doctor has agreed for Miss Taylor to return to her hotel. I hope Officer Fellini and you, Miss Taylor, are agreeable to that.

Tenika and Officer Fellini looked at each other and smiled.

"Well I must go now but I will be in contact. Ciao."

"Ispettore."

The Inspector turned towards Tenika. She had her hand extended towards him. He moved towards her and held her hand. They looked at each other for a few moments.

"Thank you" Tenika said with a soft voice.

Pietro Maldini smiled briefly at Tenika.

"No problem, it's my job. Please get yourself well and stay safe."

Tenika smiled back.

"I will."

The Inspector turned and left the room. Tenika looked at Var.

"Right what do we do to get out of here?"

"Well, the first thing is that you need new clothes because your old ones were taken away as evidence. I can go back to your hotel and get a new set for you."

"Oh Mariangela that's really good of you."

"We had better check whether there is any procedure for leaving as well."

"Hmm good point Owen, we don't want to upset anyone. Owen, could you press the red button for me?"

Owen pressed the button and a nurse arrived within a couple of minutes. Tenika asked her about the procedure for leaving and she said that a doctor would come to see her in about an hour and check her over and talk with her about the dressings for her wounds. She would then be able to leave.

Mariangela got up to leave the room.

"Where are your clothes in the room?"

"All my stuff is on the left hand side of the wardrobe. You will see a full length white dress there. That's Chanie's and everything to the left of it is mine."

"Ok, I'll be as quick as I can. I'll ring the station for a car to collect me."

With that Mariangela left the room and Owen's thoughts began to move to going home.

"I wonder whether it might be possible for us all to go home together. If they were to release Chantrea's body tonight perhaps we can get back soon. I will need to talk to the insurance company again. It's good though that Officer Fellini has already spoken to them because things may be on the move. With luck they might have spotted the possibility as well."

"I would like to go home with Chanie" Tenika said softly.

"And I am sure she would like that too" said Var.

The hour passed rather slowly. Officer Fellini returned with clothes for Tenika and finally the doctor arrived. The female doctor checked Tenika's temperature and blood pressure and asked Tenika if she had pain in her head or side. Tenika, of course, said she didn't although she still had a dull ache in her head and every time she twisted her body she had pain in her side. The doctor checked the dressings on her wounds and said a nurse would provide her with some more to replace the existing ones every day. Tenika hated having the dressing on her head but the doctor said it was necessary for a few days whilst the stitches healed. The doctor implored Tenika to rest for a few days and try hard not to bang her head on anything. This was a suggestion Tenika was very willing to follow. Finally, she said that if there were any problems she should ring the hospital or come back to the ward. The doctor smiled and told Tenika if she was happy with everything she could go. Tenika smiled, assured her that she was fine to leave and thanked her for the hospital's care.

"Oh, by the way, could you see that the flowers are given to a patient who will appreciate them?"

The doctor looked across to the colourful array of flowers brought in by Var."

"They are beautiful, yes I will make sure that happens. Thank you."

"Right Mariangela, let me have the clothes. I am off to the bathroom."

Tenika got out of bed and winced at the pain and stiffness still in her body.

"I think I had better come with you" said Mariangela smiling.

Twenty minutes later Tenika returned to the room dressed and looking refreshed.

"I feel so much better now" said Tenika smiling.

"Now how are we going to get back to the hotels?" queried Owen.

"No problem, I have asked for two cars to come here and they have arrived. We can all go now if we are ready?"

They all nodded at each other and began the slow walk along the corridor to the lift which would take them down to the ground floor. It didn't take them long to reach the front doors of the hospital and the two police cars waiting for them outside. Var and Owen got into one whilst Tenika and Officer Fellini got into the other. Within a few minutes they had arrived at their respective hotels and were returned to the familiarity of their rooms. Tenika sat down on the leather sofa and closed her eyes.

"Would you like a coffee?"

"Yes please" Tenika answered without opening her eyes.

Mariangela picked up the phone and spoke with reception. As she did so tears again rolled down Tenika's face as the trauma of the past few days began to catch up with her. Mariangela spotted the tears and went to the bathroom to get some tissues. She sat down next to Tenika who looked at her with tear filled eyes.

"I thought I was going to die. I really thought I was going to die. I had lost Chanie and I thought I was going to lose my own life. I have never felt such fear and despair. I would have done anything to get out of that barn. When I hit Maria with the stake I could have killed her and I wouldn't have cared. I was so wild."

"You mustn't feel guilty about what happened. You did what we all would have tried to do, save ourselves. There is nothing wrong in trying to preserve your own life when someone is trying to take it from you."

Mariangela took hold of Tenika's hands.

"Chanie used to do that. I so miss her."

There was a knock on the door and the receptionist was there with the coffees. Mariangela took them from her and gave one to Tenika.

"You have been so good to me Mariangela. I don't know how I am ever going to be able to thank you enough."

"You don't have to. I have wanted to do it and it is all part of the job."

"I'm getting hungry."

"Well that's a good sign then" smiled Mariangela.

Later that evening Tenika and Mariangela walked the short distance from Palazzo Abagnale to the Vittoria hotel. Tenika was so pleased to get out into the fresh air albeit for only the few minutes it took to walk to the corner of Tasso Square. Inside the Vittoria, Var and Owen had booked a table in a corner of the dining room and Var ordered Tenika to sit in a corner seat such that it was virtually impossible for anyone to accidentally hit her head with a passing tray.

"Where is your dressing for your head?" queried Var.

"You didn't think I was going to wear it here did you?"

There were smiles around the table as people could see the real Tenika begin to come through. Headstrong and determined, she was going to manage her own recovery. Drinks arrived at the table and quickly Tenika brought the group back to why they were all there. She lifted her glass.

"To Chanie, we will always be here for you."

Tenika's toast was warmly supported by all and followed by a silence as Chantrea filled their thoughts. Tenika felt it best to move those thoughts on.

"So Owen, have you been in contact with the Inspector?"

"Yes, briefly. There is no release tonight but he is very confident for the morning. We have advised the insurance company who say there is a possibility of a flight back tomorrow evening. They are in contact with the repatriation company who themselves are in contact with a local undertaking firm here. They say everything is dependent upon the police and the protocols

377

being met early in the morning. Otherwise it will probably be the day after next."

"I know this is not the best moment for this question, but have you thought about what happens when you get back?"

"Tee, it's a reasonable question and one Owen and I must deal with. We haven't thought that much about it yet so, at the moment, Chantrea will rest at an undertaker in Guildford until we have agreed how to move forward. We will also have to talk with Ronald. He is entitled to have his views heard too."

So it looked as if the next day could bring the beginning of the end of the tragedy. Food arrived and the conversation moved on to other things. Var was interested in Mariangela and her family and, although subdued, they talked about the attractions of Sorrento, the hotels, the bay and, of course, the weather. The evening passed without any further painful events for Tenika and finally it drew to a close. They were all rather weary from the emotional rollercoaster of a day and needed a good night's sleep. As they made their way out of the dining room Tenika put her left arm round Var and pulled her tightly towards her.

"It's so good to be back with you" she whispered into Var's ear.

Var turned to Tenika.

"Can we agree that you will never give me another fright as I had yesterday evening?"

"Well, I'll try."

"Mmm I suppose that's as good as I am going to get."

Tenika kissed Var on both cheeks and then did the same to Owen. Var then hugged Mariangela.

"Thank you Mariangela for being so caring for Tenika and respectful of my daughter."

"No, thank you for allowing me to be of some help."

Mariangela shook hands with Owen and then she and Tenika turned towards the main doors of the hotel whilst Var and Owen moved towards the lift. As Tenika and Mariangela walked slowly back the short distance to the Palazzo Abagnale, Tenika linked her arm into that of Mariangela. It was a sign that Tenika now saw Mariangela as being someone who had crossed a line and had become an insider to her experience. Mariangela had seen her at her lowest, had shared her tears and felt some of the pain. She was a friend now, not just a police officer.

Within minutes they arrived at the hotel. As they did so, they passed the Armani shop and Tenika briefly reflected upon her comments to Chantrea about checking out the clothes and the lack of prices on them. They went through the main doors and made their way up the stairs to reception where they made their greeting to the night receptionist. Then, on into the lift up to the top floor where Mariangela opened Tenika's door with a new key card.

"Hmmm you do think of everything, don't you?"

Mariangela smiled.

"Perhaps Tee tomorrow will be your last day and you will be able to go home and recover completely."

"As much as I love Sorrento, I think I would like to go home now."

"Tenika, can I ask you something?"

"Yes, of course."

"When Ispettore Maldini spoke with Var about you, she said something about finding you before you ran out of diamonds in your hem. Do you know what she meant by that?"

"Yes, when everyone was taken out of Phnom Penh the army took all the valuables from the city dwellers. Women took the diamonds from their rings and sewed them into their hems. Those diamonds became their only valuable asset that could be used in tight corners perhaps to persuade guards to give them more food or to escape some form of hard labour. Sometimes women were betrayed by those to whom they gave a diamond and were executed. Var came near to execution on one occasion. She was on her knees with a gun to her head but somehow avoided it going off. So, if a woman ran out of diamonds she had nothing to bargain with when things got sticky."

"Well I am glad you had something left in your hem that got you through yesterday.

Tenika smiled at Mariangela.

"I think I was down to my last diamond!"

"Let's see what happens tomorrow and don't forget I will check on you at eight in the morning."

"Do you know, you're better than an alarm clock."

"Why?"

"Because I have to get out of bed to turn you off."

THE LAST DAY

Tenika had a restless night's sleep. Whilst she could sleep lying on her left hand side, if she moved onto her right the pain in her skull would wake her. Twisting in bed also gave her some pain on her right hand side from the knife wound and she never could sleep on her back. She got up early and washed herself as best she could then replaced the dressing on her side and put ointment on her head wound. She dressed and sat out on the balcony, as Chantrea had done, watching the activity on the road below slowly increase. She closed her eyes and listened to the distinctive scooter engines begin to wind their way round the nearby roads. The sky was clear blue again albeit with a cool feel to the air. She looked at her watch and it was nearly eight. Mariangela would be knocking on her door any moment. Tenika came in from the balcony and walked across to the door. As her watch showed eight o'clock there was a knock on the door. Tenika opened the door and Mariangela looked at her with some surprise.

"Buongiorno, you are up early. How was your sleep?"

"Buongiorno Mariangela, not the best night's sleep I've had but better than I would have had in the hospital. Do you have time for breakfast? I have a favour to ask of you."

"Yes ok, by the way I popped back to my flat to get something for you."

"What was that?"

Mariangela held out a woollen hat with purple flecks in it.

"Oh Mariangela it's just the job and the colour is fabulous."

"I knew you wouldn't use the head dressing so this is perhaps the best next thing. So let's go to breakfast and tell me what favour you want doing."

A short time later at the Vittoria Owen and Var had finished breakfast and had returned to their room. It was just after nine o'clock when the phone rang. Var picked it up.

"Hello."

"Buongiorno Mrs Park, it is Ispettore Maldini here."

"Buongiorno Ispettore."

"I want to let you know that we have this morning signed the release paper for your daughter's body. That document is being taken over to the hospital now. I also know that the Coroner has agreed to sign his document for the body to be taken back to England. This document will be signed in the next hour. It too will be with the body for collection. Can I also remind you that your daughter's passport will need to accompany her on the journey so if it is with Miss Taylor please arrange for it to go to the hospital as soon as you can. Your daughter cannot leave Italy without her passport. I know it might sound odd but it is the rules. We will be informing the Embassy soon that these documents have been signed and they will be able to confirm this with the repatriation company in England. Do you understand that part so far?"

"Yes Ispettore, fully."

"Ok, then I suggest you get onto your insurance company now for them to make the arrangements for the transfer of your daughter and your flights. Please remember the undertaker cannot remove your daughter from the hospital unless all documents are with her. Once the repatriation company has confirmed the timing of the transfer with the undertaker in Sorrento, then they will contact the hospital to check if everything is in order."

"Thank you Ispettore for being so helpful. We will do as you say straight away."

"I hope everything goes well for you today and, if I don't see you again, please let me express my sincere sympathy for your loss and hope that your daughter's spirit stays strong with you."

"You are very kind and I am sure Chantrea's spirit will remain strong with us."

"Goodbye Mrs Park."

Owen immediately contacted the insurance company who said the repatriation company would be in touch with the local undertaker to check the availability of the body and documentation. In the meantime flights would be checked for available seats and they would try to bring Var, Owen and Tenika all home on the same flight given Chantrea and Tenika were on the same policy and the police in Sorrento had asked through the Embassy for this to happen if possible. As soon as the local undertaker confirmed the necessary documentation was available the flight will be confirmed and they would be contacted again.

Var reminded Owen of the need to get Chantrea's passport to the hospital. Owen rang Tenika at her hotel to check if he could pick it up. She confirmed it was in the safe and he said he would be over straight away to collect it. This he did and took it to the hospital and insisted that someone from the hospital mortuary came up to reception to collect the passport so he could be reassured that at least this document was in place. Owen asked if the coroner's release certificate could be checked for its availability. He was assured it would be done and Owen left the hospital reasonably happy that he had done as much as he could.

Owen took a slower walk back along Corso Italia relieved that soon Chantrea's body would be back in Guildford and they could then move on to a funeral. Ever since he arrived in Sorrento he had been in a bit of an emotional haze and hadn't really taken in the beauty of the town, its location or the people. Now, as if the world around him was slowing down, he began to take in the bustling activity along Corso Italia. The sky had patches of fluffy white cloud and there was a cooling breeze but it was a sunny day and still warm by UK standards. As Owen walked along the road one of the shop keepers was arranging his wares outside on a stand. He caught Owen's eye and warmly greeted him. Owen was rather taken back by this friendly gesture and he only managed to mumble a similar response. Suddenly the people of Sorrento became different to the dark figures he had been carrying around with him ever since arriving. He walked past the cathedral where he and Var had been spending some of their time in quiet reflection and soon he had arrived back at Tasso Square. Owen walked slowly across the square taking in the hazardous movement of people and vehicles across it. He began to see the beauty of the architecture and the happiness of people chatting happily in the various cafés around the square. This wasn't a place to be hated, rather one to feel a little sorry for because the actions of one person could so easily impact upon the reputation of a whole town.

Owen returned to the Vittoria and found Var sitting in the public area near to reception and Tenika was sitting next to her wearing her newly acquired woolly hat. Tenika got up and kissed Owen.

"Everything go alright?"

"Yes fine. You know, I have just realised that I came here with a burning anger inside me that Sorrento had taken Chantrea and I now realise how wrong I was. It was that Maria woman who took her, even if helped by an accomplice, and not the town. As I have walked back from the hospital I've begun to understand why you like it here so much."

Tenika smiled at Owen.

"Let's have a coffee and then we are going out."

"Are we? By the way, where is Officer Fellini?

"Oh, she's had to go back to the police station."

Tenika ordered two coffees and a tea, Owen much preferred tea, and they sat and chatted about the idea she and Var had come up with earlier. They decided it would be good to plant something in memory of Chantrea so that if they did return her spirit would be alive in the form of the plant. Var told Owen that they had thought of a caper bush because Chantrea liked to use capers in cooking and it only grew to about one metre in height. Owen enquired where they had thought of planting the bush and Tenika told him of the conversation she and Chantrea had at the Piazza della Vittoria and the small public garden that sat in it.

"Are people allowed to just plant things in the garden?"

"Probably not" replied Tenika.

"Could we get into trouble?"

"Probably."

Owen looked at Tenika and then Var and suddenly saw the funny side of it all and broke into a laugh.

"They'll be throwing us out of Italy next" he roared.

"Don't worry, we spoke with the Ispettore this morning, because he knows the Mayor very well, and asked him to contact the Mayor to see if he would be agreeable. We're waiting for a reply now."

"Ah, so I am safe, for the moment!"

"Yes, we had to use Var's mobile because mine was in my bag at Maria Aquila's house and I do feel rather cut off without it."

At that moment Var's mobile phone went off. It was the Mayor's office. Tenika listened intently to what was being said but her beaming face said it all. The call ended and Tenika looked at Var and Owen with a big smile.

"The Mayor has agreed for us to put a capers bush into the public garden at Piazza della Vittoria and wants us there at twelve. It will only take us fifteen minutes to get there so we have plenty of time. So let's drink up."

Just then one of the reception staff walked across to Owen to tell him there was a telephone call. He walked off to reception and took the call whilst Tenika and Var continued to talk about the planting. After a couple of minutes Owen returned.

"Right, it seems everything is in order for us to leave today. We have all been booked on a British Airways flight leaving at six o'clock and we will be picked up at three."

"And Chanie?" asked Tenika.

"She will be with us on the flight."

"Good, I'm pleased about that."

"Then we have a busy afternoon ahead of us" said Var.

At eleven forty five, Var, Tenika and Owen left the Vittoria and began the short walk to Piazza della Vittoria. As they crossed Tasso Square they felt more positive and their talk was a little more relaxed. Their walking pace was slower than normal due to Tenika's condition but this was a journey Tee was not going to miss. She held firmly onto Var and Owen and determinedly covered the short distance. On arrival at the piazza they could see a group of people in the public garden. Tenika spotted Luciano Albero and standing next to him was an older man but with very similar features whom she assumed to be the Mayor. There was a gardener in green overalls and she could also see a plant in a pot by the side of them.

Luciano Albero recognised Tenika but his expression told volumes about how her face looked. He welcomed her and kissed her gently on both cheeks, then introduced her to his brother, Alexander, the Mayor. He followed suit in kissing Tenika who then introduced Var and Owen. The Mayor easily slipped into the beginnings of a welcoming speech but which then took a compassionate turn as he sympathised profusely with Var and Owen for their loss of Chantrea.

"You know I thought it was such a good idea to plant something in remembrance of your daughter and that you chose Sorrento to do so makes me very proud. I understand you wanted to plant a caper plant because Chantrea liked to use them in her cooking. The gardener here has found one just for you to plant. Where would you like to put it?"

Var and Owen looked around the garden for what they thought might be a good spot. Tenika had an idea. She walked to the back of the garden and turned to the others.

"What about here. This spot is in line with the opening to the garden and Chanie will always have a good view across the bay."

"That seems a perfect spot" smiled the Mayor.

He looked at the gardener who nodded in agreement and began to prepare the ground to take the plant. As he was doing so, Luciano took Tenika to one side.

"I hope I did not offend you and your friend when you came to visit me. I was so anxious about the rumours and what they might do to the company. I am deeply troubled by what Maria did to you, Chantrea and Luke Adams. You have my sincere admiration. If you return to Sorrento please let me know, I am sure Rafael would like to see you again as we all would."

"Ok, thanks Luciano, I will do that."

The gardener had completed the task of planting the capers bush and they all stood quietly looking at it. Then the Mayor turned to Var.

"You know Var, this is a beautiful spot. People have sat here looking across the Gulf to Vesuvius and Naples for thousands of years. You daughter will join those spirits for the next thousand years."

Var took the Mayor's large hands into hers.

"Thank you Alexander for this respect. It means a lot to me."

"Thank you for asking me. My office will always be open to you if you return to Sorrento."

"Thank you. I shall remember that."

"Would you like me to take you back to your hotel in my car?"

"That's kind of you but I think we shall need the air."

"I understand."

The group exchanged their farewells and then Var, Tenika and Owen began their slow walk back to the hotels. Owen walked Tenika back to the Palazzo Abagnale and then she made her way up to reception where she was met by Officer Fellini. Tenika smiled at her.

"Hi, I wasn't expecting to see you here."

"I thought you might want a hand with packing. I have to pack as well, it's back to my flat for me. Oh, and by the way I thought you were having a restful time instead of walking round the streets of Sorrento?"

"Mmm, yes you are right but I had to do something for Chanie. Look, I do need some help so, come on."

It was rather fortuitous that Officer Fellini had turned up to help Tenika pack. It meant that she could deal with her own things and leave Mariangela to pack those of Chantrea. Tenika didn't really have to pay any attention to Chantrea's clothes or touch them. That would perhaps have been too emotional a task for her. It also made the job that much quicker and Tenika's side still pained her if she twisted too much or put a heavy strain through her right side.

Soon though the job was done and everything was packed in the appropriate bags. They had a short time remaining before the car would arrive to take Tenika along with Var and Owen to the airport. So Tenika sat on the white leather sofa and Mariangela on the bed and both reflected that this had been one holiday neither would forget.

"Oh, were you able to do my favour?"

"Yes Tenika, all is in hand."

"Ah good."

The phone rang and Tenika answered it. It was reception informing her that the car had arrived. Tenika stepped out onto the balcony one last time and looked up towards Tasso Square. She felt as if she was saying farewell to an old friend and certainly hoped to return one day.

"Right, time to go" said Tenika firmly.

She looked at Mariangela, smiled and held her arms out. They hugged each other warmly and Mariangela gave Tenika a kiss on the cheek.

"Thank you for looking after me. I would have been very alone without you."

"I am sorry it has been with these circumstances. Will you return?"

"I hope so, I do like it here but I do need to let all that's happened sink in."

"Ok, have a good journey and I hope to see you again Tenika."

"Me too."

They made their way into the lift to reception where Tenika paid the room bill and thanked the reception staff for all their help. Then it was down the stairs to the front door. As it opened Tenika could see a silver Mercedes van with tinted windows. Its side door was open and she could see Var and Owen inside. The driver took the cases from Mariangela and Tenika turned once again to her to say goodbye. As she was about to get into the van she heard a voice call her name.

"Miss Taylor."

Tenika turned to see Ispettore Maldini standing behind her.

"Ispettore, am I in trouble again?" Tenika said with a smile.

"No, no I just wanted to let you know that your clothes and hand bag including your mobile phone will be sent on to you and to say goodbye as well."

Tenika approached him and kissed him on the cheek

"Thank you for believing in me."

"I never had a doubt."

The Inspector raised his eyebrows and smiled and Tenika smiled back. With that Tenika got into the van, the sliding door was closed and it drove off along Corso Italia heading for the airport.

"What are you doing now Officer Fellini?"

"I'll just get my case and I'll come back to the station with you."

A few minutes later they arrived at the police station and the Inspector made his way to his office. When he arrived he found a soft package on his desk. There was a note pinned to it which said 'To my favourite Inspector'. Maldini opened the package carefully for it to reveal a new white shirt. The Inspector sat down and shook his head.

"Oh Miss Taylor, I will not forget you in a hurry."

The journey to the airport went without problem. The conversation in the van was muted. It was one of those situations where the journey had begun and there was a desire to get it over with as soon as possible. Owen had been contacted again by the insurer. He had been told everything was in hand regarding

Chantrea, they need not do anything. She would travel to an undertaker in Guildford who would then contact them. All they had to do was present themselves and their luggage to British Airways check-in for their boarding passes. This they did and were pleasantly surprised to find they had been booked in Business Class. As a consequence their flight was relatively peaceful. Var and Owen sat together whilst Tenika sat alone. As the flight took off and passengers settled down to relax, Tenika began to chatter.

"Right Chanie we've got three hours, do you remember those daft times at University? You thought I looked frightful when we first met ...."

ONE MONTH LATER

"Hi Var, hi Owen."

Var came out of her kitchen and hugged Tenika warmly. Tenika kissed Var on both cheeks.

"Owen is in the back garden at the moment. How are you? All healed up now?

"Yes, pretty well but more importantly how are you?"

"We're getting there. As you know the funeral was perhaps the worst part and sometimes I think that Chantrea will walk through the door or phone us. Other times I feel she is still here with us in the house but we just can't see her or touch her. What about you?

"A bit of a struggle for me too, that's why I've come over, I want to talk to Chanie at the church."

"Will you have a cup of tea first?"

"Mmm yes please."

"By the way, there is someone else here to see you."

From the lounge walked Sokhong. Tenika immediately went to her and hugged her firmly kissing her on both cheeks. Then Owen came in from the garden and hugged Tenika as well.

"It's good to see you and you are looking so much better."

Thanks Owen, I hope you are feeling better as well."

"Well it's not been easy but time will help and knowing you are well has been a comfort."

Var brought them all tea and they sat down to chat over the usual topics of conversation. They were happy to include Chantrea in the conversation. She remained part of the family but simply wasn't there to speak for herself. They were able to laugh at things and at each other. They were all healing.

At one point Tenika turned to Sokhong.

"You know I wasn't able to say much to you at Chanie's funeral. It was all a bit too emotional and public but I need to thank you for the card you sent to me in Sorrento. Throughout the time in that barn I just kept thinking of you holding my hand. I thought that if I could see my hand in yours then I would stay alive. It was the darkest moment of my life but your thought kept a spark of light in my mind, something to cling to. I don't think I could have done it without you."

"Tenika, I also never lost sight of your hand. I knew that so long as I could see it, you would stay alive."

The two women were emotional and hugged each other. Both had tears in their eyes and both understood the darkness that had been encountered and survived.

When tea was finished, Tenika bid Var, Owen and Sokhong farewell. She kissed them all at their front door and began the short journey to St Benedict's Church where Chantrea was buried. Leaves were falling from the trees surrounding the church and there was a scattering of brown leaves across the graveyard.

Chantrea's plot still stood out as being fresh amongst others that went back well over one hundred and fifty years. It was a good day weather-wise too, dry and sunny at times. It was also a good day for a conversation with a loved one in a glorious church yard. Tenika walked over to Chantrea's grave, unrolled her mat and sat down at the side of Chantrea.

"Hello Chanie, I haven't seen you for a while. I don't know about you but it's been all go since coming back from Sorrento and your send off. The scar on my side is looking good and my head has healed pretty well now although I am still a bit anxious about bumping it so I have a new range of woolly hats to protect me when I am out, and to be honest when I am in! I've still got the woolly hat given to me by Mariangela. She said I could keep it through winter and give it back to her when I next go to Sorrento. I think you would like her Chanie. She is a bit like you, thoughtful and intelligent. We exchange texts and occasionally send a photo of what we have been up to. By the way, they caught the bastard who attacked you. He was found from the contacts on Maria's phone and then they found minute specs of blood on his shoes. I've always said men who don't clean their shoes properly are a bit dodgy. Anyway Chanie, he will not be troubling you or anyone else for a very long time.

I've received my clothes and stuff back from the police in Sorrento and I think yours has arrived at your mum's as well. I even got my handbag and mobile back. Apparently Maria put them into her car with me on the basis that we were both going to die so it didn't matter about hiding them. God, she was a mad bloody woman. It was all jolly well packaged but I've thrown the lot out Chanie. I hope you don't mind, I only want to keep good memories of Sorrento.

Did I tell you that you have become a bit of a star in the press?   You have even been in the national press and they managed to get a good picture of you. I have to admit they were quite nice about you, and they dug out all sorts of lovely quotes from people you had known half your life."

Tenika stared down at the ground for a few seconds.

"Look Chanie, the real reason I've come to see you today is that I need to tell you something. Although I've been telling people I'm alright and bearing up, the truth is I've been bloody awful. I can't tell you just how empty I feel with you not being around. I come home from work and I don't know what to do. I so want you to ring and tell me you are coming over for dinner. I feel so odd walking round the shops alone at the weekend. I know it's crazy, you're somewhere else enjoying yourself with your ancestors and I am moping around not knowing what to do.

Sometimes I sit at home and think about some of the things we have done together, Paris in the rain, those two daft guys we met in Barcelona, our times at the theatre and just walking along the South Bank on a sunny afternoon.   Those are such good memories and I am glad I've got lots of photos too. Var is going to let me have copies of some of your photos too. She is so sweet. The problem Chanie is that although our memories are so good and strong, they only push back the pain of losing you for a short time. I miss you so much and every day at the flat reminds me of you. I wish now that we had moved in together ages ago. I don't know why we didn't to be honest. Perhaps we were afraid of being second in the queue for the bathroom in the morning. There are so many things we could have done together.

So, since you have moved on to a new life with new people I feel I need to do the same. I am going to give up the flat and find somewhere else to live. Like you Chanie, I need a fresh start with new surroundings. Now don't get concerned, I am not going to lose contact with you. Oh no, you don't get rid of me that easily. I will come to visit and talk to you. I promise you that and I am going to look after Var as well. You know how important my mum was to me and how much it meant to me when she died, well I think I might appoint Var as my new surrogate mum. I know you will support me in this and you know that I can say to Var the things I want as I would have done to my mum. I think it will work just fine.

So, there we are. It's all change. You have your new life and new friends and I must do the same. Life will never be quite the same for either of us Chanie."

Tenika set about cleaning the grave, removing old leaves and giving it a general tidy-up.

"Oh, and I have brought you a little present. I know how much you like Percy so I thought I would leave you one of his poems. I know it's one of your favourites and you can read it when I'm gone but remember I will see you soon."

Tenika took out of her bag a small laminated card with a poem printed on it. She also took out a kebab skewer and pushed it though two prepared holes in the card. Then she pushed the skewer into the ground in front of the gravestone such that the card sat upright. She stood up, looked at the card and smiled.

"Bye my precious Chanie."

Tenika then turned and walked slowly away thinking about the words on the card.

The fountains mingle with the river,
And the rivers with the ocean;
The winds of heaven mix forever,
With a sweet emotion;
Nothing in the world is single;
All things by a law divine
In one another's being mingle;--
Why not I with thine?

See! the mountains kiss high heaven,
And the waves clasp one another;
No sister flower would be forgiven,
If it disdained it's brother;
And the sunlight clasps the earth,
And the moonbeams kiss the sea;
Chanie, what are all these kissings worth,
If thou kiss not me?

Tee x

(Sorry Percy!)